COMRADES

aflame books

COMRADES

MARCO ANTONIO FLORES

TRANSLATED BY LEONA NICKLESS

Aflame Books
2 The Green
Laverstock
Wiltshire
SP1 1QS
United Kingdom
email: info@aflamebooks.com

ISBN: 9781906300067
First published in 2008 by Aflame Books

First published in Spanish as *Los compañeros*
by Joaquín Mortiz in Mexico in 1976

British Library Cataloguing in Publication Data
A catalogue record for this book is available from the British Library

Cover design by Zuluspice www.zuluspice.com

Printed in Turkey

The companions died one by one,
with lowered eyes. Their oars
mark the place where they sleep on the shore.
No one remembers them. Justice.

Giorgos Seferis

FOR AURA MARINA
MY WIFE

CONTENTS

1

BOOZER

1962

I started down the steps. The first thing I heard was the bongos. My eardrums were throbbing: four hours in an airborne submarine. The sun had all its reflectors on full blast and through the dense water vapour, the shimmering steamy air, I could make out white, black and brown faces. When the plane touched down I tried to stand up, but the seatbeltcrampintherightball held me down. I took it more calmly, unfastened the safety job and looked out the window: picture postcard palms. I took out my comb: smoothed back my hair, slick: with one quick flick, unstuck my dick, freed it, eased it, rel-eased it. I buttoned up my shirt with the yellow collar: torturous: new: flashy: yolk yellow: sported for the first time today. Tremendous commotion: bongos, shrieks, let me through, get up, we're here, ("Get up – arise and hear the sweet serenade that I, your lover, your belovèd, sing to you": song from a Cantinflas film of my childhood). I drew out my briefcase from beneath the seat in front of me, placed my own in an upright position, rushed to put on my tie and at that moment dropped the tie pin. Everybody was standing up, grabbing handbags, shoulder-bags, carry-bags, cameras, baby bottles, dummies, overcoats, sweaters, wide-brimmed Mexican hats from Jalisco via the flea market in Mexico City, everything including the kitchen sink / Excuse me / Get a move on mate / Let me out I'm baking / So bake then, who gives a toss? / Let me get down my vanity case, young man / Come on brother, get a move on / Quit pushing, you only make it worse / Me bent over, arse in the air, trying to find the tie pin for my yellow shirt with the yellow collar that was as tight as hell and rubbed my neck bringing up welts because it was new, brand new. Jesus, what a heat and the bloody tie pin rolling off into the corner and sticking to the side of the plane / I saw it / On my mother's life! / Sod your mother! So if you saw it why didn't you tell me? Oh well, too bad! It's gone, lost, adios-ed. So long! I stood up, tie in hand and with great difficulty put on my corduroy jacket / Just one second more, Miss, can't you see I'm getting my things together? / Yes sir, but everyone else has left and the plane has to be cleaned because it's returning directly to Mexico City. There are so many passengers nowadays, you don't realise / (**Oh, go to hell! Sod off!**) / Yes, ma'am. I'm on my way, I'm just getting my briefcase / Okay, but be quick / I'm in a corduroy jacket and the heat here's frying my balls. Maybe I can still find the pin. My mother gave me it. I squat down again / What a lousy filthy plane / Sir, please, everybody else is off the plane now / oh well, the pin will just have to stay here. It can't be helped. At the door the stewardess with her flat shiny face: irritable, pugnacious, dyke, whore, female sailor with a lover in every port: / See you again, sir / (**You'll be lucky**) / Thanks for everything / (**For what? For the delays, the waiting, the hassle, the fuck ups? What a hypocrite!**) / See you! / Both together: in unison: feigned laughter: fake: very fake.

I started down the steps.

On the first step I stopped and took a deep breath. A great blast of hot air burned right down to my diaphragm searing my lungs, nearly suffocating me. I surveyed the horizon: Land!: Land of Rodrigo.[1] Palm trees, bongos, black women with massive arses, tight little buns, big brown bums, bongos, tape recorders, flash guns, everyone milling around, grab that bag for me, hold this suitcase, bongos, maracas, gourds, vocals, "the Martians have landed and they're dancing the ricacha", Martians my arse! big randy black women hot from the sun (and hot for other things too), glass doors at the back of my eyes, imprinted on my myopic retina, an immense doorway with a notice above it, a tall neon sign: Rancho Boyeros Airport. My shoes pinching: new. I put my foot on the second step, then I felt them: tight all over, the buggers.

I started down the steps.

"I've spent my entire life – *sounds like the start of some bloody mariachi song* – trying to get you to be a decent man and make something of yourself. I'm not always going to be here – *Thank God!* – to keep you. You have to find the right path. All those political meetings – *wish the sodding clasps on this case would meet* – aren't going to get you anywhere. You've got to think about your family, your sister's good name – *God, she's the biggest slag around but does the old bawd ever say anything about that?* –You ought to go to mass, otherwise what will people say? That you're not respectable – *mass my arse. (It came out in verse, it could be worse. A poet and I didn't know it).* – You have to get to be somebody – *Christ, I'm an absolute nobody* – That's why I've made sacrifices all my life. I've taken the bread from my own mouth so that you can eat – *oh so that's why she's so skinny, the fat old lump of lard* – You have to repay all my efforts. What's all this about you going to Cuba and not going to university? Who said you could go? Where's it all going to end? – *You in hell, I hope* – You've always been a good boy. It's those friends of yours that have corrupted you – *Oh God the wicked little pervert with his big bad friends* – Listen to me, will you? I'm not talking to the wall."

This bloody suitcase won't close, I shouldn't have packed so many things, I'm already sweating and on top of it all there's my mother slagging me off. What a nag, the old hag. (It came out in verse, it could be worse. A poet and I didn't know it). Maybe I should take out a few things: perhaps the Indian *capishai* poncho from Huehuetenango. What am I, some kind of bloody

Indian that I go around with this crap, pure jingoistic romanticism: folklore: anyway it won't be any use to me in all that heat: what a dumb arsehole / Bad son, my arse, bad mother, that's what I say / If I go on pressing on this lid I'm going to break the marimba records: more folklore: that's if they aren't already broken. I sat on the case and tugged the straps hard, the clothes, squeezed tightly together, began to give up the struggle, jacket pressed against trousers, trousers to shirt, shirt to underpants, underpants to shit smear, shit smear to *capishai*, until slowly the edges began to come together to the accompaniment of the cracking of records / So do I really care? / The first strap reached the outermost hole and I fastened it. The leather trembled as it was imprisoned, it tensed, ached from the pressure, owwww! The second was easier. I stood the suitcase on end, armwrestled with it a bit, tried to bash it around a few times to settle everything inside, but, hell, the bugger weighed a ton. I dragged it to the doorway and rested it against the wall outside my room, it rested, I rested, resting, ready, prepared, all packed, waiting. I took the last papers out of my wardrobe and began to tear up receipts, school reports that had been around for a thousand years / What in the bloody hell are they doing here? / bus tickets, address books of people vanished into the past, photos, her, photos, her, photos, her. I tore up the last one of her, I dried my sweat and took out my jacket from the wardrobe: new: corduroy: baby-cack coloured. I had to get a move on so as not to prolong the drama / From here I can hear my mother's weeping, soft, slow, anguished, offended, fucking me up. I put on my jacket in a nervous sweat. God it's hot. Bloody suitcase. Packing knackers you out / One last look around the room, like Julian Sorel with the serial music from Fantomas: the walls as always, motionless, yellow / what a poxy poofter colour / silent. I picked up my briefcase and went out. The long damp winding corridor awaited me / like something out of a film, my fellow conspirator. At the end, standing in the doorway / Frankenstein in miniature / my mother and her tears: the pair of them together: as always: like a Sunday afternoon soap. I lifted the case almost dislocating my shoulder and began to walk.

These steps are endless.

Bongos and their FRENETIC rhythm. Welcome! Constant movement. This way, that way, every way. People sweating from every pore of their body: armpits, bald pates, penises, tits, bellies, palms, soles, souls? Ah! souls, arseholes, melting, running, dripping, pouring sweat. Warm welcomes, fiery embraces, fevered clinches, open up for pity's sake, we're boiling, broiling. The doors are shut tight and the maraca band's buzzing like bumblebees. The security and immigration blokes haven't arrived, they're still downing a hair of the dog in the Tropicana or the Red bar and us in this chilly Havanan winter crapping ourselves from the heat. From the womb of the plane there emerged a baggage trolley loaded high with suitcases, briefcases, all kinds of cases, bags of every variety, handbags, shoulderbags, backpacks, frontpacks, sidepacks, you-name-it-it-was-therepacks. The trolley with the cases of every colour appeared from beneath the plane / it's left the plane / I know, I saw it / so if you saw it, why am I bothering to tell you? / I only just remembered / we were standing together, weren't we? / When are we ever apart? These steps are endless. The trolley shotoutattopspeedtowardsthecustoms. I'd arrived. I'd really arrived. The pilots descended from the exit at the front of the plane, wiping away their sweat, took a shortcut and submerged into the distant building, swallowed, engulfed, devoured by the tiny concrete scale model. The maraca band buzzed like a beehive, the skin of the blackbongodrummersfaces: smooth, taut, glistening with sweat: bingbong, bingbong, bingbong, bingbong, bingbong, bingbong, bingbong, bingbong. This shit would drive anybody round the bend. Them, dancing, shouting, cha-cha-cha cha-cha-cha-ing. Me, purse-purse-purse perse-perse-piring. Them, boogying up and down, shouting, shrieking, howling. Me, all on edge, fingers twitching, nerves a-jangling. I put my foot (in the shoe that pinched) on the last tread of the (endless) steps.

Your passport, comrade.

Bloody bureaucrats.

At the end, in the doorway, my mother / My mother! / God, this corridor's long. I'm sweating blood: my armpits reek. I lifted the case, arm wrestled with it / more total idiocy / put it down

15

again slowly, as if I were thinking twice about it, took out my handkerchief from the rightarsepocket of my trousers which weren't corduroy and wiped the sweat from my face / the plane won't wait you fool / My mother waiting at the door. I wrung out the handkerchief, dried my hands and put it back, fingering the snot: making it crackle. I began to go to pieces: nerves: to pull the snot apart. It crumbled, broke up, reassembled, coalesced, assumed other forms, became a small octahedral ball. The slimey snot began to take on a firm consistency, separated and from the centre emerged the jam that my mother had spread on my crisp bread, the passage was becoming the cloister of a convent, long, misty, damp and at the end the headmistress of the lousy school standing waiting, waiting for me. Why had I been happy when I got up on that first day of school, I wonder? What was so special about it? Mother, all apprehensive, bathed me, more attentively more carefully than usual, using bath salts and talcum. My little willy moved nervously attempting to stand up under the Mennen-scented bath water. I choked, gobbling down my quickybreakfast. At the door waiting, lurking: on guard: on the look out: my aunt with her big bag at the ready. 7.15 a.m.: Flowers: May: special day: great cliché, (it came out in verse, it could be worse). We walked quickly towards the bus stop, a number 10 stopped, the only one that went out to the back of beyond which is where we lived. I watched her, very calm, proud, fond of herself, holdingmyhotlittlehand: old maid. On 5th Avenue and 9th Street she rang the bell with a great flourish. I felt my legs trembling as I got off the bus. My aunty gave me the big bag with my school things, its weight stopped me dead, held me back, my hands were like lead / great cliché / The urge to pee came over me. God I was going to pee if I didn't get to a loo soon. Come on, said spinsteraunty. Ok, let's go, said piddlernephew. The school door looked more like a witch's castle: massive light brown wood, wormeaten, half open, creaking, overwhelming, terrifying. Wait here for me, I'm going to get the Head. All the monsters of the sick dreams of a frightened child began to surround me, to run around me. They stopped to survey me surprised / Why don't you come in? / What are you doing standing here? / Come and play with us / classes haven't started yet / The boldest tugged at my bag / I'm peeing myself. I began to walk, full of fears, on the edge of tears. It came out in verse (again) it could be worse. (You know the rest). I went past the bathroom and was about to go in, the suitcase was heavy, I was sweating, the desire to pee was a bugger, my mother blocked the door like a barrier.

I handed him my passport.

I began to walk, the case was still heavy in my hand. I put it down again and went back for my briefcase that I'd left leaning against the wall. As I bent down to pick it up a spot rose before my eyes. A spot transfixed by time as proof of the punishment imposed by myself on myself, for all that I was, for all that I always had been: the idle bugger, the gobber who ruined walls with his filthy spittle. At the very edge of the walls on the skirting board a series of stains marked my sedentary, idle presence. Marks that bore witness to my solitary youth. Bitterloneliness, solitude, full of stylised masturbations: with banana leaves, with soap, with the toilet roll, with my aunt's face cream, with her panties: fetish. Loneliness heavy with lies and books that choked my brain in the heat of midday in my restless slumber, noises, murmurs, factory whistles indicating the end of the first shift, noises of cars returning home for lunch, noises of my mother setting the table for the second meal of the day, the sleep of the idle sod, the night owl, the solitary youth: midday. The stains were there all in a row at the foot of the walls, ineradicable, indelible, unspeakably vile: "Dirty little sod, look what you've done to the walls." My mouth was always sweating. Saliva poured from me at a thousand miles per hour. Instead of thinking, I salivated, instead of bathing, I salivated. When I was alone, I salivated. Instead of going out into the street, I salivated. In company, I salivated. All day long I salivated like a horse foaming at the mouth. Saliva ran from my brain, my hands, my dick, my arse, my nose, my nails. I ejaculated saliva. I shat saliva. So all my room and its adjacent domain (the corridors outside) were full of saliva. Ancient stains that marked my passing, the passage of the conqueror of the skirting boards. For years I filled the outside of everything with saliva until she came along. She whose inside I filled with saliva. I took the briefcase and lifted it, went back to the suitcase and lifted it. Suddenly I felt lonelier than ever, more wretched than ever and with an instinctive gesture I spat. The gob slid slowly, slug-like, down the wall. My mother, with her huge walrus body blocking the doorway so that I couldn't leave, looked disgusted. I handed him my passport.

The case weighed more than I'd expected and the briefcase weighed more than I'd expected. Everything was unexpected. My hands were sweating and the corridor was darkening, densifying, interminating. Along it she had come with sweating hands. My mother was out. "Mother, leave me alone, let me live." She was a virgin, it was her first time. It can't be true. Yes, it is. That's why I cried in the Hipódromo when you pulled down my panties and touched me there. No, it can't be true. Yes it is. It disgusts me to feel you so close, with that hard thing sticking to my skin. It disgusts me but I love you, I want to be with you. It can't be true. Let's go back to my place, my mother's out right now. She won't be back until tonight. No, I can't, I'm afraid, it disgusts me, I can't stand feeling you so close rubbing that big hard thing against me, it makes me want to cry. I hate you when you put it so close, let's go to your house though. Her hands were sweating as we went along the corridor, the long long passage. I can't. No, I'm not going to your room, oh, alright then, let's go. It can't be true. You must come to my room, my mother's out, she won't be back 'til tonight. "Mother leave me alone, let me live". *"It's a sin. You know that it's a sin and you should wait until you're married. The priest told me that you left school early yesterday. Where did you go? You came back smelling of perfume. I sniffed you, when you were asleep. Who were you with, you wretch?"* Walk fast, we mustn't waste any time. I'm afraid, it disgusts me. The passage grew darker and darker, my mother standing at the end. The case was growing heavier by the minute and the briefcase too. My hands were sweating, her hands were sweating. Our hands were sweating. But I had to leave even if my mother threw a fit. I had to leave. She had to enter. My mother was out and she had to enter my room. She was a virgin. The cases were heavy and now I was right in front of my mother. Close, almost up against her. I could feel her breath in my face. She smelt of wax. Down her cheeks slid old tears reeking of wax. You can't leave. I didn't say you could go. Don't go son, you'll break my heart. I handed him my passport. He checked it with a bored, impeccable bureaucratic expression on his face. Hugs, smiles, peals of laughter, weeping, sighs, murmurs beside me. An intense heat was permeating every pore of my body and from them poured sweat, I seemed like a fountain. For your edification, dear reader, my hands were sweating, my arms were sweating, my chest was sweating. Her tits were sweating but she kept talking, incessantly, like a mad thing / look pet, you're making a helluva din, you know / my bum was sweating, her bum was sweating. She looked at me and sweated. I looked at her and sweated. The man with my passport leafing through it impeccable, impassive, expressionless, very officious official, very civil civil servant, checking / Bye then darling, look after yourself. I just want you to know I'll be waiting for you in my house in the VEDADO, you know, on 1st AND 21st, you know, FACING THAT LITTLE PARK, ON THE OPPOSITE CORNER, you know, SECOND FLOOR. Bye darling / That girl there wiggled her arse at me! I saw it, I swear it, it was sweating. I took a mental note of the address, although not disposed to go there and smiled at her: both of us smiled in unison: a modulating cadence: randy chorus. My hands were sweating. My Ass-wan dam was sweating. This silly bugger is in no hurry with my passport. Passpoll, Pasepoli (he was the adjutant of the Count of Nevers, Henri de Lagardère, the hunchback) The functionary began to function, automatically, accurately, precisely: / What is the purpose of your visit to Havana? Is this your first visit? What organisation are you with? / ICAP, ICRAP some kind of crap. If I'd known the hassle I'd get I wouldn't have come / Listen, young man. You'd better supply all the relevant information. Is the heat affecting you? / Heat, what fucking heat's that then? Oh God, here's the tie pin that I lost, what a prat I am. All that fuss in the plane and it's here in my pocket all the time. I didn't lose it after all / Sir, I'm talking to you.

Listen, take this man to the Riviera and contact ICAP. I think he's got a bad case of sunstroke. Inform Mirna, the dark girl from ICAP / Sunstroke, what bloody sunstroke? Give me back my passport / No way! This remains here until you leave Cuba, lad / So that's what all this waste of time's about. **Stupid bastard** – When I picked up the case and the briefcase my hands were sweating more than ever before.

When I put the case and the briefcase down on the floor my hands were sweating more than ever before. Her tears were an endless river of mucus. Ever since I can remember she's been crying. Ever since my father left her because of her mother. Because of her damned mother, my damned grandmother, the damned old grandmother of all my cousins, the mother of my mother and of my aunt and the damned wife of my damned grandfather. Damned tyrant, dyke, Doña Barbara of the Matamoros district, who dominates her tribe, her family, my mother and everything that's within her reach and who's to blame for my father not knowing me and for me not knowing him. Ever since then my mother's been crying. I know her ways by heart. How she cries when her ulcer hurts, how she cries when I come home late, how she cries when I misbehave at school. But I was not familiar with this kind of crying. Now her tears smell of wax but also of solitude, of old age, of abandonment. Now she'll be alone forever. "Mother, let me live." What am I going to do? I have to go away and her rank tears are blocking the doorway. She looks older by the day. I just hadn't noticed before. Let me go. I won't let you, you can't go and leave me after so much sacrifice. It's only for a year, Mum. I have to go for training. I didn't make all those sacrifices for you to be a communist. I've heard it all before. So why bother to answer? Let me go. You're heartless. Let me go or the plane will go without me. Heartless. One way or another, today or tomorrow, I'm going. "Mother, let me live". I took her by the shoulders and they crackled. Her blouses had wide bell-shaped sleeves and were always clean and starched: they crackled. When I took her by the shoulders she crackled. Don't you dare go. Don't force me, Mum. I'll do anything I have to. I'll call the police. Well, call them then but let me get by. I'll curse you. Fine! Look, I curse you. She wept and bowed her head. I saw her first grey hairs. I'd never noticed them before. Gently I pushed her aside and kissed her first grey hairs. I opened the door and picked up the suitcase. It slipped from my grasp. My hands were sweating. They were cold and full of tears. I picked up the suitcase again and when I reached for the briefcase she was already holding it / I'll go with you to the airport / Alright, Mum / I've already called a taxi, it's been waiting for a while / All that buggering around, for this. I opened the door for the last time and went out. I put the case into the taxi through the rear door that the taxi driver was holding open and I sank into the leather seat with a lump in my throat. My mother locked the door of the house still clutching the briefcase tightly, got into the taxi and said:

"The airport, please driver."

The airport was full of people. Mirna – the dark girl from ICAP – still hadn't turned up and there was I in this corduroy jacket broiling in the heat. I must have looked like an idiot, standing in the midst of all these people milling around, with a tie pin hanging from one finger, a briefcase hanging from the rest and an immense suitcase in the other hand. The sweat was getting into my every cavity. I didn't know where to go. I was: I felt: I'd managed it: I was: alone. Completely alone! And people passing, pushing, shoving, elbowing, being a bloody nuisance, swearing. It was baking hot. I had a new, thick, corduroy jacket on and it was spring, she told me, go straight down this pavement here cross three streets and at the end of the last block is the lawyer's office, say that you've come for the five quetzals[2] and come back the same way. I'll be waiting for you here in Concordia Park. I walked a few metres but it was useless: I was a little lad lost in the vast world of big folk and Mirna still hadn't appeared. I placed the briefcase between my legs so it couldn't get nicked, put the suitcase down on the red-hot floor and slipped the tie pin into my pocket. I drew out my handkerchief to dry my sweat and dropped the five-quetzal note. Now I'd done it. I didn't even know when it was I'd lost the money. I started to cry, people were pushing me, mind out the way littlefiveyearoldlad, running, midday, such a great big park and her not there. Why did she say she'd wait for me here? What if she did it to lose me? How am I going to tell her that I lost the money when I took out my hanky to dry my sweat? Well sweat's sweat. How about me going to the bar for a daiquiri? And what about Mirna? Screw Mirna! The problem is, it's the first time that I've been on my own in the street. Each month she waited for me round the corner from the lawyer's office. Why does the lawyer send her five quetzals every month? Why did she get the idea to send me from here this time? Anyway I'm going to have to move, I can't go on standing on this spot forever. That'd be really stupid. Okay then, I'll see if I can find her myself. He headed for a sign: Cubana de Aviación. It was like he was carrying his entire house on his back: bloody great suitcase: little case: big jacket: short trousers: hot little willy. He asked for Mirna from the ICAP / She's over there / Where? Over there? / Yes over there, can't you see I'm busy? / But I'm lost / Yes, but what can I do about it? That's the Police Station over there, opposite, go and tell them. They'll look for your mama / No, I'm not going over there, I'm frightened of the police / Well then, what do you want me to do about it? / He walked towards the airport doors. I'm going to a hotel. They're calling your name, you berk. Where? Over the loudspeakers. Can't you hear it? Oh yeah, that's my name alright. Here mama, here I am, but don't spank me, the money got lost.

He took the suitcase and the briefcase and hurried off towards the exit following a dark girl who was showing him the way.

The airport was crowded.

People were arriving and departing, strolling around, embracing, weeping, shaking hands, chatting, laughing, perspiring, bearing their luggage and their grief. People arriving, departing, seeing off, being seen off, smoking, peeing in the loos, crapping in the same, purchasing duty-free cigarettes, cigars and liquor, buying porno-magazines prohibited in their own countries. People buying plane tickets and others selling them: people changing their money for the currency of some other place that also has an airport and other people doing the same dumb things in that other airport in their own country. Others waiting for the comrade carrying the goods to get off the plane: morphine: coke to rub on your prick: fabulous buzz when you fuck like that. My mother trying to carry the briefcase for me / Let me have it son, I'll help you / Other people coming in and going off in taxis whilst police (they're not people) indicate by whistle blasts where exactly you have to enter or exit so as not to block the traffic. Some in transit, some in transport, some arriving, others departing. People shoving, heaving, stinking, farting in secret so as not to reveal the perpetrator, (silent but violent), kids running up and down / Let's go and watch the planes taking off and landing. Maybe one will stop in mid-air / Me carrying the suitcase, the bloody great heavy suitcase, and paying the taxi driver / Whew! It's hot, isn't it sir? Cheerio, all the best! / People drying their snotty noses after crying and bidding farewell to their nearest and dearest (God, another awful cliché), people weighing their luggage, others pushing theirs in trolleys, excuse me, mind your backs. A beaming twit at the check-in: / May I have your ticket and your passport, p-leeze? Place your luggage on the scales. Lovely! Everything that you have. Lovely! You do know you're only permitted one small piece of hand luggage? Lovely! / Of course I do, you idiot. (Lovely!) I'm depositing the luggage on the scales and my old girl's starting to shriek: / Carry the briefcase on board in your hand, son / the fop, fairy, poofter, pansy for the airline-with-the-greatest-experience-in-the-world is inspecting my ticket scrutinising it as if it were a fake, stamping it, tearing bits off. How could a man waste his life doing such a crap job? My mother is snivelling. The fop, fairy etc. is returning my passport: ticket stamped, sealed, mutilated, accepted / Now proceed to Immigration, p-lease. Joey! Is there any excess to pay on this gentleman's luggage? No? Lovely! / Excess is what this sweetie must get up to with his boyfriend. Lots of people talking to the queen of queers from Pan Am. ("It's great to fly with Pan Am. It's great to fly with Pan Am.") Well son, it's God's will (my mother) / God's will, sod that! It's MY WILL. Now I've got to try to get to the Immigration window for them to stamp, check, accept, authorise my journey. I took my briefcase and my old girl, one in each hand and set off for the Immigration window to find out if there was a restriction order on me for being a thief, an embezzler or a communist. To them it's all the same thing. More people running / Oh heck, I left the car on a double yellow line so I'll say goodbye here / Look after yourself, you hear me / Bye Dad, come back soon / Your passport please / I handed over my passport to the villainous swine. He stared at me like he had Baby Face Nelson in his sights, studied my fingerprints and then went back to staring again, his eyes probing, scrutinising me closely, Sherlock Holmes "Elementary, my dear Watson". He turned the passport over three times and began to flip through a card index, he went back one, two, three, four, five, six, seven weeks and couldn't find a thing, zero, zippo, zilch. He checked it, one, two, three, four, five, six, seven times and the villain still found sod all. He turned the passport over a few more times, went back to staring at me intently / my mother is trembling, I can feel her hand on my arm shaking / He smoothed down the pages of the passport and stamped it: Exited Guatemala the such and such date nineteen hundred and such and such. He looked me straight in the eye and returned my passport. I still held my briefcase. I no longer held my mother. She followed me to the glass doors which separated those who were departing from those who were left behind. She started to weep again. "Mother leave me alone, let me live." Now comes the worst part / Well, mum, this is it / The heat, excessive, exhausting, excrutiating, execrable. Whenever I'm afraid I get the urge to take a leak. Now I desperately wanted to pee. I measured the distance. If I'm going to pee I'm going back home. I'm not leaving. Tears poured down my old lady's cheeks, her sobs were heartrending. I was all choked up, my briefcase slipping from my sweatsoaked hands. My mother opened her arms to hold me / Well son, so you're leaving me at last / I had to hold on to the briefcase, if I dropped it everything would fall out. People, pushing past, uncomprehending / Excuse me / What a bloody nuisance these people are / Why do they stand in the way? / Move out of the way, lady / As I opened my arms, tears began to mist my eyes. I saw her young, adult, old, dead, a girl in the arms of my father, the father I had never known, who came, fucked her and left her; I saw her beautiful, old, fusty, wrinkled, loving me, loving my father, alone, unappreciated, weeping, suffering in silence night after night, always abandoned. Her head was beginning to go white and I bent to kiss her first silver hairs / Will passengers for Mexico City board the plane through the central gate / Oh, hell, it's time to go. Old lady, loving me. We have to leave everything for something we don't have and maybe never will. Still, I'm young, perhaps I'll be back soon. Abandoned, alone, lonely, dried up, both inside and out, menopausal, with no other son to love / Last call for passengers to Mexico City / I hugged her tightly and kissed her first silver hairs.

The last thing I heard was her sobbing.

I started to climb the steps.

2

SKINNY DOG AND RAT

1967

Tunnels, tunnels, tunnels filled with sulphur and seawater that at night warm and swell and snake beneath the mountains surrounding Guatemala de la Asunción. Tunnels congested with gold and silver and blood and the bones of the Lords of Xibalbá. Tunnelsveinsofmountains, tunnelsabodesoftheancientlords, tunnelspoolsofvirgins. Mountains with caves congested with waste and memories. Mountains custodians of the horizon. Volcanoes riddled by dust and violence. Today I bathe in the torrent of lava from your womb and then I shall flee forever. I shall bear imprinted on my face the colour of your burn. I shall die in an alien land far from your roots.

Yes I'll flee. I'll leave here. I've no choice. Death haunts my eyelids. I'll go on fleeing as I've always done, from my parents, from the school, from the teachers, from the university, from the police, from myself. Now I'm condemned to death and forced to flee once more: "red wall: communist bastard: traitor: guerrilla agent: committed communist: all for Guatemala". We've got to fuck off before they blow us away. Well anyway, what choice have I got?

Sad husky bray. The sad bray of a car horn. A car with a sad horn and two passengers on board. Passengers on board: friends: mates. All the safehouses where I used to take refuge have been raided and I've nowhere to sleep. I've got to take the plane in the morning at seven and I've nowhere to spend the night. A cheap hotel is dangerous. The parks are dangerous. My friends' houses are dangerous. I'm going to spend the night with him: friend: mate: childhood: adolescence: manhood: friend. He's driving scared: he's watching me with frightened eyes, with panic, with pride, his friend is a revolutionary, pursued, cornered, condemned to death. How did I get embroiled in this danger? My wife must be all nervous waiting for me to come home to supper. Although I let her know, she won't go to bed. And me in the car all night with this nutter. What makes me accept everything he suggests? Why does he get into these scrapes if afterwards somebody else has to pull his nuts out of the cracker? And what if the police stop us? They're raking the city for him. If they manage to grab us I'll say he threatened me, that I don't know him, that he forced me into the car at gunpoint. If not, it'll be me who has to pay for this irresponsible jerk's actions. There I was working peacefully in the office and he appears out of the blue: you've got to hide me at your place I told him. He almost crapped himself. Finally he agreed to drive me around in his car all night. I had to phone Chayo and spin her a yarn about having to work on call all night. He had to ask his wife for permission, she's got him right under her thumb, he was trembling all over when he phoned; to think that he used to be the gang leader who taught us to drink. That first time he forced us, threatened us. I didn't want to but Boozer and the Lad supported him and so that was it. And now he's shit scared, he looks like a frightened rat. I'm so nervous I can hardly drive and that irresponsible bugger sits there calmly smoking and watching me. What the hell's he looking at me for, that's what I want to know. He looks bloated, paunchy, years older than he really is. Not even the shadow of the carefree, witty, devil-may-care Rat of our school days. Now he's all crows feet, double chin, lines around the mouth, a brow irreparably furrowed and a huge belly, a massive beer gut hanging over the steering wheel that makes it hard for him to drive. I feel ridiculous: him watching me and me driving him. My stomach hangs over the wheel, it's really grown enormous. I ought to go to a gym and do some exercise. Yeah, I will go, I've got to get this belly down. I can scarcely breathe. If we had to make a bolt for it today they'd catch me in two shakes. I'd like us to have to make a run for it so the fuzz would grab this fat paunchy bugger. How could he have let himself go like this? The fact is he's got sod all to do all day, he goes from the office to the house and back again; he sits on his arse at the office and lies around at home, I bet he doesn't even fuck the wife so he doesn't over-tire himself. In the car all day and at all hours: down-payments, deposits: the house mortgaged by his old folks and paid off by this bloody idiot. All his salary must go on paying deposits and instalments on the music centre, fridge, TV, house, car. He's turned into a deposit himself: a big bag of shite. What a hoot! Hah, and then there was that time when the commandant arrived and threw his gun down on the floor, whop / here, look after this for me mate / he said to him. Rat went stiff all over, all he could say was the commandant called me mate. That was when things were going well and everybody thought that we were taking power. That's why I had him in the house, I thought he was going to get a good job. I was even proud of the bugger and now they're on the run and I'm embroiled all over again. Who makes me stick my neck out where it's none of my concern? That first time I just got into the habit. Oh well it's only for tonight, if I manage to get out of this unscathed I'll never get into any more scrapes with this idiot, he's capable of turning me in, he's a coward. It's not because I'm a coward but you've got to look after number one, look after what you've got, what you've built up by dint of so much sacrifice, you've got to think of your wife, poor old Chayo, if she were left a widow what would she do on her own? He only thinks about himself and his "easy payments". If they catch us and take us in who's going to pay all the debts, Chayo couldn't hold down a job and my old folks are flat broke, I must have been mad to get involved with him, I should never have listened to him, I should have thought up an excuse, any old excuse to get out of it. It's not as if it hasn't happened several times before, I just never learn. Last time I had to hide him in the house for about two months. Chayo nearly divorced me. She practically had a nervous breakdown and I lost about ten pounds in the two months. And him calm as you like; he even brought arms into the house and held meetings with his mates there. I never learn, I'm an idiot, I should have told him to fuck off today. That time the neighbours began to suspect and almost searched the house. His comrades all used to turn up armed to the teeth. Every time they saw my gun he and Chayo began trembling from head to foot, they were shit scared and she went completely to pieces when they had me at their place. The boys didn't give a toss, they came and went whenever they fancied, carrying their Kalashnikovs. "Own your own house", "Put in a colour TV", "Freeze your balls with frigidaire", "All mod cons on easy monthly instalments." What a lousy dumb life: the wife lying around all day, getting fat, bone idle, belly like a porker, having it off with the milkman or the bloke from the drycleaners or with his boss rubbing him up the right way by having him once a week (to supper I mean). What a life, I really couldn't live like that, always on the run, barely a step ahead of being killed or getting thrown into jail forever. And what about a home? Or kids? Somebody to carry on your name? The buggers aren't natural, always on the run, in hiding, stinking to high heaven, it's no kind of life all that shit, better to die in a shoot out than live like a robot, stultified, despised, growing old and fat at a desk, exploited, exploiting, bored to death, sickened, dull, gross, old, cuckolded.

"Right mate, the engine's getting overheated. What shall we do then? What about stopping somewhere for a taco and a beer? Otherwise I'm going to bugger up the car and I haven't even paid off half of it yet."

What a bummer. I've been paying for this car on instalments for eighteen months. It never seems to end. Whatever possessed me to buy such an expensive model? I'd never have done it if it weren't for Chayo's stubbornness, always wanting to be one up on her friends. The bloody woman's always making endless demands.

"Well, let's go to a drive-in, if you like. That way we won't have to get out of the car."

He's always the same, hiding, keeping out of sight. You can't even have a bite in peace. It must be a guilt complex or persecution mania. Personally I think he's nuts.

"Whatever you like. It's all the same to me. But I'm hungry so let's go somewhere nearby."

"Okay then. When you get to Parque de la Industria take a right so that we come out on the extension to 6th Avenue and we'll look for something nice. There's nothing even remotely decent round here."

When we turn on to 6th we can make for the centre. There ought to be somewhere there. This bugger's always noshing. He can't stay silent for a second without feeling hungry. Worse if the cops get us because we've stopped to fill our faces. Nowadays they're suspicious of everybody. But this limpdick doesn't look dodgy so it'll probably be okay.

"Why don't you turn here on to 6th towards the centre, Cafesa's just before the Town Hall, we could grab a bite there."

Whip's mistress, the Viking, lives over there. The "boyze" go there a lot. Oh God, what if there's trouble and it ends in a shoot-out? They'll grab me just because I'm dumb enough to be in the wrong place at the wrong time. But my luck couldn't possibly be that bad.

"Okay then, You're right. That's a good spot for a taco."

That's where the whores hang out, maybe we can pick up a couple of big birds and spend the night in the Camel motel instead of hanging around like a pair of bloody idiots. A bunch of musicians wouldn't go amiss, either. At midnight we could swap tarts and then I could drop him at the airport very early. What's more I could fix it up with the birds for another session later on too. Skinny Dog's a devil for the women.

"You're right. Cafesa will do fine. You get good snacks with the beers there."

The car heads off northwards up 6th Avenue. The trees in the central reservation, where the hell did I learn that word? We don't say that in Guatemala. A reservation's a park for wildlife. This is a garden in the centre of the street. I really don't know what it's called. The car accelerated. Or, to be more precise Rat accelerated. He put his foot down hard and the trees began to whistle past, whoosh, whoosh, whoosh, and be lifted from the central island. That's what we call it, a central island not a ruddy reservation. Wherever did I learn that word? I think they say reservation in Havana. The trees stir, are lifted, uprooted by our velocity. Rat's always driven like a lunatic. Once we really screwed it up down in Iztapa. The car rolled over five times. The trees are getting uprooted. After the accident his old woman held a mass of thanksgiving. If she'd only known that we'd been travelling totally rat-arsed with a couple of tarts in tow she wouldn't have done a thing. Zilch! They made all five of us go down on our knees and then this daft bugger of a priest chucked holy water all over us. As we were still hungover, a drop of the hardstuff would have gone down a damned sight better. When I turn around to look, the trees are still well rooted in the central island. Chevron Station, Shell Station, Klee Pharmacy on the corner. Nestlé Co. building. I hope he notices the traffic lights on the first street in Zone 9, otherwise we'll end up imprinted on the side of one of those buses leaving the Terminal. When we left the port of San José and we passed the military checkpoint, we were all singing our heads off, boozy, oozy, hands in the glands of juicy-arsed floozies, ripe and randy, reckless, feckless, their cracks on our laps. There were two of them and five of us and they could take it. The night before we'd had a right skinful, we queued for a shag, one after another, fucked them sandwich fashion each of them in turn, full frontal assault, fixed bayonets, firing with precision, bringing up the rear, the last man swimming in a sea of slush, slurping through a swamp of semolina semen-olina. We boozed until 5 a.m. Then, pissed out of my skull, I started bouncing a coconut filled with sand off the head of Bigbonce who was stretched out paralytic from so much rum. Over and over again until finally the coconut shattered. Rat crashed out under a beach hut. We never did work out quite how he managed to get under there. At seven I began to come round. I climbed out of the car and dimly made out Rat and Bigbonce staggering along holding each other up, singing volubly. The Lad and Boozer were already taking the sun lying in holes in the sand rat-arsed, shitfaced and hungover with a beer in each fist getting a tan with a horny whore lying alongside. Both well out of it. The Nestlé Co. building next to the Shell station and opposite the Oasis: a hairdressers with an advert for Andrews Liver Salts on the side wall, perfect for drunks. Opposite INVI: the National Housing Institute: El Sótano nightclub: great government scam: housing for the poor (fairy tales). Underneath it, El Sótano nightclub: boneyard: trap for the dimwitted. That's where, a few nights ago, I had the last meeting with the rep for my Section, we sat near the mirrors at the back and began to discuss the propaganda for the movement. Conspiracy used to be so much more enjoyable in the past. Now it's all longwinded so you get bored, tired, disillusioned, scared. Petit bourgeois prejudices, says the rep, but I'm already fed up, worn out, drained. Every year that passes I feel more exhausted. My nerves can't take it any longer. Always on the run. Always watching the car behind. And the one in front. And the one that overtakes us. The burst of machine-gun fire could come from any of them. And at night you can't sleep. I keep my pistol under my pillow ready, cocked, every single car that stops or passes beneath my window makes me jump out of my skin. If anyone stares at me I think he's an informer. I'm overwhelmed by the urge to shoot him. I can't have a girlfriend or love anybody because I can't let anyone get close to me. When I go into a bank, a shop, a café, wherever, I've always got my hand on my ammo-belt, cocked, ready to start shooting. The other day, during an engagement, I nearly killed a comrade because of my nerves. They ought to give me a year off on the Black Sea, at a Romanian health resort or in some place like that. My petit bourgeois prejudices won't go away for anything. My petit bourgeois desperation is torturing me. I got up, opened the car and ran desperately to the shop for a giveusabeerasquickasyoucan. Afterwards I went and sat on the beach for a quick wank. About eleven, Rat and Bigbonce came back totally shitfaced, they fell around, hanging on to each other, hiccoughing, playing the fool, hooting with laughter, sweating, reeling, staggering, they took another swig, lay down beside me, passing the bottle around: we gargled with it, it was warm but who gave a toss. Rat went for a dip. The sea had it's way with him. It dragged him, rolled him over, turned him round, screwed him, fucked him, bathed him. He didn't feel a thing. We were doubled up with laughter. At twelve o'clock he gave the order to leave. The bugle sounded, tarara, tarara, tarara! The bulls came forth into the arena in their bullfight costumes, marking, attacking the sand with their hooves, snorting, hooting with laughter, galloping around. The cries of the maidens, damsels accompanying the matador imposed a sense of tragedy upon the afternoon. Our rodent friend dedicated the bull of the afternoon and came forth snorting on to the hot sand: barefooted. His banderilleros ran as one: in unison: eager. Opening the door they hurtled into the mobile bullring piling in amidst shrieks of joy and fountains of beer, one foot on another, a head under somebody's arse, one tit against another / Get your foot off there / Ow, you're squashing my boob / Don't be so stubborn, I'm going in the front with Rat. No, that's my place / Get your bum off there kiddo, I'm sitting there / You're going on my lap, stop messing about / It was midnight, twelve on the dot when the car took off crammed with trollops and drunks. It headed off straight between the palm trees that lined the road out of San José. In the front rode Rat and the Lad and behind the two torrid tarts sitting on Boozer, Bigbonce and me. The Kativos Paint Co., one more block and we'll be at Cafesa. All this thinking has given me a thirst. Right now a fizzy drink would go down a treat. The

M.A. Ayan Industrial Gas Plant, Pinsal Paints, Infom, the Tecún Umán Universal Technology Co. Tecún Umán, our Indian of feathered fame, "green, green, he of the tall green feathers, green, green, green", that Miguel Ángel Asturias[3] is a right poofter, all that crap he wrote about Tecún, he's a fat sentimental blackmailer: "he of the green feathers, green, green", he must have been pissed out of his skull when he wrote that crap. Now we're there. The car was swerving up the highway, the heat was intensifying by the minute but all I felt was the car suddenly begin to turn over and over, poom, poom, poom, chas, chas, crash. The windscreen shattered, shards of glass flying under the impact. I grabbed hold of a shrieking strumpet. Then silence. At Vecesa, the car did a U-turn at the lights, Rat drove into the Cafesa car park slowed to a halt and let out the clutch. He switched off the ignition. Silence.

"Okay. We're here mate. What do you fancy then?"

That's what the tarts in El Salvador say. What do you fancy then, love? Well, what do I fancy? Shit, so many things I'd like. Peace, tranquillity, rest, that the entire police force drop dead, that we take power soon, that my nerves will last out another five years; perhaps by then we'll have a liberated zone and I can rest in the highlands lying around all day never doing a damned thing, instructor in Marxism to the Indian twerps of the free zone, getting up whenever I like, stuffing my face with whatever I fancy and getting my leg over with a nice bit of Indian crumpet. Well, what do I fancy? Perhaps to sleep a whole night without waking with a start, without thinking about the cop whose face I blew away, the dumbfuck blew his whistle and approached the car window. I reckoned he was on his own so I stopped. He came right up to the window of the panel / Your driving licence, sir / I put my hand into my breast pocket while he was gazing at the sky distractedly and scratching his balls, with a smirk that stank of an easy bribe / Here's my licence / Bang! the shot from the .45 rang out; all I saw was the Nazi helmet flying through the air and the cop begin to crumple. I jammed my foot to the floor and took off like a madman / Comrade, the killing of the

35

enemy when it is not absolutely essential, constitutes an act of murder / But the car was loaded with propaganda and my driving licence had expired, it was Services' fault, they hadn't renewed it and if the cop had taken me in to Headquarters things would have turned ugly. For that reason I invoked my independent judgement as a field operative / I consider that the comrade's evaluation of the situation was accurate, he is exonerated of all responsibility. The death of the policeman was necessary / So what do I fancy now?

"I think I'll have a ceviche and a Coca Cola with ice."
"Don't you want a cold beer?"
"I've got to be on the ball all night, I prefer to keep off the booze."

Now he's really screwing it up. If he doesn't get a skinful he won't get into the mood and he won't agree to having a couple of girls. We'll have to stay in the car, like it or not. If I'm the only one to fill up with beer I'll get paralytic and then he'll have to drive. Then the fat'll be in the fire. What a cock up!

"We'll if you don't drink I won't either."
"Oh, alright then. But just the one."
"One ceviche, one hamburger and two beers, but make sure they're really cold, please."

"The pause which refreshes". This guy's got a real habit. After the first drink he just can't stop. I reckon we're well on our way to getting into the swing. Let's get our skates on, then I'll soon overcome my fear. Maybe afterwards when he's half cut I'll persuade him to go to the cathouse. That way there'll be no problem about where to spend the night. I'll have a good fuck with Concha and everybody'll be happy. It's ages since I had a bit on the side. After the first beer I'll see what happens. He always did like his booze. He's a real tippler. The snag is I like it too. But it'd be madness to get a skinful today. If we get tanked up the cops might catch us and then we'll really have screwed up. They'll shoot me right there and then and they'll kill Rat just for being with me. But when it's a matter of booze the bloody idiot just doesn't think. I'll knock back just this one beer and stop right there because otherwise things might turn nasty. He looks as if he's playing dumb but I know him, when the first one hits his stomach he'll lighten up, he'll forget they're looking for him and then I'll take him to La Locha and once in the whorehouse that'll be it. Nothing else will matter. If he thinks I'm going to get pissed, he's off his rocker, I'm drawing the line at one. I'd better talk about something that'll loosen him up, get him in the mood, otherwise he won't want to drink.

"You heard that they killed the Lad, didn't you?"

Now he's well and truly nailed me. He's going to tell me all the ghastly details. As if he didn't know that I'd heard.

"No I hadn't heard. Poor guy."
"He was killed in combat, so I heard. Strange you didn't know about it."
"That's life, mate."

Yeah. That's bloody life. What frigging combat. They caught the Lad because he was a fool. "Report from the Revolutionary Headquarters. It is the painful duty of the CDR to inform the Guatemalan people that, on the 1st of March 1966, Comrade ... lost his life in combat with the forces of repression that cover our country in blood." What combat? What fucking combat? They got him because he was a bloody idiot. I can't see why we need to hide the fact that he was out drinking visiting his mistress in Marta's Bar and that when he was blind drunk he started shouting dangerous inanities / Up the FAR[4] / I wipe my arse with cops / Bring on a few of them. I'll show them all / In a few seconds the bar was surrounded by five cop cars. "It must be exciting to die in combat, don't you think? I've always imagined how the Lad died. According to the communiqué from the FAR he fell fighting in the mountains / *What bloody mountains? They beat him to death in the 4th Precinct* / after walking for five days 'the valiant combatants were forced by conditions of extreme thirst to come into the open to reach / *the nearest bar where the cops fell on them* / the river'. That's what the report that I read said. Poor chap. Terrible isn't it? Do you remember what a bugger he was at school? Always stirring up trouble. How could they have broken him so young? He was a looker too, wasn't he? Do you remember when we used to go to the brothel every day. He had a really sensational mistress. Rosa, the best whore in El Hoyito / *It was because he screwed around that they managed to kill him. The bugger is that he didn't die straight away, he was wounded and taken to the 4th Precinct and there they tortured him for four days consecutively until they killed him. His father's in the military but, however hard he tried to get him released, they wouldn't let him go. It must be terrible to be beaten to death. But every man meets death his own way. He had balls. He must have resisted like a man right to the end. I hope so. None of the safe houses that he knew about fell. I had to organise the withdrawal from one of them where we were storing a load of propaganda, that's why I had to kill the cop when he stopped me. But I did it out of rage too, rage that they'd caught him, I loved him, he was my friend. I knew he wouldn't come out of it alive, it was too much to hope for. It was a foregone conclusion. The Secret Police Chief had warned his mother. "You'd better know right from the start that, when we catch him, he's a dead man." It was out of pure rage that I blew off the cop's face with my .45. The worst thing is that now it won't let me sleep* / But with women he was shy. He didn't have a single girl in his last two years at school. Do you remember that, whenever we went to discos, he'd get absolutely pissed and wouldn't dance. Well, I didn't dance much either but he wouldn't dance, not even once, even though the birds gave him the come on. They were always after him and the daft bugger was always avoiding them, then, when he was really sloshed, he'd insult them and we'd have to leave the party fast. He never had a girlfriend until he was at the University. I can scarcely believe he's dead / *Neither can I* / I hope he died quickly from a bullet without suffering much. It would have been worse if they'd caught him alive and tortured him and torn him apart like they do with those they take prisoner. He probably wouldn't have held out for long, what do you think? He was brave but not that brave / *God, how he carries on. It's the beer talking. I'm the same too /* or maybe he was, you know. I remember that, whenever there was a punch up, he never made a run for it. I'll never forget that time when Swine Zendejas wanted to beat him up. Swine was one of the class bullies. The Lad bit his nipples and hung on and afterwards he slit open his schoolbag. Swine didn't dare go near him in case he got stabbed. The Lad was a brave bloke. And now he's dead, I can hardly believe it / *Neither can I. But he always lacked discipline and that cost him his life. When we worked together in the Resistance I had to criticise him severely and the bugger refused to offer any self-criticism, he preferred to accept the sanction and practically refused to speak to me again. That's why I requested for a transfer to Propaganda. I can't believe that he'd quarrel with me over such a stupid issue. Now he's dead and we never did make up our differences after we'd been such close friends /* And you. Why don't you say anything if you were such close friends!"

"Call the waiter for a couple more beers, will you?"

I knew it, he's getting tanked up and into the mood. One more beer and I'll take him off to the Pussy Palace, we'll stay there 'til six in the morning, then, rat-arsed, I'll take him to the airport, boot him out and it'll be, sod off – see yah mate – preferably later rather than sooner. The snag's going to be Chayo, she's going to give me one helluva bollocking, but at least I'll be free of this character. I'm going to spend the night shagging even if I have to pay for his fuck myself. Who's going to think of looking for him in a room in a cathouse? Afterwards I'll fob Chayo off. I'll say that a friend from work invited me back to his place for a drink. No problem. I'll stop her sulks with a trip to the pictures or a good fuck. It's just a case of getting out of this without creating any greater problem. Also this beer's beginning to take away my fear. I drive like the devil and if a copcar spots us, there's no way they'll catch me.

"Shall we drink them here or shall we go somewhere else? It's up to you."

What's the matter with him? Where does he want us to go now? I knew he'd start knocking them back seriously. That really was an excellent beer. Another like that would go down nicely. Anyway, it's early and I suppose he's got his papers on him and they're in order. I can't see any reason why things should go so wrong that the cops catch us. Anyway, he'll pay for everything and it won't cost me a cent.

"The snag is I haven't got a bean. I changed all my money into dollars and there's no way I can spend them or I'll be really screwed when I get to Mexico."

He's always such a sponger. He's been the same ever since we were at school, you had to pay for the cinema, his billiards his fucks, oh ... and his fags. He never ever bought any, it was always: lend us a ciggy, mate. The sod is that it's not two notes for a fuck any more and if we stay all night it'll cost me an arm and a leg. At Grace's its twenty-five a night plus booze and food. That's more or less forty a head. Bloody hell! that's eighty altogether. God, that's half the instalment on the car. I'll have to sign an IOU at Grace's and pay her off a bit at a time. Another monumental cockup. How can I explain the deficit to Chayo? Still, I'd rather spend the cash than get caught with this walking stick of dynamite in my car because I'll be spending fuck all if I'm floating in pieces down the Motagua River. Then there'll be sod all instalments on the car, sod all everything. Let's see, I've got twenty in my wallet and fifteen hidden away in my cache. But I was keeping those fifteen for a drink tomorrow to get rid of my hangover. I know, I'll leave my watch with Grace and get it back with the first instalment and then I'll owe her the rest. All this higher finance does your head in. Well, whatever, let's have a good night of it. Perhaps that little Salvadorean girl's still there. She gives a great blow job. Maybe she'll do a good striptease for us, but that'll be another twenty, damn it. Still, let's get going.

"Never mind. I've got some money and even if I haven't I've got good credit. How about going to the brothel for a bit?"

Now he's screwing me again. He knows all my weaknesses. Whatever we decide he's determined on a bonk. The bugger is that the whorehouse is always stacked out with grasses. All those bloody informers are pimps or they're the bodyguard for the Minister of Finance or some other whoring minister or his sons. Still there's no way all the narks in the country could recognise me. We'll grab a couple of scrubbers and get them to give us a good striptease behind locked doors. Afterwards we'll shag each of them in turn. We can spend the whole night fucking them rigid. But what if one of them is the mistress of a grass? Yeah, yeah and maybe the earth will open and swallow me up. The whole thing's a potential balls-up. Still we've got to get to the broads well tanked up. Another couple of beers wouldn't go amiss.

"Okay if you like. But let's have another couple of beers first."

Now I've got him. Now it's me giving the orders. Like before at school. He who pays the piper calls the tune. I'll sound the horn so he'll see it's me making the decisions. Beep beep beep. What a poofterhorn, I'll see if I can change it for another at the end of the month. But after this booze up I won't have a single cent left. Where's that damned waiter? The bugger's taking his time. This dumbfuck's staring at me like a prize idiot. He thinks I'm going to order another couple of beers. Fat chance! We're going straight from here to Grace's. She's got a place on 12th Avenue now, just round the corner from the Faculty of Economics, right near the Barracks. Skinny Dog's going to shit himself when we approach it. I won't say a thing. I just want to see his face as we go past. But what if they stop us? This bugger's quite capable of starting shooting. No. I'd better turn into 18th Street and go straight on to 12th. Beepbeeb, beepbeep. That sodding waiter still hasn't appeared. Ah, here he comes at last.

"The bill please."

"What was it you had?"

"One ceviche, one hamburger and two Gallo beers."

"Ok. Let's see ... that's forty, eighty, one twenty ... one sixty, sir."

"Here. Keep the change."

"Thank you, sir."

Vrac, chas, vroooomm, vroooomm vroooomm roomm roomm. I switch on the lights, put her into reverse, release the handbrake. Clunk. This daft bugger keeps looking at me. Why doesn't he say something? What time is it anyway? Bloody hell, one thirty, half the night's gone already. We've got five hours left. Well, five hours will pass quickly enough. We've already been together for, let's see .... six, seven ... almost seven and a half hours. I should have eaten more. Hell, I've turned up the wrong street. I said I was going to go up 18th and now I'm heading towards Industrial Park again because my head's full of all this bullshit. Maybe I'd be better off not spending all this brass and just pull the car over to the side somewhere. The snag is that nowadays there's a patrol car lurking on every corner and they can intercept you just about anywhere in a matter of seconds. They stop you wherever they see you, even worse at this time of night. No, it'd be best to go to the cathouse. Why can't I stop thinking? I'm tired of trying to solve the problem and this dumbcluck doesn't help, he just keeps staring at me like an idiot. I think he must be asleep already. God I hope he's not going to carry on like this all night. Could it be because I didn't consult him over where we were going? Touchy on top of everything else. Good grief, we're at Montúfar already. I'd better cross here and go up Liberation Boulevard. Alicia, the bird who was the Lad's mistress has got a bar next to the Social Security Building. We could have a couple of drinks and while away the time making small talk with her until the dawn. She'd be chuffed to see us. If we get talking about the Lad she'll shut down the bar. Skinny Dog can nod off for a bit while I give her a good feel up cause she's a touch too old for fucking. It's been almost thirteen years since the Lad was her lover and she was already pushing it then. She used to turn up every Good Friday at the student demo for the boys to fuck. As many as fifty used to ball her. Her greatest pleasure was to appear with the 'Honourable' on the main balcony of the Medical School. The last time I saw her she was all tarted up, with a huge fat belly. She must be forty-eight to fifty. Right, there's the Social Security Hospital. I'll go around the block and come back on the other side. This sod's asleep. When we get to Alicia's I'll wake him up.

"The Baron of Ventimiglia and Olones are trusty friends, they will help me to plan my revenge. Olones has a redoubtable sword. He bade me await him here in the caves beneath the Cerrito del Carmen with all my band of stalwart men ready to board. I have my red scarf around my brow, my belt of stout leather and my pirates' boots. They have to help me because, when they killed the Red Corsaire and the Green Corsaire, I placed all my men at the disposal of the Baron of Ventimiglia to attack Van Guld, but the villain escaped us through Aguas Vivas in Escuintla and thence vanished. However fast The Ray sailed, we could not reach the old Fleming who had killed the brothers of the Black Corsaire. From that time hence I had not seen The Corsaire nor Olones. Moko came to tell me that it is already known that they have killed my second in command and that they are willing to help me in my crusade for vengeance. For that gesture I am indebted to him and await him here. Together with Olones's men and those of the Black Corsaire, we form a great host and can attack the 4th Precinct. That is where they are holding the Lad captive. We shall rescue him and in the process we shall put to the sword all the murderous police of that accursed barracks. Night is drawing on and there is no way that we can see the lanterns of The Ray approaching, even though it has wondrous lights that may be seen from many leagues distance. The boat should dock, near La Candelaria whence the warriors may come on foot. But no harm should befall them, for patrol cars rarely pass this way; moreover, they are well armed, bearing their blunderbusses, their sabres and pistols. Only the Black Corsaire wields a sword. And this because he is noble and learned to fence in Ventimiglia or in Macondo, I do not recall.

43

He is not just any old pirate like us. He respects the laws of buccaneering, he leaves his barque moored in the centre of a town and wanders at ease. He denies no man his greeting and for this reason is greatly praised. This Black Corsaire is a fine fellow and resorts to piracy and pillaging only to avenge his brothers. Pity it is that at that time we could not seize Van Guld, but we suffer no regrets because for sure our day will come. These caves are the coldest in the world, I tremble with cold and these devils still do not arrive. What if they are trifling with me and never come. But such doubt is folly, for the Baron of Ventimiglia is a noble man, a man of his word. So, sword in sheath, and I shall staunchly suffer this icy cold. If only I might partake of a dram but my wine sack hangs in my room at home. If my father finds it, he will drink it dry. He will leave not a drop. And the boys are partial to their liquor, especially Van Stiller, who has downed many a dram. For the time being, I shall have to rub my balls, maybe that will warm me. Regretfully, I left my cape behind, else, enveloped in its warmth I might, perchance, avoid this dire cold. I know! I'll make a shadow with my sabre. By the light from the moon I can make a fine shadow on that wall of the cave. On guard, slash, slash, one, two, a parry below and a deep lunge to the fore, like Henri de Lagardère, Count of Nevers. And if I play the hunchback like him and play hopscotch and jump like a clown and throw the stone and hide my hand, perhaps then I won't feel the cold, I'll curl up here in the cave. They say that the boys come to these caves to bonk, as they're so dark. They reek of stale urine. The police are never far from here for they say that La Llorona appears and madness stalks the air. But the Corsaire has ruined everything, he has made no appearance and here I lie curled up to keep out the cold. And when day dawns? What then? And the sun rises over the sea, 'life is more pleasurable, on the sea I love you much more, with the sun, the moon, the stars, on the sea all is joy, for a shell is our shelter'. Damned Corsaire! I should have brought my overcoat to cover myself. The sun rises earlier over the sea and the police will start to patrol the Cerro del Carmen so the boys will not be able to get through and I, alone with just my few trusted friends, will not be able to attack the 4th Precinct. But what if The Ray should be shipwrecked? That Van Guld is a bastard. If he had got wind of it he would have sunk the boat with cannon fire. Just one volley and not even a shadow of the little boats would remain. The worst is that the boys from Las Tortugas will blame the death of the Corsaire and Olones on me, especially Morgan, who is such a great friend of theirs. Then my luck will really have run out, for they will pursue me to the ends of the earth. Especially now that Morgan is the friend of the Queen of England. What can that bright light be? God, don't shine it into my face, it was not I who killed the copper, it was his fault. I didn't want to fire, but he was going to call the patrol car and my car was crammed with propaganda. He told me, you're carrying propaganda, you're finished, so I had no alternative and bang! I shot him straight between the eyes to avenge my friend. Let go of me, do you hear me, or I'll call the Black Corsaire and he's my trusty friend. Take that light away from my face. Can't you see it's hurting my eyes."

"Wake up, it's late. You fell asleep in the car and I went and knocked back a couple of drinks at Alicia's. Do you remember her? Wake up, it's gone six and you've got to get to the airport."

Bloody hell! I fell asleep and it's already light. This swine left me asleep in the car all night. God, my neck hurts. It must have been all twisted like a spring. How could he have been so stupid? He didn't stop to think that it only needed a patrol car to pass and the cop to see me asleep in the car for all hell to let loose. I've slobbered everywhere. I must have slept for about five hours. I'm all confused. I feel sick. It was a massive pissup and now I've got to drive to the airport. We've got through the night without anything happening. He's all red in the face. It's a wonder he didn't suffocate. I didn't realise I'd left the car hermetically sealed. I'd better not say a thing, he must be mad as hell. Brooom, brooom, from 2nd Avenue I'll reach La Aurora airport in five minutes and then I'll be rid of him. My gun's left a mark on my chest, I slept on top of it, it's marked me here on the side by my heart, where I carry it, in the last five years it has been my only faithful companion. I ought to give this thoughtless berk a damned good punch. How could he leave me asleep inside the car? It's the first time in years that I've slept so soundly. Just five minutes more and I'll be free of this coward and I shan't stop 'til I reach "Mexico oh my belovèd, should I die far from your charms, tell them that I only slumber and carry me back to your arms". I wonder if the cash I filched from the Section funds will last out. When the boys find out that I've disappeared, they'll set up a revolutionary tribunal and condemn me to death. There'll be two trials. Anyway, I'm never coming back. I asked for leave over and over again. I needed to rest, I couldn't take it any more, and they always came back with the same old story: you are indispensable, comrade, and me with my nerves shot to pieces, never able to really sleep, just a couple of hours nap and back to transporting all that shit, distributing propaganda to the coast, the highlands, the mountains, my knuckles rigid, gripping the steering wheel, the machine gun cocked on the seat beside me, terrified that all the police in the country were after me. I COULDN'T TAKE ANY MORE. I was a nervous wreck, when I saw that he'd fallen asleep I said to myself I'll go into Alicia's on my own and, if a patrol car finds him asleep and there's any trouble, I'll say I didn't know he was there, that he must have got in at some time or other when I was drinking and that I don't know him from Adam. Well, here we are on the last stretch. Hincapié Avenue. What a stupid name. 'Hinca-pié' – foot of an Inca. What bloody Inca? Atahualpa? No it was Moctezuma. Who cares? All those Indians are the same. Load of wankers. I want to watch this prat's face when we pass the Airforce Base. I'll take out my machine gun just so he can see it and he'll think I've gone round the bend. Another five hundred metres and we'll be at Aurora airport. PanAmericanannouncesitsnextflight. We're here. At last we're here.

"Well mate, we're here."

"Right, we're here. Thanks for everything mate, really."

"No. It was nothing, you know that. That's what friends are for. Drop me a line, do you hear?"

I can't believe it. I've got a lump in my throat. How could I have left him asleep in the car? They could have caught him and he'd never have got out of it alive. What a shite one can be when one's afraid. It was a lousy thing to do. I'll never forgive myself. We should have spent his last night having a good time drinking together.

"Give me the key to the boot. I'll get my suitcase out."

He looks old. Old and paunchy. After a night on the tiles he looks ten years older. He didn't treat me so badly, really, he drove me around all night. Maybe I will write to him.

"Here mate. Have you got enough dough for the first few months? Look. Here's fifteen quetzals. Maybe it'll come in useful."

"Thanks mate. I'll go and get my stuff."

Bang! The car door. He always slams it like that. One day it'll come off in his hand. I've given him all my reserve cash for the month, but it doesn't matter, he's my friend, when we got drunk for the first time it was together. And I've got a future ahead of me. What's he got? He's going to have a rough time in exile. So what do fifteen quetzals matter? He's a great mate in spite of everything. He's given me his last few notes. He always keeps the odd one or two hidden away in his wallet for emergencies, like an old miser. I know him like the back of my hand. He's a good mate. Oh God I'm going to cry, like a great poofter. He was the only one I could always turn to, always rely on. Who cares if he's got old and fat and cowardly? What does that really matter?

"Here are your keys, mate. Look after yourself. Say hi to Chayo. I'll write you. Bye mate."

"Bye mate, look after yourself. Write me, do you hear?"

3

THE LAD

1966

Bitter liquor: molasses: caramel: malt vinegar: water: firewater: rot-gut: hooch; booze: A dance through baroque palaces filled with clouds weighing less than a glance. Noon-day transparency: blue morning suffused with honey. On the clouds sea shells of all sizes in pastel pinks, blues, greens. The smallest: pretty: delicate: set in ivory boxes and at the bottom of each little box the dancer spinning to the music. Always her: the ivory box full of semen, of shells reeking of the piss of drunks. Soaked in piss, seized, jailed, broken, arrested for an act of folly, beaten: squeal from an informer, punch from a grass, pistol whipping from a soldier: stoolies, narks, killers, bastards.

He was looking at the light, aligned carefully, vertically. The light that filtered through the bars was burning his eyes. Light from the long alley, misty, damp, silent, stinking of old food, of dried shit, of congealed blood. With the background music from the bar ringing in his ears he took a few steps and received the first blow in the face, frantic, insulting, humiliating, agonising.

A second punch filled his mouth with blood. The taste of blood is like liquor, it scrapes the throat and the larynx, becomes molten lead in the oesophagus falling to the stomach like a torrent of lava: gastritis: acidity: diet: ulcer: major trouble. From the first drink he began to see crazy visions. He'd never drunk hard liquor before, this was the first time. All because of the stupidity, demands, pressure, obligation, imposed on them by Rat: / we've got to celebrate the end of the exams / Cooked tripe in a filthy bar reeking of drunks' piss, beer fermented in rats' bellies, puke in every corner, old snacks covered in cobwebs hidden beneath the tables, in the corners, in the doorway. Rat, small, sly, black thing that ran between your feet, that stood on two stout legs, who got pissed from the age of twelve, who led us by the nose almost by force. The blow made him stagger more than usual, he felt that the blood was going down down through his whole intestine, burning his rectum, his colon; his anus closed automatically sphincterised. I can take it. Even if they go on beating me like this with all their strength, with all their hatred, with all the zeal of their hands, feet, rifle butts, I can take it. Where did I end up? In a cheap bar. This is where I'll disappear. The famous disappearances of Easter Week when Rat began to drink: he disappeared into a bar, his mother into the church, and his father into the brothel: text book cases: twelve years old. The second blow didn't hurt so much, his head was numb, his skin was numb, they forced him out of the bar at gunpoint, his head began to spin, the alcohol didn't taste so strong, he assimilated it better. Anyway, it wasn't a blow from a pistol butt, it was a punch. His lip began to swell. We must be fools to let him order us around like this, pressurising us here, forcing us there: Rat isn't one of those who commands, he isn't even any good at fighting, but he's a scoundrel, a bastard with the gift of the gab and dead persuasive / men, real men, drink liquor / I'm falling, this is my third glass and I'm falling off the chair. What a lousy dump! God knows how he gets to know these shitty dives. "Los Gavilanes Bar." Damned rodent, perverter of adults: he pushed the swing door of the bar with all the certainty of an expert, a connoisseur and greeted everyone confidently. A load of foul-smelling drunks, bearded hippies, eyed us, mistrusting, distrusting, like they were looking at the cops: grasses: fuzz. A long-haired tart served us what Rat ordered / a bottle of Indita rum and a plate of pork scratchings / At a first quick glance, half nervous, half bold, not wanting to get a real eyeful by staring but, nevertheless, fancying my chances, I thought she was a bit of all right. Nice arse, small tits, quite tasty. As the booze hit me, I saw her better: thick moustache and two or three bristles on her chin and skinny legs, like on the pork scratchings. She began to rub against my chair, randy, abusive. I was dead nervous. Then she got bold, rubbed her pubes against my shoulder. That was when all hell was let loose. A hard feverish packet made me rise from the chair and I landed him a good sock to the jaw, pork scratchings, three hairs and all, lousy Indian snout, sodding queer, bloody madhouse. Now I'm going to fall. My head's spinning: like the big dipper. It all went wrong and I can feel the vomit rising. This is the School of Medicine, at least it looks like it. Now I really am falling, don't worry boys, I can take it, don't hold me, I won't say anything. The blow the soldier gave me at the bar door really threw me. Now I couldn't feel my chest or my ribs. The soldier: Indian bastard: Mayan face: had the punch of a mule, the kick of a mare in season, each pistol blow made the earth sway. How does he make the earth move like that? The clouds changed colour, pink, light blue, white, violet. He was hitting me as if all his sex, his life, his soul were in it / Communist bastard / Everything began to go black, black like his mouth, he didn't stop hitting me and cursing me / Communist bastard / Everything black, black, deep, deep. I seemed to be floating in a tunnel of sound. A hollow sound that was unfamiliar to me, that seemed like an interplanetary sea. I felt my body squeezed and gelatinous, deep husky voices came from who knows where: sometimes moans and contractions shook me all over. The sea of time, space, infinity, ejaculated calm into my time tunnel, my secret dark enclosure. It was almost always calm there. I was alone, completely alone but at peace. Sometimes for fun, I would kick the walls of my alabaster sphere. It was the strangest place that I have known. Everything sounded like a bell that was hollow or made of platinum or of salt and from time to time the whole area was bathed in a viscous, creamy white, aseptic, odourless liquid that was accompanied by moans, peristaltic movements that made me nauseous, little cries of pleasure, long deep, spasmodic, animal cries that disturbed my silence. I don't know when the noise finally settled into my silence. An unaccustomed touch, a prolonged moan and a hollow voice / easy now, señora / took me from my peace. I suppose the noise and the handling enraged me and I began to kick out furiously. Then came the worst part, because my sphere became angry and started to push me out, to expel me, offended, incensed, violent. Him hitting outside and me inside until I dug my heels into the walls that contained me / There's a problem, señora, nothing serious, just that the baby isn't coming in the normal way, head first, it's coming feet first. We'll have to use forceps / Really they wouldn't ever have got me out, but some shiny polished tongs came to the help of my sphere and seized my legs. It was all over. I fell into space and began to turn, to shout, to shriek, to bellow with rage. I've been doing that ever since. Afterwards they threw water in my face, on my chest, on my feet, on to my whole body: whilst an immense deformed being shrieked / it's a boy, a male, another man in the family. You're not much of a man, two or three drinks and you're pissed, lift him up boys you're not much of a man, you're not much of a man, two or three blows and you faint, why did you get into all this? Hit him harder, it's a boy, a little male, congratulations señora / In this new place, full of unknown beings, began the solitude and the prodding, rough things that they passed over my face and body, strange instruments that they put into my mouth so I'd suck the viscous liquid, their hands on my face / wake up, wake up, we've got to get you home / and the water on my face. The sudden, cold, wet contact of the jet of water made me open my eyes, it flooded my nostrils drowning me; they had me lying over a fountain and the jet was falling straight on to my face. I tried to sit up but I couldn't. I didn't have the strength, my head was spinning and the liquid was going up my nose, I felt that my throat was blocked and I was choking. I was desperate, something hot was rising from my stomach / So young and look at the state he's in / voice of some religious old bat: in the distance: someone talking in the distance: straight out of that

Neruda poem: blasted pious old bag / So young and so drunk / At least I wasn't dead. I wasn't drowned, I could hear the fat-arsed, censorious old biddies criticising me. (Someone singing in the distance and she's not with me.) That poem again. I began to come round / I know that fountain, it's not far from my jail, so we must be near the Avenida Centroamerica and 16th Street / My head was rolling, dancing, leaping, spinning like a Ferris wheel, like a roundabout at the fair; I couldn't stand up, the water was forming puddles and my clothing was soaked, the stench of the puddles was getting more rank, it reeked of drunks' piss, a light began to infiltrate high above me, a carefully aligned light, incomplete, divided into strips. I tried to sit up but my body was burning, aching, shivering. They had beaten me all over, there wasn't a single part of my body that didn't hurt. Once again the viscous sensation in my cheeks, when I stuck out my tongue and felt the bitter taste I knew everything / Maya with his rifle butt / I tried to drag myself towards the bars, but I was tied hand and foot, always that feeling of being tied hand and foot, when I gave her the first kiss I knew that we were alone, that there was nobody around, that her grandmother had gone to church and her grandfather was in the rear courtyard and that she wanted it, but still I felt tied hand and foot. I dragged myself to get to the light. But she was my cousin (your children will turn out like pigs, with big heads and bulging eyes) and fear tied me, immobilised me, stopped me from taking her, from possessing her. She put her hands on my shoulders flirting with me, my instant erection stopped me, I had to fuck her, I couldn't stand it any more, I tried to squeeze one of her tits, I lifted my hand slowly but it was tied, then I dragged myself slowly towards the bars of the cell, I was beginning to feel sick again, the miasma that was emanating from the piss started to drive me back into the tunnel, I could hear nothing, my head was hollow, full of worms which began to crawl into my nostrils, into my ears, into my arse, into my eyes, they began to block out the light, the earth full of worms was falling all over my body, I tried to cry out and nothing came from my mouth, a pressure on my abdomen was silencing me, was stopping the sounds on my tongue, my cries grew faint, were lost in the silence. Gradually I was retreating into my vacuum, calm descended upon me, a vibration came from deep within me, from down in my abdomen, from my belly, from my stomach, perhaps from my colon, heat was rising up through my intestines and was beginning to burn my throat, my larynx was full of bubbles that were fighting to escape, from within came belches that tasted of alcohol, of milk, of piss, of shit, I couldn't breath any more and my eyes began to water, I could no longer contain the eruption, from my mouth poured a torrent: lava / Bloody hell lads, what a great puke, it almost went on my trousers / He's got that shit all over me. How disgusting! / Wash yourself down in the fountain / Look how they've left the trough of this fountain, we get our water for cooking from there / Call a copper / Those boys are pissed / Take him straight home / Help me to lift him / God this bugger's heavy / Look ... tunnel, voice, half-digested pork crackling ... Take me home and leave me at my door / The tunnel lengthened, shrank, had neither beginning nor end, the lights of the Avenida del Cementerio began to glitter with an unaccustomed velocity, my eyes filled with shadows, with pink and blue seashells, that began attacking my hands trying to bite them. Shells and ivory boxes were falling all around, I pushed them away from my body and played with them, a pair of breasts was calling to me from the bottom of the smallest box but the multitude of shells that were raining down prevented me from squeezing inside to fondle and suck them. The shells filled with blood, with mud, with vomit, then poured out their contents on to me, bathing me, until they were immaculate once more, between them they lifted me on high and raised me to the sun, which fractured into a myriad miniature suns and the stars shattered into millions of refulgent shards that penetrated my brain one by one, invaded my veins and strummed on my nerve chords producing a deep pain that swept through me from head to toe and back again. Excruciating roller coaster. When the first blow smashed my head the light over the bar seemed to shatter. All I felt was Efi beside me firing, that was the last thing I saw amidst the splinters of blinding light that were penetrating to the marrow of my bones, I felt myself falling again / Hold him tight, he's slipping out of my hands / We're almost there. But there's a lot of light round here

/ Yes the old bat's going to see us / worse if she's standing in the doorway waiting for him / Get a move on / The sounds weren't reaching me, I could only guess their voices, their murmurs. I hadn't heard anything for ages. Only a dull intermittent whistling, I had forgotten that sounds existed, had forgotten their texture, their tones, their intensity, their modulations. I didn't know what ears were for any more. Perhaps the first blows had ruptured my eardrums. Perhaps that bloody Maya had left me stone deaf. Or perhaps it was the punches from Napo or the beating they gave me with the hose in the solitary room with the one single light. The light began to filter in slowly, fearfully, through the cracks, stroking them, fingering the bars and the urine on the floor. The light felt no revulsion. But the sounds didn't dare to enter the enclosure full of viscous liquid. There, you didn't need sounds, nor lights, nor parks, nor bars, nor her breasts. There it was all peace, solitude and eternal soothing, calming, beneficent darkness. Damned forceps that force me from my alabaster sphere. Now the void and this silence that crushes my eyes and my throat. Don't speak, you don't need to say anything, just hold me in your arms and kiss me. Me, tied hand and foot and her blue eyes boring into the very depths of my nerves. I felt her whole body clinging to mine hurting me, exciting me, rousing me to erection, making my blood race, then I broke the bonds and blood began to gush from the liquid furrows that the ropes had cut into my wrists, my body began to ache, especially my lower belly and my balls. I had come. I looked at her timidly, ashamed, not daring to say a thing, doing nothing, quiet, stiff like my trousers on which the semen was beginning to dry. She didn't realise what had happened. I felt disgusted. I moved to unstick my penis from my underpants. The cold came through the bars of the cell and I untied my feet. I stood up. I was saturated, soaked in urine, reeking of piss: piss. Water was flowing in and out of my entire body, beyond my control. The water – urine flooded the cell. Each time I lost consciousness they doused me in it to bring me round. The warmth of the urine began to infiltrate my ears, my skin, my eyes, but it was silent or I was unable to hear what it said. Urine doesn't speak or perhaps I don't understand its language, or what's worse, perhaps that bloody grunt Maya has left me stone deaf for life. Maybe it's because it's very early or very late or because I've had it, or because there's nothing around me and the earth is beginning to fall on to my mouth, filling it with fistfuls of tears, or because those buggers didn't hold me up properly and dropped me when we got to my place or perhaps because in the tunnel there were no sounds or because Maya broke my eardrums or because my mother is going to shout at me when I get home drunk and I don't want to hear her or because when I gave her the first kiss and I came I didn't hear anything or because when I was coming on her an intensely pleasurable heat invaded my body, or because finally I was not born to hear. The fact is I've heard nothing for years.

4

BOOZER

1942

Granny always takes a bath early. I heard her get up a little while ago and go into the bathroom. I've been all excited since last night. She's going to take me to the pictures. To the matinée at the Palace. I've got to get up soon so that Mama can give me my present, and my aunty too. I wonder what I'll get because they didn't even want to give me a piñata and today's my birthday and I'm five. They haven't been a bit nice to me. They said we're only going to give you a few little presents because we're in Holy Week and it's a sin to have a party. I'd hoped they'd get me a piñata so my friends could come and play, but no way. Why did my birthday have to fall on Easter Tuesday? It's real bad luck. From the moment she gets up Granny starts singing. Why can't she sleep after six o'clock? The last time when we were wrestling on the sofa I asked her about it, she laughed and told me that old age spoils everything. I don't think she's so old, she's still young enough to beat me when we fight / I can't sleep more than six hours my lad, I'm old now and I wake up early to pray / Why is she always praying? Does she have lots of sins? I don't think so, she's good, she buys me things, she brings me sweets and she takes me to the pictures. Today she's going to take me to see Jesus of Nazareth. Yesterday she showed me the poster. I read it for ages and ages, finally I made out what it said: José Cibrián is Jesus of Nazareth. How can that be? How can Jesus be José Cibrián? However much Mama explained it to me, I still couldn't get it. Jesus is in the church and now he's become another man / He's an actor / Mama says. The only good thing is that José Cibrián is more handsome than the Jesus in the church. Now it turns out that he's in the cinema. That's the only bad thing. Whenever we pass the picture house there's always a load of people going in or coming out. I can never see the people it's so dark. What I don't get is how Jesús Cibrián can be over there if Jesus is in the church. How does it work? What can he be doing in the cinema? He won't be able to perform any miracles there. I was so excited I could hardly sleep last night. Mama came to bless me three times / Go to sleep darling, it's very late. In the name of the Father the Son and the Holy Ghost, Amen / She made me recite three I Believes, that's the prayer at night, the worst thing is it's very long, not like the Our Father or the Hail Mary, those are really short. I have to do the Our Father in the mornings when I wake. In a little while Mama will come in and make me pray. I'm fed up with all this praying, all day and every day. I think Sundays is enough, more than enough. But Mama's very stubborn. I know all the prayers by heart already but she's stubborn and insists I recite them all day and every day. The only one that doesn't stick in my mind is the I Sinner, its long and hard, it's confusing. But the one that really gets me all on edge is the I Believe at night. What a funny word that is, edge. Sometimes Granny uses it for one thing and then other times Mama uses it for something else. The other day when I was standing by the door there was a tremor and Granny shouted at me get away from the edge come into the middle of the courtyard because the wood's very old and it might fall on you. I didn't understand a thing but I ran out before the edge could fall on me. Everything was shaking and I was scared. The other day when my friends came to play and we were playing Off-Ground Touch Mama came in and shouted boys all this noise is driving me right to the edge. I almost pulled her into the courtyard so that the edge wouldn't fall on us, but I was already dead, I'd just got caught and they'd tapped me on the back three times: / one, two, three releaster / and when they grab you and they tap you three times and they say one two three releaster it means you're a dead man and you can't move until the game is over: that's Off-Ground-Touch and Mama simply doesn't understand the rules, she absolutely insisted on me moving and getting out of the living room / Look what you've done to the armchairs, your granny's going to come in and get cross. And the worst of it is it's me she tells off not you. Clear off, you're driving me mad, you've got me all on edge / Really, I don't understand them, I just don't understand those words, they always get me confused. Whenever I ask her anything, Mama says when you're a big boy you'll understand. But the I Believe gets me all on edge. The Hail Mary doesn't. It's the shortest and I can say it in two ticks. That's the one I have to do at midday. Now Granny's singing. Whenever she turns on the shower and the water starts to splash like it was raining, she starts singing. It's always the same song, I know it off by heart / Ramona, hear my song of love, Ramona, have pity on my pain / such an ugly name for a woman, Ramona. Ram-ona, Rat-ona. It's even an ugly name for a man, and for a woman it's worse. The only thing I like about the song is the music, it's lovely, it's like another song Granny sings; I can't remember the words because she sings it softly and I haven't listened carefully, she sings that one at night when she comes back from work, I think it's called Alejandra. Now that's really a pretty name, it sounds like big stones plopping into water. Alejandra sounds like the band sounds in Centenario Park on Sundays. That's where I heard it. Granny takes me there on Sundays. At three o'clock all the musicians go into the Concha Bandstand with their green uniforms and the things they play and, after a little while, they're blasting away. Then they play Alejandra, I look askance, (what a funny word, my aunt taught me that one / You mustn't look at people askance you must look at them straight in the face), I look askance at Granny and she squeezes my hand. I see her eyes go all shiny and she murmurs the words of Alejandra. But the morning song is Ramona, what lovely music, it's like a heap of flowers, even with Granny's shrill voice it sounds pretty. She's already started to shout, the water must be falling on her big titties, the other day she was getting dressed and I went in and she had her titties out, she didn't see me and I stood in the doorway having a look at her, I felt a sort of cramp in my tummy or lower down. Now the song's started / Ramona, hear my song of love, Ramona have pity on my pain / her eyes go shiny when she sings that one too. On Christmas Eve when we've eaten loads, really late after the midnight tamale, when I'm nearly falling asleep, she and Mama hug each other and weep and sing Ramona together, my aunty just watches them really really seriously and then afterwards her eyes go all shiny and she runs out of the dining room / oh Mother, you two are the limit / then my granny and Mama both cry together, they hold each other tight and they hug me really hard, they squash me against their titties and sing at the top of their voices ever so sharp / Ramona, hear my song of love, Ramona have pity on my pain / Granny's stopped singing now, she's going to come out of the bathroom and Mama's going to come and get me up. What a hassle, she always comes and gets me up when I'm getting sleepy. Why doesn't she come before? Before, I lie thinking and thinking, I'm not a bit sleepy, I hear Granny get up, go into the kitchen and light the stove, she just blows on the embers that stay hot all night with a bellows made of cornhusks, then she throws on a few coals and starts to blow and blow, the ashes fly and fly like grey dust, then she puts the coffee pot on top and goes off to take a bath. Now she's out of the bath. I'm going to get up and see what the outfit looks like that I'm going to wear for the first time today. There's no way they're going to dress me as a girl. Yesterday, the men started appearing on the street dressed like girls, all in purple. I asked my aunty why they dressed like that and she told me that they were penitents who have to carry Jesus because it's Holy Week and that's why they wear those long purple skirts. I think they look like girls with those long skirts that come right down to their ankles and their hoods with the point behind. Just like girls. But my new costume's a real man's outfit. A jacket and trousers in blue, just how I like it. Granny took me to buy the material and she bought the one I liked, a really pretty blue. Last night they brought the outfit here, the tailor on the corner made it for me. I'd been going and trying it on for days and it fitted me like a glove: but it was only tacked. Last night they brought it, but Mama wouldn't let me put it on / You can't wear it until tomorrow, it's late now so what's the point? / that's why I couldn't sleep. She doesn't understand. Did she think I was going to wear it outside? I only wanted to see it on me in the mirror. It's got short trousers, that's how I like them. My aunty bought me the socks. Now those she did let me try on. They're very long and checked and made of wool. They come right up to the knee. They look lovely on me. I've never had any as pretty as that before. Mama bought me the shirt and the shoes. She wouldn't let me try those on either. I could only try them on in the shoe shop / Up to the ankle young man / Mama said to the shop assistant. The man just looked at me. They're black and shiny with black laces / High, madam? / Yes, little patent leather boots / The old guy fitted them on me and made me walk on a purple carpet. Good, Granny's combing her hair now. She let's it down, it comes right down to her bottom, and then she begins to comb it. Gosh, it's long. She combs from the roots down to the tips to get rid of the knots. The drops of water drip and drip on to the floor. She does it for half an hour until it's dry. Doesn't she ever get tired, I wonder. Afterwards, she starts to plait it. It must be very hard to make plaits. When she's combing, she doesn't sing. She just looks at herself in the mirror, swishes her hair from side to side, and combs and combs for ages and ages until it's dry and she's got all the knots out. After that she starts to plait it. First, she divides her hair into two parts, then she makes a parting in the centre and divides each of the bunches into three. Then, she grabs one of the bunches and begins to plait, she passes the strands one over the other over and over again until the three make a kind of rope and her mop of hair starts to become a tight neat braid and you can see the three strands all interwoven in it. Now I'm getting sleepy and the sun's right up. When she does it wrong she undoes it all again and starts to comb it through to get it smooth. What patience! Then she starts the plait again. What a bore! And every day it's the same. I think that's Mama coming to get me up now that I'm starting to get sleepy. I'm going to pretend I'm asleep. Last night I had a very ugly dream, I dreamed that Jesus unnailed himself from the cross and grabbed a big stick and was hitting José Cibrián and Granny and all the people were running away like they do when they leave the cinema in a big crowd. Jesus was naked and his willy was all bare because the cloth which hid his willy had fallen down and he came out of the Palace and went running all naked and covered in blood up 6th Avenue, chasing José Cibrián whose head was also bleeding from the blows, after that my Granny grabbed me by the hand and her head was bleeding too and Jesus's willy was swinging from side to side, it was huge and bare like the dirty old man who was peeing on the post on the corner the other day. I think I woke up sweating and crying, but I reckon I went back to sleep then because I don't remember what happened after that. Here comes Mama to get me up. What a hassle! But I'd better get up quickly 'cos Granny might change her mind and not take me to the pictures. There's always lots of light when she opens the door. She can't do it like other people, little by little; no, she's always got to bang the door and open it suddenly so the bright light hurts my eyes. Afterwards, I go on seeing little stars and yellow shadows and it's very hard to make her out. I can only see her shadow against the light. It's always the same, here she comes with that boring old prayer / Ave María Purísima, in the name of the Father, the Son and the Holy Ghost. Good morning, darling / I'd better go on pretending to be asleep while she blesses me and gives me my kiss. I wonder if Granny has put the water on to heat 'cos there's no way I'm bathing in cold water. I'll throw a big tantrum rather than freeze in that cold water, even if I don't go to the pictures. Anything they like, but they're not going to bath me in cold water. No way! / Have a happy day, my little prince. Wake up and receive your hug / I'd forgotten that they all have to give me a hug. But it's going to be difficult for my Mama with that big belly she's got. How big it's got. And when I ask her what's the matter with her, she asks me if I want another little brother. What's that got to do with it I wonder? She must be ill, that bump's not normal. Oh well, it's her problem, she can give me my hug even though she's all swollen up. Anyway, she won't carry me. She hasn't carried me for days, she says she can't now / Can't you see I'm very fat / Always some excuse. Anyway, I don't care two hoots if she carries me or not, because my Granny carries me when I want and we have little fights and play tug of war. We always tie in the fights. Sometimes she gives in, I climb up on to her big belly I put my knees on her arms and I say do you give in and she says yes, then I jump on her belly and I shout I won. But in Bumpsadaisy she beats me, with each bump on the bum she bowls me over and she shouts bump bump bump, beat you, beat you. Then she lifts me up off the floor and she gives me a kiss and she carries me. So it doesn't matter if Mama can't carry me any more because of that great big belly she's got. What I don't like is that she's always crying. Why ever does she cry so much? / Happy Birthday my little darling / I love it when she hugs me like that but I don't like how she's always crying. She cries at everything, even when she's singing she cries. I really don't understand that. When I sing I feel happy. There's a song that I like best of all and which makes me all warm when I sing it / come on spotted cow, don't be stubborn, have you got a date with the little white bull, moooo / when I go moooo at the end I can feel like bells in my head. But Mama cries even when she sings. She always cries with the same song and she's always singing it, I even know it by heart / Love, love, love, born of God, for we two, born of the soul / Whenever she's in the washroom scrubbing the clothes she starts singing it softly, afterwards her face is all soapy from wiping her cheeks with her hands covered in soap. She ends up all smeared. Now it's my birthday, she shouldn't be crying. She ought to be happy and singing without any tears. I've got to get up right away if I want to go to the pictures / Good morning Mama / Poor thing, always crying, I hope she'll take my pyjamas off fast because I want to do a wee wee / Is my water hot yet Mama? / Yes your Granny put it on to heat up early / Dress me quickly Mama, I'm going to the pictures with Granny / well let me take off your pyjamas then and you can go to the toilet / she always notices. Why is she laughing now? I don't understand big people. When they should be serious, they laugh, and when they ought to laugh, then they

cry. They're like words, they confuse me / Come here, I'll put
your sandals on so you're not walking around barefoot / the
water always makes my willy tremble. When it comes down here
over my tummy, warm and delicious, I feel a little shiver in my
willy. And in my bum too. When the water goes down over my
back and trickles in between my buttocks I feel a little tremble
all over my body. The warm water's delicious. That's why I like
it. The last time that Granny went out early she didn't heat up
my water. Why is it Mama doesn't soap my willy any more? Now
she gives me the soap and tells me to soap it myself. I like doing
it, I feel a little tingling feeling in my little bag down there /
Hurry up and soap yourself, the water's getting cold / On top of
it, she's rushing me. If I told her that I'm taking my time because
I like the tingly feeling, she'd tell me off. She doesn't like me
playing with my willy. The other day, when I was rubbing it in
the wash house and I was doing it really nice, she beat me / You
filthy, disgusting, little boy, that's a mortal sin / she wrapped
my hands in corn husks and set fire to them and afterwards she
took me to church with my hands all bandaged. Her face was
very red and angry / You'll go to hell if you go on doing those
dirty things / Afterwards, when she had to cure the burns on my
hands, she cried. I don't understand anything. Anyway, I don't
tell her I like soaping my willy because she might burn my
hands again. I'd better hurry because it's getting late and they
won't take me to the pictures. Granny must have finished
combing her hair by now. Now she has to put on her girdle. The
other day, I put it on and danced in it, it's like an overcoat on me.
It's got a lot of wires inside. I can't imagine how she can walk
around in that thing. It stretches and it's made of rubber but it's
got strips of iron inside it. Granny says they're whalebones but,
afterwards, I asked my aunty what whales are and she said
they're big animals that swim in the sea and toss water out of
their heads. In the evening, my aunty brought me a picture, she
called it a coloured print, to show me a whale swimming in the
sea and, sure enough, it had a big jet of water coming out of the
top of its head. And it didn't look anything like the bones that
are inside Granny's girdle. I still don't understand. When she
climbs into it, she snorts, she blows, (like a whale my aunty

says), she sweats and she goes all red. A whale in whalebones, that's what I say. She's so fat, poor thing. But she doesn't ask me if I want a little brother. Anyway, what do I want a little brother for? My friends come here to the house to play, so I'm not so alone. She begins by putting her feet into her girdle and then she starts to pull it up, moving from side to side. It always gets stuck on her bum and then all the puffing and panting starts. I had a shock the first time I saw it. I thought it was a penance or a punishment that they'd given her. Afterwards, it made me laugh. I'm already up when she puts her girdle on and I go and spy on her in secret. Mama says it's a sin to spy on people. For Mama, everything is a sin. I'm not afraid of sins any more. Perhaps that's the reason why Mama cries so much, for people's sins, because everybody is a sinner. Now she's going to put powder all over me, it gets on my nerves. I hate it when she covers me in powder as if I were a girl. My friends say only little girls are powdered all over. After bathing me, she puts talcum everywhere, on my arms, on my chest, on my willy, in the crack of my bum, on my legs. She leaves me all white all over. What a horrible habit, she takes no notice when I tell her I don't like it. I told her I don't like it and she said / I don't care. It's so that you'll smell clean / and it makes me sneeze too. Now I've started sneezing. She thinks it's for another reason / You've caught a chill, it's having a bath so early / It's the powder, Mama / How can that be? Talcum's deliciously refreshing. Let's go to your room. I'm going to dress you / Always the same story. Why doesn't she bring my clothes to the bathroom and dress me here? I have to go outside and get cold. That's how I catch a chill. I think Granny's got her girdle on now because there's no puffing coming from her room any more. She must be almost ready. I've got to hurry up 'cos she might leave me behind. She's only got her bra, her petticoat and her dress to put on, / Mama, Granny's ready so dress me quickly / Wait a minute / Who can have put the presents on my bed? As if it were a surprise. I know all about it already. In this parcel are the socks and in that other one the shoes and the shirt. They couldn't wrap up my suit, of course / Happy birthday to you, Happy birthday to you, Happy birthday little darling, Happy birthday to you / They're both hidden, behind the door as if they were little girls. Granny's dressed now and I'm still in my birthday suit. I get a faceful of titties each time they hug me. Makes me want to bite them. I'm almost suffocating under so much titty. I've got to open the parcels. As if I didn't know what's inside. My shoes and shirt are fabulous / Do you like your presents darling? / Yes Mama, but hurry up and dress me 'cos Granny's all set to go / How handsome you look, my little prince, a proper little man / Let me comb your hair darling / we ought to have bought him a little tie / He's very tiny to wear a tie / But he'd have looked smarter / He's cute as he is / I must look like a girl, men don't look cute / Don't go and get yourself dirty when you're having breakfast / It would have been better to dress him after breakfast, he's going to get stained / I'll undress him if you like, Mama / Just put a bib on him and a serviette on his lap and give him his breakfast straight away because it's getting late. The cinema is going to be full and we'll have to sit at the back / At last I'm ready. Mama cleaned my teeth. As if I couldn't do that myself. It was fine when I was a baby, but I'm five now. She even put perfume on me. What a nuisance she is with all those airs and graces. She thinks I'm a sissy. Well, I'm ready at last. Granny's just got to get her coat and we're off. Oh, and her handbag, otherwise we won't have any money and we won't be able to pay for the seats. Mama and my aunty are looking at me like idiots, why are they looking at me, I wonder. As if I were a scarecrow / Look after him Mama / she doesn't need to, I can look after myself. See you! / At last we're off. It took forever. As usual Mama started crying when she kissed me. Why ever is it Mama cries so much?

5

SKINNY DOG

1967

The plane purrs slowly along the runway to the end where it stands drawing out its last breath on the asphalt. The people on the airport terrace grow smaller by the minute. The plane thunders, snorts, revs up for the last time, begins to rotate to get into position for take off. Tanks full of fuel. Ailerons raised. Turbines roaring. Zuuuuuuuuum, zuuuuuuuuum, zuuuuuuuuum, zuuuuuuuuum. Passengers are requested to fasten their seat belts and observe the no-smoking signs.

In this house you don't notice the smell from the tunnels of salt water. Being in another country is like being a snake and shedding your skin, like always having dirty hands, like being in a music box that moves to a different rhythm. I brought the tunnels with me in my suitcase and placed them in the corners of this wretched room on Ángel del Campo, in the Colonia Obrera district of Mexico City. It was the only cheap one I could find. I paid the first rent with the 15 quetzals that Rat gave me when we parted at the airport.

It's a fact that man needs personal satisfaction. He needs to fulfil himself as an individual. Don't start on about scruples and all that rubbish. Stop avoiding the real issue. The individual should function where he is most needed. We are all revolutionaries but not all of us can be combatants, the revolution can be fought in many different ways. Not only by killing. The Party should have understood this at the time and not forced all of us into the armed struggle. It was a colossal mistake to submit to the pressure of the mercenaries. You see, what did it achieve? Now they're all dead, every one of them and we're suffering in exile. Don't talk bullshit. You drunks make me sick, always justifying yourselves. No need to be offensive.

The plane purrs out its last spittle on to the earth. Its noise is like an old old song that I learned as a child: "Pastries! Pastries! There's apple for the priest and lemon for his niece, there's pear for the mayor and one or two to spare. Pastries! Pastries!" But I always carry something with me deep within my skin: the salt water, the green hills that circle and protect Guatemala de la Asunción, the squat settlement, compressed, crowded into the valley, the jade palace in the centre of the main square constructed by a venal, bloody tyrant.[5] The jade palace furrowed by tunnels that connect with the Cathedral and with San Francisco. The dictator Ubico couldn't escape through them on October 20th because Pipo was hiding and wasn't there to show him the way. The shooting in the early hours had frightened Pipo. When the dictator sought him, he was hidden, and so Ubico had to abandon power. Mad Pipo, keeper of the Cathedral catacombs. When we left La Juventud High School, we used to go through the Central Market to pinch fruit. The stallholders shouted at us, cursed us and went purple with rage / You bloody kids / quick nick an apple / Grab them, girls / Call a copper / If I catch you, I'll cut your balls off you little sod / but they never caught us. We had our techniques and good strong legs. After fleeing from the gossipy old birds, we'd creep up to the windows of the catacombs and call out his nickname. The sound went bouncing over the nets of avocados, the baskets of the women traders, the insults of the Indians, and echoed through the ancient vaults: Piiipooo! Piiipooo! The madman hurtled out of his catacombs foaming at the eyes wearing an enormous straw hat that covered almost his entire body, armed with an antediluvian broom / I'll kill you, you bloody kids, I'll kill you / he'd pursue us until old age caught up with him and he fell exhausted. I spent hours tossing and turning in my bed unable to sleep, trying to forget his face distorted with anger. When eventually I'd be dropping off, I'd hear Piiipoooo and once again I'd be fleeing, dodging in between the fruit sellers and their mounds of oranges and aubergines, the second-hand merchants, the cooks and pork-scratching vendors, pursued by that lugubrious howl that reverberated through the catacombs which only he knew, where once upon a time there were, there are, there always will be interred all the bishops of Guatemala de la Ermita, and where lie blanching, rotting, crumbling to dust the bones of the first reactionary tyrant that the country ever had, by whose hand the Liberals were crushed and the bloody apostolic Catholic Church of Rome prospered. Piiiyyyypooouuu, Piiiyyyypooouu ... When I reached 5th Street and 7th ready to collapse into Central Park, Pipo was left far behind, abandoned, a faded blur on the distant horizon of 8th; disorientated, crushed, clutching his great hat in his hand and repeating / Bloody kids, bloody kids /

That's why I took off, that's why I came here into exile, to forge my own life and not go on living on hand-outs. You know that the Party comes to be one's father and mother, you can't shag who you like any more or go to the pub for a quick one, or take a mistress, or even a wife, or children without receiving a critique, your personal performance has declined comrade, how the fuck could it do anything other than decline if all they give you is fifty quetzals to train on? Who can live on fifty? Ah, but when they received a ransom payment the wife of the Head of Finance or Administration appeared in a new dress and all the accessories. But not just that, members of the Party Central Committee had a private car and a chauffeur and one hundred and fifty smackers a month and diplomatic travel for them and their families every year. Yeah, the lazy sods turned up in Moscow or Prague or Havana wanking around at conventions and such like crap. Who wouldn't want to become a revolutionary for a life like that? At least the blokes from the FAR do some real fighting so they've got some right to do it but that bunch of shite are just sucking the tits of the Party machine. You're just saying that because you're against the Party. I got sick of all that crap, that's why I came here. I want to have a wife, children, a career without some arsehole telling me what I have to do. It's easy to say that now, you're just a bunch of bitter, resentful petits bourgeois with chips on your shoulders. Why didn't you complain when you were there? Now you're responsible too. You, because you were Baldy's favourite. Anyway, I'm not responsible for anything. Why should I pay for corn that I didn't eat? Did I handle any cash? Was I a leader? Did I travel at the expense of the Party, or send my family round the world at the expense of friendly parties? Don't come to me with all that crap, everything's rotten. Yeah that's what you can't stomach, not having travelled. That isn't what this is all about. What we have to determine is who is responsible for the defeat, the chaotic rout. That's easy, it's Moscow and Havana.

Central Park is a kind of racetrack for Crazy Horse / Crazy Horse, Crazy Horse / cray-zee-horse, zeehorsey, horsey horsey. Crazy Horse lived in El Gallito in a ramshackle house devoid of windows; in the middle of the big dining room which opened straight on to the street, our equine loon had hung up his hammock. It was there that Equus Manicus slept. When we went past in the mornings on our way to school we used to wake him with shouts of / Crazy Horse, Crazy Horse / By day he carried baskets around the Central Market / Carry your basket lady? Anywhere you like for a quetzal, yes ma'am I'll carry it for you / They always gave him the biggest heaviest baskets because Crazy Horse could really cut it. He was almost six feet six and had a stride of nearly equal magnitude, his baskets weighed a ton and were full of magical things. A modern Pied Piper of El Gallito, he was always pursued by a bunch of kids shouting Crazy Horse, Crazy Horse, Crazy Horse. He'd just look at them surreptitiously out of the corner of one eye surveying them, watching them, eyeing them briefly as he stopped for a second. When he had handed over the basket and received his quetzal he started the race through the streets, his calves swelled, the veins in his neck and forehead distended and as he ran he hollered dementedly, giddyuuupp, giddyuuupp. He sprang over the puddles and the ruts, wheeled round corners like Maquinita. (Maquinita was another lunatic, this time one who thought he was a car. He hung around 5th Street or the Shrine of Guadalupe thrumming like a car, vrooom, vrooommm. He pulled away in first, and after ten metres changed into second, chas chas chas vroomm. When he reached an intersection he let in the clutch, took the corner in first, leaning inwards as if banking with the camber and sounded the horn, beepbeep, beepbeep. He turned right, keeping close to the wall and, coming out of the bend, he changed into third, going happily vrooming off again being a car.) Yep, like Maquinita, Crazy Horse would bend with the basket on his head holding it with just one hand whilst with the other he'd strike himself on his flank, chas chas chas, as if with a whip, like a riding crop on a frisky horse; and, with his mouth, he'd simulate the gallop of a stallion, clip clop clip clop. I almost mistook him for a horse. He had a long thick muscular neck just like one. His cap seemed to perch between two long ears that stuck out of imaginary holes. He had a long protuberant Indian mouth with which he whinnied like a foaming colt. He trotted elegantly on legs with glistening calves clearly visible beneath his trousers rolled up to the knee. When he caught somebody, he went berserk. Woe betide anybody who got caught during the chase. Then Crazy Horse took off the cord he used as a belt and beat him with it; then he tossed him into the basket and began to run through all the streets neighbouring the Central Market. Proud of having caught someone, he reared up like a pure-blood stallion. He trotted, thrust out his chest and spun around. I always wanted to know what Crazy Horse carried in his basket because, after a journey with him, the unfortunate occupant vanished as if by magic from the bunch of kids who endlessly pursued him. Some said that, inside the basket, he kept silver mice that nibbled your willy, others that there were poisoned sweets in there and that those who disappeared were dead. I always thought that he kept light inside the basket, but I never let myself get caught to find out if I'd got it right. Crazy Horse remained engraved on my memory. Years after his demise we were all skating in Central Park and, as I came down the slope on to 7th Avenue and 8th Street, I saw our phantom horse with his basket of greens slowly pawing the ground, trotting majestically, his trousers rolled up over his glistening calves and, in my head, I emitted a long silent whoop of challenge Crazy Horse, Crazy Horse and then I put the wind behind my wheels so he wouldn't catch me.

I left my suitcase on the pavement at the airport exit. I was dizzy. An hour and twenty minutes of the throb of the engine, boring into my brain. Some bloke came up to me / Taxi Sir? / So what alternative did I have? I didn't know which direction to go in, nor which bus to take, or even if the bus went anywhere near the district that they'd mentioned to me / Yes, please / It'll be seventeen pesos sir? / Jesus Christ that's a fortune and I'm flat broke. Well, I've no option / Okay. Here you are / Where to sir? / Colonia Obrera / He eyed me askance, with a suspicious, distrustful look, shitty Indian face, all Mexicans have shitty Indian faces, their Indian blood comes out even in the blond ones, touch of the tar-brush, they can't avoid it, can't conceal it, their slanty eyes can be hidden by their gringo or Italian or German or whatever blood that has been begged, stolen or maintained by dint of adulation and mixing over the centuries, but they can't lose the Indian mouth, it hangs on them like an affront, twisted downwards, like a rope or the flat droopy nose of a turkey that hangs on them as a reminder so they don't get above themselves, so they never forget their place. Suspicious, this taxi driver. And me, squashed, sunk, dejected, rejected, declining, reclining, looking out of the window, surprised, shocked, reading the names of the streets, the bunch of weird names everywhere. Fray Servando, Teresa de Mier, San Juan de Letrán, Niño Perdido ('lost child', who lost what kid?) / Which part of the Colonia Obrera sir? / This 'Sir' business is getting right on my tits. Why can't they say comrade or mate or any other bullshit? They have to add 'Sir' to everything. They've got arselicking in their blood / Take me to Ángel del Campo, if you'd be so kind / We Guatemalans are like that too, guilt-ridden Indians. Kind? Why is he being kind? Kindness my arse! I'm paying this bloody redskin seventeen pesos. The worst thing is he's going to want a tip too. Here they all expect a tip. They're a pain in the arse. The chocolate Indian at the airport kept trying to carry my suitcase as if I didn't have arms, I shot him a look that froze him to the spot / No thanks, I can manage / He stared at me gobsmacked / Okay. Don't be like that. I wasn't going to ask you for any money / I left him standing babbling some bullshit or other / Before Bolívar or after? / What happened before Bolívar? Before him there was this useless bunch of fat-lipped Indians. And after him? The same / I asked you if it's before or after Bolívar Street / Look here's the bit of paper, it says Ángel del Campo, Angel in the Field, between Isabel the Catholic and 5th of February Avenues, number 69. Bloody hell what an address. Well it should be easy to remember Isabel the Pope's tart doing a bit of soixante-neuf with an angel in a field on February the 5th. I shan't forget that in a hurry / It's right here, sir / Stuff the sir bit. He stares at me with his Indian snout anticipating his tip, I just said see yah and grabbed my suitcase. The big green metal door told me everything I needed to know about the place, the sadness, the poverty, the loneliness, the mediocrity, all that was cheap and nasty. There was no bell. I rapped on the door twice with my graduation ring. It echoed, reverberated as if it were totally hollow inside. A few faint steps, shuffling along brought me face to face with an Indian girl. In this country of Indians every one of the buggers is a fat-lipped Indian even at the presidential level where they all burp caviar. What a thought! The door was opened slowly, timidly. An Indian girl peeped out. I christened her La Totoneca. I'm going to give her one.

It's the sodding Cubans who are to blame for the cockup. Why did they have to stick their noses in where it didn't concern them? According to Fidel, he was going to be another Bolívar. Oh yeah! Some Bolívar that bugger turned out to be. He just got a mass of people embroiled and then washed his hands of it all. When he saw it was all going wrong and the gringos tightened the blockade and that no way were the guerrillas going to win then he started to pull out. At the beginning, everything was great, fabulous. Travel, plenty of the readies, R and R in Varadero, months and months of swanning around doing sod all as a tourist in the Hotel Presidente or The Habana Libre. More like the condemned cell you mean. If you like. But, at the end of the month, you went to the Party rep, collected your month's allowance and then it was out on the town boozing, and pulling Cuban birds. After he saw that he wasn't getting what he wanted, the pressure started. He wouldn't take in the relatives of the comrades who'd been killed / They were a burden on the Cuban State / as if they weren't the very ones who had got them killed in the first place. They put on the pressure in the University, in the residences where the scholarship students lived, in the hotels. The Cubans looked at you as if you were betraying the cause because you were studying or resting. They made you feel like a coward and a traitor because you weren't going into combat in the mountains. So what the hell did they offer us scholarships to study for? Remember that when the first students graduated they demanded that they returned home to fight in the mountains. Yes, that's how Pliny and Onion got killed. Only a handful resisted the pressure and beat it to Europe and remained in Paris or in Prague. The other poor sods are pushing up the daisies. Just think about it! Some bloody offer. A real bargain, eh? And right from the start they were sticking their noses into everything. When Blondie, Macho Man and Boxer got to Havana in 1960 they were pushed into it immediately. Yeah, absolutely right, without knowing if conditions were right for armed conflict, without making any prior study, with sod all, they just gave them money and arms and sent them back. It's a wonder they weren't killed there and then. Yeah, well, Blondie and Boxer did get killed. But that was afterwards, several years later when Blondie came back from Mexico and was fighting in the 13th of November Movement. Yeah, right. Poor sod. He was a good bloke, dead brave, had balls, so I heard. Don't change the subject Foxie. You're a right anarchist. You couldn't be from anywhere but the

13th to be such a bloody Trotskyite. I'd rather not be one of the Party apparatchiks. Those blokes are all talk and no substance, just a load of hot air. That's exactly where the problem with the Cubans started. They didn't want any theoretical study, six months training and straight into the mountains as if all that shit were as easy as falling off a log. Yeah, even the girls who'd gone off to study were pulled in when there was no one else. Don't you remember Judy, that gorgeous great raunchy creature that was studying medicine? She was about to graduate and the stubborn bastards sent her off to train and after her giving up five years of her life to study they sent her back to be killed. And didn't that bastard the Indian force all those who were in Moscow to go back too. Ginger, for instance, you knew her didn't you? There's another one who went home only to get killed. Those shites are just like vultures looking for corpses. No. Sharks, more like great whites. Bloody hell you lot, we've nearly finished all the booze, there's only half a bottle left. You've knocked back a bottle and a half. That's why I'm getting so smashed. Stop interrupting. You won't let anybody speak because you don't like us talking about the Cubans, you were one of their supporters. That's not so, what happened is that for years Havana was like Mecca, like paradise to the revolutionaries of Latin America. You fought to get recognition or to get invited to a celebration. Imagine! Lots from my section were utterly traumatised because they didn't get an invite. Macho Man, for instance, is still in shock and resentful because he didn't get to travel to Havana. Whatever those buggers said was what went down. Yeah, even the Party submitted and when the Directorate finally wised up the Cubans had almost destroyed it. Those fucking Cuban bastards ruined everything, didn't they? If they'd not interfered perhaps it would have been a different kettle of fish. Maybe the revolution wouldn't have been put back fifteen years like it was, right? Who knows? What I'm sure of is that they're responsible for all the blood that was shed, all the lives that were wasted, because of their fanaticism, their petit bourgeois desperation. They're a load of arseholes, right boys? I need another drink, all this rage has made me thirsty again. Tough! It's all gone. Okay, let's piss off.

It takes balls to find work in Mexico. I woke up at six, or to be more precise, the roar of the traffic woke me up. Christ, the deafening din started up at I don't know what time in the early hours. I'd landed up in one of the worst areas of Mexico City, two blocks up from the Calzada de Tlalpán and two from the Viaducto Piedad. From dawn onwards the race track started up with its lethal, mind-rending roar, zzzzuuummmm, zzzuuummm zzzzuuummm, zusss, prac, prac, pa, pa, pa, zzzuuummm, gears grinding, clutches shrieking, brakes squealing, horns blasting, patience fraying, maniacs swearing, the Tlalpán train shaking the earth to its core. At six I could stand my exhaustion no longer. Totoneca had been washing clothes in the sink in the passage for two hours. Splish, splish, as she threw water over the sheets with an empty gourd, shicky shicky shicky, the scrubbing of the wet cloth against the stone scrubbing board. When she let me into the hallway yesterday / Good evening, sir, if you please, can I help you / I want a room / I'll go and get the mistress sir / She darted inside to fetch the old bird who owns the place. The old bat emerged. She had a face that could curdle milk. She looked me up and down as if I were a criminal or a lunatic escaped from an asylum. As soon as she heard me speak she demanded my passport. I tried to tell her I was from Chiapas but nothing doing. She wouldn't even let me get a word in. The old crone was wise to everything. So there was nothing for it but to come straight to the point / A double sir / said the old bugger / we don't have any singles so when another guest arrives I'll put him in the other bed / but where, I ask myself / That's two hundred and seventy-five pesos a month with use of bath and shower, you do your own washing / Bossy old bag. Let's see, two eights are sixteen, five eights are forty, shit, twenty-two dollars for a grotty double room, daylight bloody robbery / There's plenty of takers, so if you want it there it is, if not... / did I say anything? / Okay I'll take it / Totoneca helped me make up my mind. From a corner she peeped out at me, half timid, half provocative. She'll do my washing and on top of that I'll bonk her regularly, that way I'll get my money's worth. There she is now in a corner, calmly washing the clothes, occasionally she casts a quick glance towards where I'm sunning myself. The hall door banged behind me as I left. Now, which direction do I take? The first thing I have to do is get to the Immigration Office. It's on Abraham González and General Prim Street. Where the hell's that? What bus goes there? I'd better take a taxi in case I get lost. Anyway I've got to get there whether I like it or not, so I'd better save time and spend a few bob whilst I find my way around the bus routes. Long, endless, in-ter-min-able queues. I had to speak to the Head of Personnel, the Head of Immigration, the Sub-secretary. What a neverending load of crap and the money going like water / you have to fill in a card for an appointment, put your name, profession, nationality, migrant status / mine was interesting / the business that's brought you, what you intend to talk to the official about / so what's the point of talking to him then? Better to write the whole bloody thing down once and for all / and time flying by and the money running out, days and days on end wasted in this damned great house. The solitude depressing, the problems of conscience accentuating, and the government offices getting farther and farther away, multiplying like rabbits. Every day I meet a load of other Guatemalans doing the rounds of the same offices / Hi mate, how's it going, did you get to see the Head of Immigration? Did you get a permit to stay? Boat's calm reply / Yep. Got it. God, you wouldn't believe the difficulties I had getting over the frontier / Little Bear had to sell his gun for four hundred pesos in Tapachula to get here, he had to carry his one-year-old daughter on his back with his wife pregnant and him with kidney trouble, his feet were all swollen and he had to walk forty kilometres and in Tapachula he had to pawn his pistol for four hundred pesos. He came to my house in Ángel del Campo that afternoon after we met at Immigration and all he told me was that he'd been through hell and that his wife was about to give birth and I had to tighten my belt and give him some brass so he could take her to the ABC, that American hospital on the Toluca road, so his wife could give birth and the child would be born a Mexican citizen. Weeks of trudging back and forth before I could get to see the Head of Immigration / By an official accord between my government and that of our friendly neighbouring state, to wit, your government, the Secretary of the Interior on the instructions of our President has resolved not to accept any further political exiles not accredited by his Chancery / Look sir, if I am forced by your government to return to Guatemala I shall be killed but before leaving this country I shall attribute the total responsibility for my death to your government / This being the case allow me to consult with the Under Secretary to the Ministry of the Interior in order to come to a decision in relation to the issue under discussion / and a week passed, one, two, three, four, five, six, seven weeks passed, one, two, three, four, five, six, seven weeks and one, two three, four, cha cha cha boom. Back and forth, up and down, begging and pleading, shouting, demanding, seething, fuming, ranting, abusing, and endlessly plodding, traipsing, hoofing hoofing hoofing it because there's no money left for the bus. On and on and on and on / Look sir, give me a work permit, my situation is really untenable, I've no money left to pay the rent / The Mexican government respects free enterprise and the free contracting of labour but the law is the law. First, obtain an offer of employment in writing, duly signed and sealed by the manager of the company extending to you this offer / vicious, pernicious, malicious circle. The company won't give you a job offer unless you possess a work permit from the Ministry and the Ministry won't issue the work permit if you don't have the offer from the company. Mexican bloodymindedness carried out to perfection. Catch 22 with chilli / The Mexican government is heedful of international treaties regulating the rights of asylum and, moreover, concedes this right, albeit in an anomalous form, but, nevertheless, it does concede it. What more do you want? But we must also respect the internal laws of our country, and so should you. In consequence, obtain an offer of employment and we will give you the permit / Utter pig-head-ed-ness-aaaaarrrrgghhh. Sick of it all, I left. Then I went to Cuba's Latin American press agency to slag off the Ministry of the Interior and to denounce the pressure that the Mexican government was using to starve me to death and thus force me to leave the country. The following day the Head of Immigration received me immediately, if not sooner, and informed me that on the instructions of some lawyer or other he would personally attend to my case and I should sign the document that they had prepared informally to legalise my stay in Mexico (Oh my belovèd, should I die far from your charms, tell them that I only slumber and carry me back to your arms) in which it is stated that having been persecuted and condemned to death by terrorist organisations of the Guatemalan government under the presidency of the Right Honourable Jesús Méndez Montenegro and thereby suffering persecution (blessed are the persecuted for they shall inherit the earth of Mexico fair and belovèd) which put my little life at SERIOUS risk I had to remain in Mexican territory, (how kind, how kind, how frightfully kind) whilst my new immigrant status was being processed. Really to find work in Mexico with these papers takes balls. I got lost three times today. I must have walked like twenty kilometres. This city is frigging enormous, vaster than my vision of the unemployed, jobless, redundant, fired, sacked, dismissed, discharged, severed from work from life. There's no way anybody will commit himself when he casts eyes on these lousy papers / You have to bring us your FH10, these documents have no validity, if they catch you working with these it'll be me that gets it in the neck / I knew it, I just knew it, it's all a big joke / Have you brought your federal tax returns and your cards? / Cards? What bloody cards? Christmas? Birthday? Playing? Up your sleeve? On the table? / If your papers aren't in order / More crap. Order: two tacos and a beer: Order: money draft that never arrives: Order: Law and Order / Your papers must be in order, if not, there's no work / if there's no papers, there's no order, if there's no order, there's no papers, if there's no papers there's no work and there's no work if there's no papers and if there's no work how the hell do I eat and how the hell do I pay for the room in the street where the Pope's tart Lizzy's screwing with an angel in the field? So: I hoof around for twenty kilometres a day. Protein intake: sod all: one meat taco and a coffee every twenty-four hours. I'm training to be a fakir. Every day I discover bones I didn't know I had: a nasty shock that, I beg your pardon, what did you say? / Look Mr Immigration Director, everywhere they say that if I don't possess an FH10 they can't offer me a job because they'd be sticking their necks out (**and he who sticks his neck out gets**

his head chopped off). In addition, the Federal Employment Office can fine them / Always hassling those damned people / But I cannot give you an FH10 unless you change your migratory status / (**birds are migratory, aren't they?**) More and more papers, paperwork, red tape, plodding, tramping, slogging back and forth from office to office: an application to the Secretary of the Interior which / you have to hand in to that office over there / come back in twenty days young man and we'll see if your case is resolved / twenty days? / Well maybe twenty or a little longer, we've got a lot of work on and as you NEVER SHOW ANY APPRECIATION FOR ANYTHING / (**how the fuck can I slip this dumb creep a bribe if I don't even have enough to eat? Christ, why can't he get it through his thick skull. Dammit!**) I know every brick of this lousy corner. I'm at Abraham González and General Prim. The damned military get everywhere even into the street names. I'll never forget these bloody names. Never. Every day in the early morning I do the same round. I enter the building on Abraham and start visiting offices like a berk, all these ruddy pen-pushing mules know me, they greet me, they mess me about, they mock me with their eyes, mental mooners, (up yours, lousy, Mexican faces). At midday after the regulation morning route march I take off along Bucareli. At this hour of the day, everyone's leaving work. Bucareli is thundering. People everywhere rushing, milling, swirling, spilling. Voices shouting, screaming, shrieking, buses roaring, horns blasting, diesel smoke, petrol fumes, foul farts, tacos reeking of rancid fat, gridlocked transport, jammed fast, revving clouds of choking fetid fumes, my exasperation, my exhaustion, everything, everything is here in Bucareli at midday. All this and the sun boring down, burning, broiling, searing, charring. The Excélsior comes on sale and the paperboys race down from El Caballito knocking over anyone who gets in their way. They push me aside and lope off hawking their merchandise, hollering headlines, Excelsior, Exceeeelsiooorrr, read all about it, and I slope off to the Chinese Clock to meet them. On the corner of Atenas, I just about manage to scrape enough together for my meat taco (my supper is a coffee). ATENAS: Athens, with the Colossus of Marussi and

Henry Miller and Ulysses (the James Joyce one, not the other one, because that's dead boring and I never could get to the end of it. I couldn't finish the Joyce one either if it comes to that) and the Paideia which is totally unfathomable and sat on my shelf for years and years because I never could get stuck into it and Alfonso Reyes who thought he was a Greek and was really just a thick-footed striped-panted fat-lipped Mexican Indian and Nikos Kazantzakis (that bloke really is excellent and no bugger has read him at all) and Zorba the Greek, the Piraikon Theatre and the Iliad, now there's a really boring work, and Greek blokes and birds, and that pansy, poofter, faggot, fairy, gay, homo, queen, catamite, Socrates: Athens encompasses all this and more. So much more on the corner of Atenas and Bucareli. I buy my taco and my eyes fall on a huge ham sandwich that a fat guy is stuffing down his throat and my mouth begins to water uncontrollably. Then my brain slips out of gear and I'm stuck there staring, like a loony at the bunch of gannets gorging themselves on tacos full of rank, rancid, charred, infected fat which drips down their chops, gobs, mugs, chins and points south. Then I twig, catch on, get it, that this is a collective ritual, a high mass of the masses of an entire nation in the thrall of the Great God Tacoas. The high priest is the Taco chef: Tacuarnis I: attired in his ceremonial robes: a white apron that covers his chest, his stomach and his private parts. His instruments of sacrifice of the Aztec liturgy: a huge knife and a wooden board on which he chops the meat, slicing precisely with dexterous destruction. His victim, a piece of meat, steak, topside, silverside, belly, flank, sirloin, fillet, rib, neck, entrails etc., etc., etc. His altar: a grill where he browns all the offal, large and medium-sized pieces of foul smelling entrails that this bunch of cretins cram into their gobs: bits of cat, dog, horse, or anything that walks or speaks that he can catch unawares on a corner near the temple: Tacoburgers Inc. The ceremony starts with the arrival of the first of the faithful who orders modestly, cautiously, warily, craftily, two steak tacos with chilli and a mamey juice, please. The ceremony commences immediately / Bring out two steaks! A mamey juice for the gentleman / the sacred magic words having been enunciated, the faithful takes a seat: introit, now he can await the offertory calmly, his guts at peace and his gaze lost in the smoke that ascends from the grill that reeks of the old rank, noxious, putrid, stomach-churning oil which will season the sacrificial offering. With magical ludic movements, the celebrant turns the tortillas, which are browning, and raises the steaks, which he places with virtuosic bravura, dripping, sweating, on to the wood which serves as a chopping block. Now comes the offertory of the sacrifice, he sharpens the great knife and begins to cut. With the blade he chops the meat at Supermanic speed (swifter than a bullet, more powerful than a train), turns it with his left hand time and again until no sign of the meat remains, then he seizes the tortilla violently (pure Mexican machismo this bit), whacks it down upon the wood and with the knife and his free hand (the greasy, filthy left one that he just held his dick with when he had a slash) he lifts the slices of meat and places them in the centre of the tortilla, shakes chilli sauce on to them and folds the tortilla placing it on a small tin plate / Two steaks coming up / Waiter, the gentleman's drink / Now it is the turn of the devotee. The introit has arrived, the communion of the flesh. The communicant, with supreme respect and tact, surveys the sacred dressing languidly, takes it between thumb and index finger, weighs it, surveys it once again, stretches his neck forward so that the grease may not drip upon his clothes, draws back his body lest he become stained at the first bite when the ancient rancid oil spurts from the other end, counts to three (what a lovely little mover, looks like he's doing the conga) and takes a mighty bite. The jet of oil shoots out the other end, but the adherent, forewarned as he is, does not stain as much as his index finger (or thumb). It is a custom, an age-old ceremony / I ate bloody well, mate / He chews with his mouth full, introiting it bit by bit into his enraptured mush. The high priest watches him with a deep cathartic satisfaction and awaits another of the faithful whilst the cash register begins to vibrate / two by two, that's four pesos, sir / Before I realised it, I was standing in front of the Caballito, at the end of Bucareli. After being pushed, pulled, squeezed, fingered and felt up all the way along the Avenida Juárez and doing the same in return I went straight towards San Juan de Letrán and stood on the corner of Article 23 Street for a bit, just thinking. I was weary, exhausted, pissed off, knackered, with swollen feet and backache, still hungry in spite of the taco, defeated, depressed, in need of a slash, disillusioned, desperate and penniless, wondering how I was going to get back to Ángel del Campo. There's no money left for a taxi, nor for a first-class bus, so it's trolleybus or nothing. I try to bamboozle the driver in the crush of passengers but he's got his eye on me and I have to leave my thirty-five cents in the wooden tray. I sink amidst the fetid armpits of hundreds of sour-faced bloody Indians, equally tired, who share my misery.

What we have to do is buy another Titanic (Bottle: botanic: tanic: Titanic: You can really screw up a language if you put your mind to it. I must be pissed to be thinking all this crap.) Yep, I vote for another Titanic. Parrot, staggering, puts on his shoes (whenever he has a few, he takes off his shoes, he's got weird habits this guy) and volunteers to go and buy one. He makes it clear in advance that it's not with his money because he hasn't got any, we have to take a collection. You, how much have you got? I can only put in one peso. Heck, that much! You're overdoing it a bit, aren't you? Well, I haven't got any dosh or a job. Right, I'm in for three pesos, says Blackboard, and carries on with his story. I did eighteen months inside thanks to Monkey but in reality it wasn't his fault. It was the Party's because as Monkey was such a disciplined official they put him into the Central Committee and then out of sheer bloodymindedness thrust him into the leadership of the Resistance. That was the time when we were going to bump off the Chief Justice but it all went wrong, Efi's shooter jammed and we had to beat a quick retreat with all the cops after us in hot pursuit pumping lead in all directions and, when we got to the car to make our getaway, Monkey was sitting there rigid, his hands glued to the steering wheel, unable to move a muscle or start the engine or do sod all. Efi was shouting / Move it Monkey, move it you arsehole. The fuzz are right behind us shooting to kill / But Monkey, paralysed with fear, couldn't move a finger until Pig, firing wildly, hurled open the door and knocked him out of the way. By now the police jeep was coming round the corner. So they couldn't rescue me and I was left lying on the ground with two bullets in the back: here, take a look at these (whenever we're having a piss-up he shows us his scars); I woke up in the police clinic of the 1st Precinct. But even then they hadn't learned their lesson. As a reward for this cock-up they sent Monkey to fight in the mountains and six months later he took off without any warning. He was the sub-commandant of Rabinal and they didn't even find out until he was well away in Mexico. That's why the Party people get right on my tits. They're just bullshitters. Not everybody, you know. There are only two of us left from our group, Whip and me, and if we hadn't scarpered we'd be pushing up the daisies now. There was only enough for a bottle of Palmas. I can't stand that Bacardi crap. But you lads only gave me eleven pesos, I had to put in a peso that I was keeping for my bus fare tomorrow. Let's see if one of you'll come across with it before you go home. Parrot is always such a whinger, so tight-fisted. Come on, stop messing about and pass the bottle, I'm parched, I need another drink. I was lucky the police didn't finish me off and when I recovered from the shooting I was put inside. That's why you're such a villain. You learned your bad habits in the nick. Your trouble is you're just a sodding bourgeois. I don't know what the fuck you're doing here. You couldn't be anything but a Party man, all screwed up, full of petty complexes, always prattarsing around done up to the nines, all theory, spouting bullshit round the University. I remember you, you bugger, you can't fool me, you used to turn up at the Law Faculty in Italian suits with long jackets down to your arse reeking of perfume, you used to talk bullshit in the corridors, about the dictatorship of the proletariat and the class struggle and at the first sign of trouble you were off like a shot. I was joking but if you really want us to have an ideological discussion, no sweat, I'm ready any time. The fact is you're a petit bourgeois who wanted to make the most of the situation, you thought it was going to be all so easy and we were going to get into power in two shakes. Now you're getting personal and if that's the case I'm going to tell you that the only reason you got involved in all this is because you've got a big chip on your shoulder and you feel society owes you something. You don't even know why you got into the fighting in the first place. Why did you join the FAR then? That's none of your bloody business. Listen you, I don't have to explain myself to anyone. Come on lads, calm down. We came here for a chat and to share a few jars not to fight over things that can't be remedied, (such a pacifist, Parrot). The fact is, he's drunk, and he's starting to get offensive. Oh fuck you, Skinny Dog, I could kick your arse, what I just said wasn't because you're drunk but because I'm sick of your middle-class airs of superiority. You're down to eating shit and you still think you're somebody. Now lads, that's enough, that's why we never have any success, we're always fighting amongst ourselves eating garbage whilst the enemy is getting its act together, gaining strength. Yeah, that's why we're here, fucked up, and you never learn, they don't give a toss about you any more. Forget about your organisations, they don't even remember you, you're losing more and more your sense of perspective, you imagine they're still there waiting for you to decide to go back but now there are new people there who've never even heard of you. We're not like that in the 13th of November. When I go back they'll all remember me! Look Fox don't be such an idealist, you're losing all sense of reality. Who's going to remember you in the 13th if you've been here for the last eighteen months totally isolated? Do you think it's the same people? Don't be such a bloody fool, by now all your comrades are six feet under. Wise up! Look here, Chicken, you arsehole, the fact that we're friends doesn't mean I have to put up with all your crap. I'm not going to stand you criticising the 13th because you're nothing but a traitor to the Party and, if you persist, you and I are going to come to blows. Look, Fox, I could smash your face in in ten seconds. Christ, calm down, it's not worth a punch up. No, I won't calm down. All you lot from the Party and the FAR get on my tits. I don't give a toss about any of you, bloody middle-class bastards. Right, that's it, we'll settle this outside. No Parrot, don't you start too, you shouldn't take any notice of Fox. Let's all have another drink. Fuck you, Fox! Get your hands off me or you'll be the first one to get it. God Parrot, I'm surprised at you. I can't believe you're a Marxist. Sod Marxism, sod everything. Come on then Fox. Get your hands off me Chicken, get 'em off, you hear, unless you want me to rearrange your face too. Get off, I said, I'm fed up with Parrot I'm

going to kick his teeth in. Right boys, that's it. Sod off the lot of
you and don't come back here. Every Saturday it's the same. I've
already been warned that if there's any more of this they'll chuck
me out. So piss off the lot of you. That Whip, what an arsehole,
who does he think he is? That he's the only one with a room? Look
at the state you've left my room in, you've broken all my glasses
and look at the carpet, you're all pissed out of your skulls, who's
going to clean up all this mess? The Ogre will be here tomorrow
and when she sees all this she'll chuck me out on my ear. Look at
the neighbours too, they're all standing at their windows.
Tomorrow they'll ask the old bitch to throw me out, so fuck off
the lot of you. Come on lads, let's go.

With Crazy Horse left behind on 7th and 8th I skated on and as
I slowed in front of the cathedral to cross myself I saw before me
a florid face with distinctly foreign features dripping with sweat,
so intensely suffused that his blood seemed to be about to burst
out of every pore of his cheeks. His great belly supported the
basket in which he carried / Pastries! Pastries! There's apple for
the priest and lemon for his niece, there's pear for the mayor and
one or two to spare, Pastries! Pastries! / He'd bought his hat in
his youth in his homeland: France or Switzerland or Germany.
Qui sait? Wer weiss? He was always surrounded by a posse of
sweet-toothed kids. He seemed to attract children with his
songs, his honey, his big belly and his white beard. He was the
Santa Claus of the pastry world. Five cents a pastry. When the
sun was setting and the pairs of skaters began to hold hands
and slip away along the side streets of the park, the Pastry Man
would close up his stall, put his basket on his head, fold up his
trestle and set it on his shoulder / Pastries! Pastries! We had
apple for the priest and lemon for his niece, pear for the mayor
but there's nothing now to spare. Pastries! Pastries! / The
youngest of us, those who didn't have a girlfriend yet, sat
together round the edge of the park watching the honeyed orb
slide into the warm dark basket of the night.

I'd been going back and forth to Immigration for weeks when I
met him. I was hoofing it along Obrero Mundial Street, not

knowing where to go next when I noticed them getting off a trolleybus on Universidad Avenue. At first I didn't give them a second glance but I thought at the time: doesn't that dark bloke look like Blackboard, except this guy's fatter. They went into a shop and I thought no more about it. I was heading down Cuauhtémoc Street passing the ring road when somebody behind me called out / Skinny Dog! / My entire body froze, my fists clenched, my hand flew instinctively to where I normally carried my gun. It wasn't there. I walked faster, thinking that the 'Mano'[6] had sent agents to Mexico. I looked everywhere to see where I could run to / Stop ballsing about Skinny Dog, it's us, how long have you been here? / I could never stand Blackboard, he was one of the FAR gunmen, but now I hugged him, I almost kissed him / Hi mate / God, you've got thin, now you're really living up to your nickname / That's starvation, mate I've got no contacts and in Immigration they won't give me an FH10 / That's how it always is, they really are shits these Mexicans / Christ Blackie, I thought they'd killed you / No way mate, I got over the frontier with bullets buzzing up my arse, they were that close, and there wasn't a single bloody safe house left where I could hide. You remember this guy, don't you? / Of course, but we never spoke, I saw him once with the commandant and with the Chinaman, / You were the head of the base in Zacapa, right Blondie? / Yes, but don't let's talk about that / Let's go to my place for a drink Skinny Dog / Okay mate, let's do that / From that day onwards the boozing started. They got me a job as a proofreader in a publishing house on Tlalpán Avenue and every Saturday we'd get together at Whip's place to drink and talk politics. Whip's room measured only four by five metres and into this were crammed a massive double bed, two armchairs, a writing table and chair, a small bar and two doors, one of which led to the bathroom and the other to the closet. All carpeted in blue for four hundred and fifty pesos a month. Into this we squashed ourselves like sardines every Saturday from half twelve onwards and sang, ate, remembered, imbibed and fought when we were totally rat-arsed. Each of us contributed something, a bottle, some sardines, a bit of meat that we cooked in the bathroom over a meths burner. Those who didn't have time to buy something on the way / What do we need, lads? Come to Aurrera with me, mate / Take him with you, I already brought a Titanic / but it's right opposite / get some crackers to go with this salmon / I'll go with you. I've brought my big jacket with the inside pockets. I want to see if I can "liberate" a couple of tins of sardines / The Big Chicken was the most punctual, he always went halves with Parrot on a bottle of Castillo rum, he didn't like any other kind of drink. Parrot, Vesco, Whip and I were Party members, or rather, we had been. Fox had fought in the 13th Nov. Blackboard and Blondie were from the FAR. The Big Chicken was the oldest, he'd been a Party member in his youth, back in '54, but he'd not been interested in any of it for years. That's why the boys said he was a traitor. After the first few drinks the singing started. Vesco would pick up his guitar and launch straight into Luna de Xelajú. Then everyone would sing softly and lower their heads, a whisper on their breath, their eyes would grow misty, filling with tears and they'd knock back their drinks in one gulp. After a while Vesco would put down the guitar and begin his personal lament: "The problem is a man needs personal satisfaction. He needs to fulfil himself. We can't all be combatants." These exiled wankers make me want to puke. Always trying to justify themselves. Load of drunks.

We went off draped round each others necks. *Do you remember when it was that we got into all this bloody nonsense? I can't even recall how we got sucked in in the first place.* From the tunnels you could see the water steadily dripping, at first it was tepid but on coming into contact with the sulphur it began to simmer. There were three volcanoes, Agua, Fuego and Pacaya. Perhaps that is where the cities of Xibalbá had lain. We have always been this way, deep down, we are a nation of catacombs and tracks entwined beneath the earth, each of us keeps an Indian squatting hidden deep within his breast. The lava that flowed down from the crater of the volcanoes did not burn me. For years the volcanoes had been consuming their lava and there at the bottom was I with my little Indian who had now sprung forth from my breast and was squatting beside me. There was nowhere to flee to and we were always fleeing. Gradually the lava seeped into all the tunnels until it reached the tranquillity of the stomach. Then he stopped me / *Don't you go falling over, mind / I really am going to study, I'm tired of this kind of life, this persecution, this exile. I'm going to study economics. We're always deceiving ourselves. What am I going to study? I'm always crippled by memories, by the death of so many friends, by so much fear. The fact is I'm here and I don't know what to do. I had to flee or else they'd have killed me. I think that as a professional I can make a better contribution to the Revolution.* That's a likely ruddy story. I'm finished at thirty and the Revolution can't expect anything more from me: *I think I'm going to travel to Europe for a while; maybe I could still con the Party rep into giving me a scholarship,* the holes have penetrated into our consciences, they drill into our goodwill and split the earth asunder rendering it old, sterile and furrowed, Pipo's face is deeply furrowed by wrinkles that seem chiselled by a knife, his face like a stone eroded by the constant dripping of water as if they had bound him face upwards in a convent cell from whose ceiling water droplets scored his features for all eternity. One day I saw him through the bars of one of the catacombs that look on to the street. I was alone and I didn't even think of crying out when I saw close to the grille a gigantic raisin with two little grey eyes that pierced me to my innermost being. I beat it fast and walked around aimlessly for several hours, not daring to go home and go to bed on my own and fall asleep. I thought I'd committed a sin seeing that old shattered face. Gradually I calmed down and began to sober up, I said goodbye to him and set off for my room in Ángel del Campo in the Colonia Obrera district of Mexico City. I went round Obrero Mundial Street three times and got lost in every single one of them. As I was crossing the 'Missing Infant', the urge to throw up overcame me once more, *after the second drink Whip started up the same old patter, I don't know how we got into the Party, the fact is we've got too much social conscience,* always fooling ourselves, the fact was we had nothing to do, we were idle bastards full of resentment and moreover we always had our heads in the clouds seeking social solutions to our personal problems, our class was born frustrated (*and Fidel wanted to make it the base of the covert revolution, he forgot Lenin there*) and it was emasculated when it might have been most influential. We were born when our class was on the decline and now we are paying for it, that's the price of our generation (and buckets of blood), almost all our dead were bitter, frustrated people, *they believed they were bringing about the Revolution and what they were trying to do was to save themselves by acquiring a power that does not belong to us. We have to understand once and for all that this Revolution is not ours. It belongs to the outcasts, the wretched, it's they who have to make it and the power must go to them, we can do very little to help them.* When I left the earth shook, it moved at a thousand miles per hour as Pipo ran over the clouds flourishing his broom shouting Piiipppooo, Piiipppooo and ran to see if he could catch them. Now and then the broom touched the legs before him, then came the feeling of sickness. On another cloud a drawing of Crazy Horse's basket began to emerge, whilst the Pastry Man, instead of calling Pastreeez! Pastreeeez! as he usually did, began to empty his basket in the clouds above, shouting as he did so Crazy Horse, Crazy Horse. Then he climbed into the basket, Crazy Horse threw it over his shoulder and vanished into infinite space and there behind them was I, sitting comfortably in the plane which was beginning its take-off; from my suitcase stuffed with pastries, there rose a laugh that appeared to be mine. As the plane soared, banking over the runway, I could make out three hands waving from the airport door, the Pastry Man, Pipo and Crazy Horse.

6

TATIANA

1963

You were left imprinted on the windows of the waiting room. He was growing smaller. You weren't aware when the first tear fell, you only felt its heat on your cheek. Everything was growing distant, with sadness, with a pain in your chest, a pain in your mouth, in your breath, in your words. Suddenly, you regretted everything. You, who'd never regretted anything before. You put your hand on the glass and tried to retain him, to stop him, to hold him forever. You were to blame. You'd always known it. You'd let yourself hope. You'd known it was impossible. It was an intense year. Nevertheless you regretted it. Like that time when sitting on the Malecón you told him that there was no reason to go on together, because he had to leave, had to return to his country compulsorily and you couldn't follow him, couldn't leave because your government wouldn't allow anyone to leave, because you were imprisoned on the island, because you were a revolutionary, *fatherland or death*, because your work centre needed you, because at the time of the blockade you became a soldier and swore to die rather than surrender, because there were no technical experts and you were going to be one, because he had to go because he was a revolutionary and had to return to his country to help bring about the revolution, because he was a revolutionary intellectual and even if he didn't bring about the revolution he couldn't disassociate himself from its reality, because he was an egoist who was not going to sacrifice everything for you. You said all this to him and then he, devious that he was, told you that you had to live the present, that the past and the future don't exist and that if you don't live the present you'll live the future frustrated, twisted, embittered, with grey, dark memories, with nothing in your breast, nothing in your brain and nothing on your body, no love bites, no marks on your sex, with a hymen that rots like the past which will be sad and grey and then you'll have no past or future because both will be poisoned. And you said, yes, you're right, and you took his hand and said to him, look at that house of tiles, it looks like a bath house and you took his hand and told him that was what the bathroom would be like in your house, the one that you would build together and where you would live together forever. That night you walked hand in hand to the Avenida de los Presidentes, you went some ten blocks in silence hand in hand. Havana was cool and the sun was starting to sink into the sea. When you reached G Street, the 72 bus was disappearing into the distance, leaving you behind. You'd walked so slowly that, when you reached G, it was already midnight and that was the last bus. Still holding hands, you ran and ran until you caught it up. The driver laughed but said nothing. You sat suffocated, asphyxiated, exhausted, hand in hand. You thought it would be forever. You had hopes. That was your undoing. Did you never look at his eyes? Did you never realise that he had no hope? That he always avoided speaking about it? It was like that from the first day. Don't you remember? Now, when your mind is blank, and he's fading into the distance, almost at the doors of the plane in this airport to which you will never return because in this country there will never again be anyone that you know to meet or anyone to bid farewell to. Now you can't recall the first moment, that evening, when a poet from El Salvador was courting you and you were surrounded by a group of friends from the UNEAC but feeling uneasy. You were laughing and chatting, laughing and socialising, sipping your drink and laughing heartily but you felt ill at ease and you didn't know why, don't you remember? Now that your mind is blank you must remember him so as never to forget him, to spend your life remembering, inquiring, thinking, finding out why you didn't realise from that day in the Casa de las Américas a year ago, when you were laughing and chatting with an ochre glass in your hand and a yellow flowered dress, and were surrounded by friends, you in the centre as always but feeling uneasy, don't you remember? Until you decided, made up your mind. Because you've always had a strong decisive character; you've always confronted your problems, with courage. Like now that you dry your tears and refuse to cry so that they can't see you, but so that you can see him until the last moment, when he disappears, when the Chesa plane that's taking him to Prague swallows him, the plane that's taking him far from you forever. And you'll never see him again, never. Understand this! NEVER! When the Chesa plane that's taking him to Prague swallows him you'll never see him again. You won't see him again you thought, and you took a drink from your ochre glass, you felt his gaze, on your neck and you became uneasy until you made up your mind, strong willed that you are, you resolved to look at him and you turned and looked into his mocking, piercing eyes which were watching you scornfully with derision in his pupils and then you asked yourself, why does he think I'm ridiculous? And you felt uneasy for the first time in your life and you tried to avoid his gaze to abandon yourself to the conversation and you asked Yolanda, who's that? And she told you he's a Guatemalan poet. Then you felt even more uneasy. More uneasy than ever. Didn't you see then that he had no hope and that he was never going to stay with you? You must have considered the probability of this, because of your character, your way of always weighing up the emotional consequences. You've always been very cool when analysing things, you're very mature, very serious, very controlled, you always measure, have always measured the possibilities, you must have understood, have sensed, have foreseen, that he was not the man you should love. Afterwards

Tania told you so. Afterwards she stated it, repeated it, hammered the point. Tania, your friend since childhood. The sister of your lubricious lesbian games. And you knew that it wasn't jealousy, because jealousy was only a toy of your childhood, of your adolescence, of her childhood, of her adolescence. Tania told you, said it until she was tired of repeating it, because she was, she is, an expert on men (and on women too, you thought), she's jealous, you told yourself, and took no notice. And she repeated again he's not the sort of man that stays, he's one of the leaving kind, one of those that doesn't care what he leaves in his wake. Then Yolanda said I'll introduce him to you in a moment and you started to get nervous, to seek that moment, to seek the right opportunity so that you wouldn't remain in doubt for the rest of your life, because he'd already set his eyes on you, his mocking cynical gaze had penetrated deep into your soul and you had to know him, and this had never happened to you before, you would never have believed that it could happen to you, you, the most sensible, the most self-controlled of all your friends, the one to whom this would never happen, and after three minutes you told Yolanda to hurry and he seemed to be aware of all this, he seemed to know what was happening to you, because he didn't move, he just watched you without moving from where he was standing, without moving even a muscle, without taking even a sip of the drink he had in his hand, and this made you more nervous, more uneasy by the minute. He was dressed in the same suit that he's wearing now, now that he's walking towards the plane with a suitcase in his hand, a navy blue three-piece suit, blue like the Cuban sky, like the Cuban sea, like Cuban eyes. A blue suit that made him look like the sea or the Cuban sky. And Yolanda wouldn't go ahead and call him over, but it wouldn't have made any difference anyway because he wasn't looking at her, he was looking at you, the groups of people between him and you came and went and when the space between you was empty again, he was in the same position, he had not moved a single muscle, hadn't even blinked and then you put down the glass on the little table because your hands were trembling so much that you could no longer hold it and you began to call to him. You've always had a powerful mind, you were very self-controlled, very well balanced, very mature, despite being only twenty-three. You began to call him with your mind, with your body, with your sex. This had never happened to you, your sexual organs had always been frigid, men for you were necessary but dispensable, your relationship with them was mental but never sexual; to you the male organs were repulsive, when you felt the hard, hot bulk you retreated, offended, so that it couldn't touch you, couldn't contaminate you. Only with young girls had you felt what you were feeling now. You felt that your sex was burning, was boiling with a strange heat, your hands were sweating, your sex was throbbing, you called him and his expression became more mocking, he knew it and he put off the moment and suddenly you hated him. Perhaps you never ceased to hate him, for his defiance, for his confidence, for his deviousness, for his lying, for his masculinity, for all the things you knew about afterwards or you knew right from the start and didn't want to accept. You hated him and you told Yolanda to hurry because if she didn't you would go and talk to him yourself, nothing mattered to you any more, you would have gone and would have said to him Hi how are you, and then he would have burst out laughing like he did so often afterwards and maybe he would have responded to you with one of his usual acts of rudeness, turned his back on you or thrown his drink over your yellow flowered dress or insulted you, any of these things he might have done. But you didn't go. He sensed it and came over and said Hi Yolanda how are you and she said I don't think you know each other and you said pleased to meet you and he just said mockingly Hi and you gave him your hand. Your hand was always cold but that evening it was like ice, and when you were about to put your hand in his you remembered that it was sweating with nervousness and you wanted to withdraw it and dry it, but his warmth dried it, his hand was like fire, burning, ardent and it dried all the cold sweat of your hand, and invaded your whole body with its heat, like an electric blanket that you'd suddenly plugged in; the warmth of his hand thawed your hand and your body and your sex, which was burning, for the first time you couldn't stand it between your legs, and if he didn't release it soon you would come. His hand was soft, firm, burning hot, like an electric blanket which was transmitting to you all its warmth and you didn't want to release it and you thought if I don't let go I'm going to come and he went on looking at you with those mocking eyes, with that gaze that bored into you like a drill into concrete and you felt yourself break into a thousand pieces, your lesbian past shattered, the soiled heat of the young girls was released from your skin in an explosion of shock, your sex was cleansed of their tongues, of their hands, of their clitoris and you felt clean and burning inside and out and he mockingly squeezed your hand and did something that you didn't understand until much later: he tickled the palm of your hand with his forefinger. Much later he explained it to you but you knew, from that moment, from that instant, you knew what it meant and from that moment you said yes you would go to bed with him. Because that was what it meant, that was what it insinuated in his country and he knew that here, in Cuba, they didn't know what this signified and he was taking advantage of you, and you knew it right from the first moment, you the virgin, you the lesbian, you the enemy of the male organ, you consented, said you would be a woman with him, that his gesture, his signal, his trick in your hand was not in vain, because from that moment it was as if you'd already gone to bed with him, as if at that moment you'd lost your virginity, as if his forefinger striking the hollow of your palm was his penis in your hymen, breaking it, shattering it, and his heat was blasting into a thousand pieces all your past. At that moment you were no longer a virgin, no longer a lesbian. At that time, you didn't regret, as you do now at this moment when he is getting farther and farther away, drawing closer and closer to the Chesa plane which will carry him to Prague, take him away from you forever. Forever! That word is incomprehensible. Forever. Forever. He uses it a lot. That's why it is incomprehensible or meaningless. It tells you nothing and it tells you everything. Forever, he told you in Río Cristal when Silvia got married. When after a week of looking for him you found him and you took him to the wedding to show him off. You who'd never cared about any man. You who'd mocked all of them because not one of them had been able to penetrate you in any way. You who went everywhere alone or accompanied by a girlfriend. When he disappeared, because the day that you had arranged to go to Santa María del Mar together he didn't show up and you stayed at home all day waiting and when night began to fall were still sitting in the living room of your house with your swimsuit in your hand, that was when you swore that you'd never seek him again and you'd never see him again, when you swore that you hated him because nobody, neither girl nor man, had ever done this to you before, because it was always you who stood up everyone else and you'd waited all day for him to go to the beach at Santa María del Mar and he didn't turn up, because he didn't, because he didn't feel like it, because he didn't even feel like calling you to tell you he hadn't felt like it, then you swore that you'd never seek him again and you spent the whole week calling his hotel to speak to him, because you had found an excuse because on Saturday Silvia was getting married and she'd told you to invite him and you knew that this wasn't true, that Silvia would never tell you this, on the contrary you had asked her, you had begged her, reminding her of the happy days you had spent together and you begged her to invite him, to tell him herself, and Silvia finally said yes, that she'd locate him and at that moment you knew that she wasn't going to do it, then you started to call the hotel like a mad thing at all hours and, when, finally you spoke to him, you didn't even complain that he'd stood you up and that it was the first time that anyone had ever stood you up and that you wouldn't stand that from anybody, but you said nothing to him, you just felt that your heart was going to fail, to burst, that you were going to come, when he said Okay he would go to Silvia's wedding with you. Then you called Silvia, Tania and all your ex-girlfriends to tell them what you had already told yourself, that you loved him, that the past was past and that you were happy and that he was going to be yours forever. Why from the moment you knew him did you begin to sail on a sea of hope without hope? Didn't you know, perhaps? Didn't you realise when he said to you, 'forever', at Río Cristal, that he was lying? What's happened to you? After the wedding where all your friends gave him strange scornful looks, because he wasn't handsome, not good looking like your ex-girlfriends, because he spoke in a strange way, with an odd animal intonation, with a voice that in no way resembled anything your friends were used to, because of his appearance of an old man even though he was only two years older than you, because he regarded all of them with a trace of mockery which was why everyone rejected him, for all these reasons, you pressed close to him asserting yourself through him, protecting yourself with him, feeling for the first time in your life that strange sensation of being protected by an animal, by a wild beast dressed as a human, by an animal of a different sex. You clung to him and felt his muscles, his mammalian hot blood running through all your veins, heard his breath, sensed his inner laughter when Silvia, after saying / I do / looked at you with hatred, with anger, because you were clinging to him and for that reason you clung tighter, you hurt his arm and he laughed; perhaps he laughed because the pain you caused him was nothing compared to the pain he was going to cause you, because he knew already, he knew from the first moment that he was going to go through Immigration today with a suitcase in his hand, dressed in blue like the Cuban sea, and that you were going to be left like now pressed to the window, far from the runway where the Chesa plane is standing quiet, calm, metallic grey, shining, waiting to engulf him. That's why he simply laughed, and because he liked physical pain; when he took your virginity you saw on his face an incredible serenity and whilst you couldn't understand what had happened and his penis was purple, covered in blood, also broken, he was laughing. Like now when you dig your nails into him and watch Silvia with pride, because you know that she still loves you despite this absurd marriage, you know that despite her / I do / she doesn't love her new husband, she loves you, she desires you, but now you know that you'll never be hers again because you belong to him, and she knows that you'll never be hers again because you belong to him. That afternoon, remember this, never forget it, after Silvia's wedding, he suggested that the four of you went by bus to Río Cristal to have a beer and play in the miniature castle for a while. She knew that it was not going to be the same there, because amongst the battlements, in the turrets of that miniature castle you'd kissed her for the first time, had caressed her breasts, had squeezed them, and she had taken off your brassiere and had sucked your breasts, your virgin breasts that had never known the touch of a man's mouth, because amidst the passageways of the miniature castle at Río Cristal, you'd told her that you loved her and she'd told you that she loved you and you'd rolled on the ground with your hands in her vagina and her hands in your vagina and your lips on her breasts and her lips on your breasts; that's why Silvia believed that in Río Cristal you would be the same again and that, in a moment of carelessness by the men, you would kiss in some passageway of the miniature castle at Río Cristal. And Silvia was wrong. Do you remember? Don't forget it, because that day he kissed you for the first time. For the first time in your life you felt his hard, fevered member and you accepted it, you twisted, you rubbed yourself against it, you took it, you felt it thrust hard against you and you crushed yourself against it. That day he said forever. Forever. As he lifted your skirt, as he squeezed your breasts in a narrow passageway of the miniature castle, as you pretended to escape from his arms and his hands, he said that he'd love you forever, as he put his fingers into your virgin sex and made it sweat, made your juices flow, he said that you'd be his forever. And he was right, you will be his forever. Now you understand this. Now, as you press your lips to the icy window pane of the airport to cool their fever and find on the glass the taste of the tears that you didn't want, now, as he walks away towards the plane that will engulf him and he grows ever smaller, you understand that you'll be his forever. Now you understand clearly that you won't be able to return to your lesbian games, nor will you be able to feel another fevered member penetrate you, because from the moment he penetrated you that first time he possessed you forever. Not only did he possess you physically, he possessed you completely. As he penetrated you and you felt that he was splitting you in two and you wept, you knew that you'd never do it again with anyone. From the moment you entered his hotel room, you understood it. You'd refused to do it for months. You caressed each other. You caressed him in the cinema, in the darkness of the cinema you took out his penis and kissed it, you masturbated him, you felt the hot liquid spurt into your hands and then you tasted it with your tongue. You did it at home too, on Sundays when your parents were at the cinema. But you'd never agreed to go to his room at the hotel. He masturbated you, put his tongue into your vulva, the cinema revolved. You always sat right at the front, so that no one else would be there. You always chose the cinema on the Jesús del Monte road. You knew that few people went there and that nobody sat in the front seats. That was where you used to go with the young girls every afternoon when they left La Víbora secondary school. You spent every afternoon fondling them, they spent the whole afternoon fondling you. But with him it was different. You were full, you were complete, you didn't care if anyone saw you or not. He pressed you against the fridge in your kitchen whilst your parents watched TV in the living room and thought you were both eating. You took out his penis, you stroked it, he removed your slip and took down your panties and tried to put it in but you wouldn't let him. You would only allow him to play. It was always the same, you were afraid to go all the way. In addition you had Tania on top of you, not on top physically but on top of you, advising, warning, he'll be leaving soon and you might get pregnant. You must be careful. That's why you wouldn't let him penetrate you. When he bathed your hand with that hot liquid, he became calm, panting gently, still, not moving from you and you breathed more easily because he wasn't stimulating you, laying siege to you, trying to penetrate you. Afterwards, he realised that it wouldn't be possible at your home and he pressed you to go to his hotel. He began to demand. You knew what would happen and you were afraid. You refused. He refused. You refused to go to his hotel, you came up with a host of reasons, that you were ashamed, that the lift man would see you, that you had to get permission at the front desk, that you couldn't use the stairs without being seen, that there might be a scandal and you were a soldier, *fatherland or death*. He refused to see you again. He didn't come to your home any more. He no longer met you from university. The university steps began to be empty. Empty as the eyes of the woman who waited looking down from above. The feast of San Lázaro arrived and you stood at the foot of the stairway and it seemed totally empty even when everyone was coming out. Now, without him, you could do nothing. When you were working in the factory you were in turmoil. You phoned him at the hotel and he refused to take your call. Then afterwards he didn't refuse, he did take your call and promised to come to your house. You waited for him for days on end; your father called the factory to say you were ill and couldn't go in but you were waiting for him. He didn't come. Now you really were ill. It came to the point when you hid on the corner by the hotel to speak to him in the street when he came out or went in but you still couldn't find him. He attacked you, he assaulted you with his absence. You tried to go out with some young girl but it didn't work. You tried to write, to go out with another man but it didn't work. What will happen to you now, now that you are left alone, without him, forever? Now when he walks towards the plane slowly, unhurriedly, as if avenging himself of something you didn't do. Now that he is engraving his figure on your retina with fire. Now that he is leaving forever. Remember him. Don't forget him because this is the last time that you will see him. You tried to see him and he replied finally one Sunday, if you want to see me I'm at the hotel. You made up your mind. You couldn't stand it any longer. He forced you, he assaulted you, you went to his room against your will, hating him, loving him, desiring him, your sex was trembling, your lips were trembling, you felt the sweat pouring from your armpits, from your hands, into your eyes, the lift rose slowly, it was very old, everything was old in the Hotel Presidente, the lift was old, the doors were old, your memories were old. The lift was old until it reached the ninth floor. There, everything became new. Now you had no doubts. When you stood outside number 9-13, there were no doubts left, you knocked, he came to open it, he was in his underpants, lubricious, hot as the afternoon, sweating like the afternoon, you felt dizzy, you said nothing to each other, you simply entered. You'd always touched him in the darkness, in the cinema, at night in your house, everywhere you had been together had been in shadow. On Sundays when you swam at Santa María del Mar and you saw him in bathing trunks he had no sex, he was like any other person, man or woman, and he embraced you in bathing trunks, laughing, running along the beach, he touched you, he threw you to the ground, he caught you on the sand and you didn't think about his sex; but there in his room, in his underpants, it was different, he was all sex, all sexual organ. At that moment you began to remember everything. To bathe your eyes in memory. You let your eyes record all the details of his room to avoid seeing his eyes, his sexual organ that was already growing stiff just looking at you. On your right, for you remained standing there stiff, motionless, seemingly for centuries, was the closet with a huge mirror. Before you, were two parallel beds, it was a double room; between these, a bedside table, on top, a lamp and a telephone. On the same side, to your left and beyond the beds, a door which opened to the bathroom. Beside the door, a small table where he wrote, next to the table, in the other corner of the room to your right, a chest: in front of the chest towards you, nearer your gaze, a dressing table and another mirror. At eye level, directly in front of you, a large window, at the foot of which was the little table where he wrote. The table where he wrote a poem about that afternoon. He lay back on the bed which he was using, the one that was next to the bathroom door, and beckoned to you. The silence had not been broken but now you were no longer trembling, you knew why you were there, to become a woman, to become his woman. You left your bag on the other bed, the one next to you, the one that he wasn't using. Your hands were steady. You didn't go straight to his bed, you went to the window to look out, to see what he saw every day, to discover what view he had from that hotel bedroom. From there you saw the Habana Libre, the Foxa, CMQ, the Línea Building for the scholarship students, the monument to the Presidents, you turned towards him and looked at him, that mocking expression he had had the first day had not disappeared, he was sure, lying there, watching you mockingly. Didn't you realise at that moment that you'd end up standing here, where you're standing now? That the day would come when you'd see him growing smaller as he walked towards the Chesa plane standing on the runway at Rancho Boyeros? Yes, you realised. But at that moment you didn't care. You went towards the other bed, you returned and you sat facing him, you, too, looked at him mockingly, he had to know that it was not he who was violating you, but you who consented to be violated by him, that you surrendered to him because it was your will, that he was not forcing you to surrender to him but you were giving yourself because you wanted to. You knew that he understood this because he became serious. Not a word had been spoken. Everything was silent, like now, that you feel that you are totally alone, pressed against the window of the airport watching every detail of the runway where a figure that is yourself moves, advances, slowly. Everything was silent, without him telling you, you removed your blouse and stood in your brassiere, without him telling or commanding you, you broke all your deepest prejudices, you felt yourself blush, felt all your skin flush and you dropped your blouse on the tiles of the room. He didn't move, he let you do it, now he knew that you had defeated him, that you were stronger than him, that you were all woman, that you didn't care that he knew you had been a homosexual, a lesbian, that the past was dead forever that you were all woman for him. For him and for no one else, like any other woman. Then he laughed, a peal of nervous laughter. You had defeated him before it had even started. Your veins danced with joy, with ardour, now he'd know that you were all woman. He had to know. The silence remained unbroken. You stood beside him. He made no attempt to move, he crossed his arms behind his head to raise it so that he could see you better and took off his glasses. You stood before him and lowered the zipper of your skirt, undid the button that held it, let it slide slowly, gently to the tiles. You saw his underpants grow taut, his erection was beginning, you were not wearing a slip beneath your skirt and you were left in your bra, panties, suspender belt and stockings. You sat, still on the other bed, far from his hands, unfastened the suspender belt and began to lower your stockings slowly, so that he could hear, so that he could see, so that the silk as it slid from your skin would swish gently, softly, so that his erection would be complete, so that he would get up and take you, but he didn't move, his eyes danced over the curves of your body and his erection grew to fullness, but he didn't move. He had defeated you. You had to go to him vanquished, if not you would never be a woman. You couldn't take him as you took the young girls and he knew it and you knew it. You were beaten. He was the stronger. Then your hands began to tremble again, you were in your bra and panties, alone, barely clothed, and blushing from head to foot. You stood up and remained motionless. He watched you, once more mockingly. He had beaten you. Then you began to grow calm, to enjoy your defeat, you regained your composure and felt that your veins were ready for what was to come. Your sex was wet, you looked at him and knew that he knew it. You begged his forgiveness with your eyes and he forgave you. Only then did he get up from the bed. He said hi, he took your face in his hands and gave you a gentle kiss, of forgiveness, he dried your tears and pressed his sex to your belly, then he smoothed his hands down your back and began to unfasten your bra which slid down your body caressing it until it lay still on the tiles with all the other spoils of your defeat. His hands began to stroke up and down your back as he bit your neck, then, avenging himself, he put his hands between your buttocks and began to pull down your panties. You stood totally naked, flushed with embarrassment. You were burning, panting, knowing that he would leave. You were always sure of that. You don't know, don't remember when it became a certainty, when it ceased to be a doubt. Perhaps it was when you saw Sayonara, where Marlon Brando leaves the Japanese girl that he loves, then you wept and he asked you why and you didn't want to tell him that you were sure that this was what would happen to you. Perhaps it was in Varadero, when you were swimming and you rested for a while on the beach while he stayed in the water. He couldn't swim and suddenly he disappeared, the sea covered him and you could see him dead for all eternity and your heart leapt and you were paralysed, unable to help him and you thought, perhaps it's better like this because this way I know that I'll bury him. Perhaps it was the very day that you saw him for the first time and wished that he didn't exist. You were burning, never before had you heard yourself moan with passion, with the fire of desire. You sank your nails into his back and pressed your body against his penis longing to thrust it deeply into your belly, nervously, feverishly you pulled down his underpants and fell back on to the bed in which he didn't sleep. Did you choose that bed so that he couldn't totally possess you? Did you choose the neutral one, where he never slept, where there was none of his heat or his smell or anything that was part of him? You were ready for sex. You felt his immense weight. You hadn't thought that a man would weigh so much. You had always felt his penis in your hands but you had never felt his weight on you, his chest, his stomach, his thighs on yours. He was tireless, he kissed every part of you, you could no longer think, he kissed you all over from your mouth to your feet and back, you couldn't breathe, he was like an octopus, he sucked your breasts, he sucked your clitoris, you felt the room spinning round and round until you finally felt all his weight on you and he began to penetrate you. It was the greatest pain you've ever known, you felt that he was rending you, that a red hot iron was going up into your belly, you bit your lips, and midst your tears saw him above you moving backwards and forwards, his face above you growing larger and then smaller, you felt full of something strange, you felt your body invaded, it was strange but you could take it, it was right, it was what your body had always needed and, alongside your pain, your pleasure grew. Didn't you force him to leave? Remember. Remember when he told you, when he made up his mind to tell you. Weren't you responsible for him going? Didn't you demand things of him that really didn't matter to you? Did you really care if he was a good revolutionary, if he went back to his country to die? What was more important to you, to have him as your man or lose him as a good revolutionary? When he told you, you felt that the ground was sinking beneath you, that the earth was swallowing you, that the breath was taken from your body. You had always expected this, from the moment you saw him, but you had hope, a firm hope, all that he lacked. And you loved him, you loved him intensely as you've never loved anyone before, not even your mother, and you'll never love again. And you let him go. Didn't you force him to go? Think about it. Remember the moment when he told you. It was when you were both at your brother's apartment, alone and he tried to undress you and you didn't want him to because it was your brother's place and you thought you should respect it. After that he didn't speak to you all night and later he told you you're full of prejudices and a revolutionary shouldn't be full of prejudices. So what should a revolutionary be full of? you asked him. What were you full of Tatiana? At that moment you were full of him. His face loomed large and then grew smaller above you, the pain was receding before the heat that you felt permeating your entire body that invaded all of you, like the feeling of him inside you, filling you totally. The heat inflamed you, possessed you, reduced you to ashes and you, too, began to move instinctively, in spite of all your past. The instinct of a complete, totally fulfilled woman overcame you. It overwhelmed everything and the pain disappeared totally. You began to move. You thrust your hips up and down, his weight became insignificant, nothing. Now you didn't feel him on top of you, only inside you. Your frenzy surpassed his because this was your first time, the room spun round and round, you began to hallucinate, radiant images flickering through your mind, you lost all sense of reality, you to whom reality was more important than anything else in the world. For you the most important thing was the rational not the emotional, even when you had one of the young girls beneath you, you were always thinking, rationalising the act. Not now. The heat invaded you and your thoughts melted, flowing like water, like honey, your brain dissolved and you couldn't think, you could only feel the heat, you moved, you quivered, you gasped for breath, you moaned, you panted, you couldn't think. Your brain became a brilliant dense mass which began to move at an incredible velocity and you felt a tremendous throbbing low down in your belly, a crescendo which culminated in paroxysms of ecstasy that shattered your mind, an explosion that left you in a state of utter exhaustion yet not an exhaustion that arose from the fever of sickness but one that produced a feeling of total wellbeing, your muscles rested, became limp, languorous, your body relaxed under his weight and you stretched out your limbs. Did you come? he asked you. You didn't understand him. You didn't understand what he meant. You had never been asked that question before. His sweat was dripping, trickling down over your belly, your breasts, your thighs. You were completely melded together. You were sweating from every pore. You were bathed both inside and out. Now you were another woman. The same one who's now pressed painfully against the window leaving her salty tears bathing the glass, encrusting it with saline crystals. Then he told you I'm going back to my country soon. I've got a scholarship to Prague but I'm not going to complete it, I'll do just a few months and then I'm going home. Remember it. Don't forget it. You were his and you rejected him. Was that why he left? He couldn't accept rejection and you knew it. You looked at him for a long time. Your mind was a blank, like now. You already knew it, ever since you'd known him, since you'd looked into his eyes you'd known that they were somewhere else, somewhere far from you, far from where you would be all your life because you were a revolutionary, *fatherland or death*. You knew all this and still you asked, why? Is it something I did? That mocking expression of his appeared once more on his face and separated you from each other totally, absolutely. That day there began the headache, which still won't go away. He deceived you. He lied to you. He'd always lied to you but you knew it and accepted it. Tania had told you. You'd known from the first of May when you saw him in the Plaza de la Revolución with another woman, he was kissing her and caressing her neck whilst you were marching past in the parade, he hadn't seen you, lost in the crowd. In the evening you went to the cinema and asked him, naive that you were, what he'd done that morning, he replied that he'd been sleeping. Then the following day, naive that you were, you called his hotel and they told you that he hadn't slept there for three nights. You'd always known it, you were always sure that he'd leave, that the day would come when you'd watch him departing, just like now, with his briefcase in his hand, his back half bent, getting farther and farther away from this window against which you're pressed whilst your future grows sadder and sadder. Why did you never tell him? Why did you accept everything without saying a single word? What happened to you? You know that you're paying for something. You sensed it right from the first night. He left his glass on a window sill and invited you to go to the exhibition of paintings that was opening that evening in the Casa de las Américas. He took out a cigarette for himself and gave you one too, he didn't even ask if you smoked. You strolled round several times without looking at anything. Nothing, absolutely nothing mattered to either of you at that moment, his eyes bored into yours obsessively, you felt naked, penetrated. His look stripped you naked, left you without clothes, without thoughts, defenceless, powerless, he took your hand and said, let's leave, this is very boring. You followed him. As you left, you sensed that you were making a mistake, that you were beginning to swim in hope and in lies, but you said nothing, he took your arm and squeezed it, leading you, guiding you in the direction he wanted. It was drizzling outside, the north wind was lashing the Havana night. You walked along G as far as Línea, scarcely speaking. Something inside you wasn't functioning but you didn't react, your mind was a blank, like today. At Línea you turned left, he uttered a few monosyllables, what do you do? At the corner of G and Línea you told him I studied in that school over there, before socialism it was the Lasalles College. He roared with laughter and called you a Papist bird in his Guatemalan dialect. It wasn't until much later that you understood what he'd said. Until he chose to explain it to you. Via Línea you reached the Malecón again and turned right, he took your arm and, without asking you, went towards the door of the Gato Negro club where José Antonio Méndez was singing. Fabulous, you thought and let him lead you there. You sat on the low seats of the Gato Negro and he ordered a couple of rums, you didn't dare tell him that you didn't drink. You were no longer yourself. You were another person. It was then that you foresaw it, you saw yourself standing like you are now, pressed against the airport window, helpless, with nothing left inside you, not even tears. It was then that you felt an intense pain and something began to thunder deep inside you, shaking you and your past. When he said cheers and lifted his glass, you were like a mirror, but you weren't yourself, you were someone else, this same woman that now watches him going away from her, growing smaller, disappearing into the belly of the burnished, silver plane that's standing quietly on the runway at Rancho

Boyeros. Now your entire life floods on to the window, like a mosaic of colours and lights that burst in your brain. Now you can no longer see him, he's inside the aircraft, swallowed by the Chesa plane forever. Now you're a woman with no past and no future because your present doesn't exist, because time stopped a year ago in the Casa de las Américas, when he fixed his gaze on your back and chose you for the sacrifice.

7

THE LAD

1966

You've got to seal the hole, you've got to seal it up! Put a sponge in! Push, push hard. Push until you're exhausted! Don't let them pull me out. I mustn't come out. Squeeze out the sponge on the outside so it mixes with the water in here to make a paste that will harden into a plug and shrink tight leaving me inside forever. Afterwards, lay cement in the entrance, brick it in, wall it right up, whitewash it, level it and leave it like a smooth-surfaced road. Listen to me! Push in the sponge and the cement! It's alright, in here I don't need to breathe. Here in this cave I'm calm, at peace, I don't need to eat or breathe or defecate, there's no noise to disturb me. I've grown accustomed to it in these last nine months and I don't want to come out. Leave me in here alone. Seal up the hole so they can never get me out. My cave gets increasingly more comfortable. It's been growing bigger and bigger and in the last three months, nothing has disturbed my tranquillity. Sometimes I kick the wall to see if anyone responds, but only cavernous voices echo my kicks. Don't let them pull me out. Wall up the hole. Block it, seal it, plug it, occlude it. Fend off those who are trying to open it. Don't let them remove me. Take that instrument away from the man in the white coat. He's gripping my feet. Can't you see that he's got me by the feet and he's trying to pull me out? The worst thing is, he's succeeding, he's dragging me from my cloister. My legs can't stand the strain, they're yielding, however hard I jam them against the entrance, they still slip. In the distance, far away, someone is pushing, my legs won't accept that they're giving way, even if this is the last push that expels me. Help! Mayday! Can't you see I'm too little to be on my own? Don't drag me. Clean up the urine because the cell is very slippery. When they drag me, I slip and can't hold on to the bars. Even though I jam my feet against the cell door, I slide. Don't pull so hard. You're dislocating my arms. The piss has got into my wounds and I can't stand the burning on my wrists. Don't drag me so violently. The worst thing is that they're winning. I'm being ejected. They're forcing me from my cave. Look at this water flooding out with me! I was floating in water. The light is so bright outside. It hits my eyes. They're hitting my eyes. Get him out men, says the officer, we have to go on flogging him until he confesses where the guerrillas have their safe houses. They were dragging him through urine and saliva. His wrists were cut and his back raw from so many beatings. He could not stand, to get him out the soldiers had to drag him. He leaned against the cell walls for support and they began to whip him, give it to him hard, the bastard's still strong. Yeah, he's still resisting, they came from headquarters to see if we'd topped him yet. The fact is, Napoleon has sworn to kill him and, as he can't have the pleasure of breaking him himself, he's impatient to know when we're going to waste him. Yeah, well, what you don't know is that that guy there who looks half dead right now was the one who scarred Napoleon's face over in Zone 6. Really? I had no idea, go on. Well, acting on a tip-off from a grass, Napoleon mobilised his forces to Zone 6 and surrounded a house where a group of guerrillas were meeting in secret. He encircled them and was just about to go in and grab them when a jeep appeared with this guy and two others in it and booommm, this bastard, pulled the pin and hurled a grenade from about two metres; well, it didn't kill him but it ruined his operation, they couldn't catch a single one because Napo was left lying in a pool of blood and his assistant blown apart, his guts splattered all down the walls. From that day on Napo swore that this swine would pay for it. When I knew that he'd caught him I said to myself the Lad's had his chips now, but the colonel wanted to interrogate him and poor old Napo had to suck sorrow. What I can't understand is how Napo managed to recognise him so clearly in the dark at the very moment when the grenade exploded. Anyway, when he got out of hospital he went straight to this arsehole's mother's place and told her when I get my hands on your mother-fucking shit of a son I'm going to kill him and, by the time he gets this message, it'll already be too late. You'd better believe it, and if I find him near this house I'm going to blast this shit-hole to hell with all of you inside it. Napo's really bitter about it, he'd have wasted him by now but for the colonel fucking up his plans. He's left frustrated and disfigured for life by a scar right down his cheek. When they caught me I thought, now I'm really screwed. After the pistol-whipping from that cop Maya, Napoleon landed the second blow. Now you've had it, he told me, get ready to die and it's going to be very slowly, you son of a bitch. From that moment I realised that there was no salvation for me. Then I plucked up courage and said to him Hi Scarface and, smash, a blow, smash, another, smack. Fuck you arsehole, take him to the 1st Precinct and, tonight, we'll bust his balls. When I turned to look at him again all I could see were the bodies of the three soldiers that Efi had killed before he escaped and then, whop, a fist in my guts, a boot in the face, a blow in the kidneys from the butt of Napo's .45, and I couldn't straighten up, I can't stand, my spine hurts like hell. Right, if he doesn't get up put the boot in 'cos I'm sick of dragging him around. Alright you, get up! Boom, smash, crash, crash, boom, crack, boom, crack, everything's going round, everything's whirling, the world's spinning inside and outside, the car won't stop going over and over, bloody Rat, why did he have to go so fast? I knew this was going to happen from the moment we left San José, bang, crash, bang, crash, if the door flies off there won't be even a scrap of me left. We zoomed past the police checkpoint, the cop blew his whistle but I was the only one who noticed and then only because I was in the front passenger seat with the window rolled right down, otherwise not even I would have heard it at the speed Rat was going. Anyway, what would the boys have heard? They were in the back with a couple of whores on their laps singing their heads off. I told Rat that the copper had blown his whistle but he just put his foot down further. We were all totally rat-arsed and a mist of steam was rising from the shimmering road. All you could see all around was heat. The sea thundering in the far distance, the sound of singing, "someone singing, from afar", what a load of crap. I began to watch the speedo compulsively, 90, 100, 110, 115, then I looked at Rat; the dumb-fuck had one eye closed to keep the road in focus like he was a marksman taking aim. When we approached a bend he leaned over the steering wheel and gradually began to turn it in slow motion. When he pulled out of the bend, he breathed, I breathed, we both breathed again with relief. Then, foot hard down on the accelerator again, slow down mate. That only made it worse, he went even faster. D'you think I'm pissed, or what? You know I drive better when I'm tanked up, yeah I know that but what if the pigs flag us down, look how bollocksed that lot are back there. Behind us, Big Bonce, Boozer and Skinny Dog, drunk as skunks, were belting out some dumb song, oblivious to everything, their hands lost up the skirts of the manky randy trollops. It would have been better if I'd stayed shtumm. It only made it worse, 110, 115, 120, 130, then I held on tight and shut my mouth. I dropped the catch on my door, put my legs forward and braced my feet in the front well. If we were going to crash at least I'd be prepared, and maybe I'd save myself. Doing 130 on the straight, Rat was in control of absolutely sod all. I'll show you how much better I drive when I'm stoned, watch this, man. He began to swing the wheel from side to side / watch out, man / Tarts shrieking their heads off / We're going to crash / For Christ's sake, straighten up man / Oh my God, this is it / Rat closed his eyes. He hugged the wheel with his forearms using all his strength to control it and jammed his foot on the brake putting all his weight behind it. Then came the crash, the car flew off the road and plunged with an ear-shattering impact of metal and screams / Oh God, hold me tight luv / sweet Jesus, save me / Boom, crack / not that tight / Big Bonce cracked his skull / I won't come out of this alive / he'll not get out of this alive, he's a loser, put the boot in again. The boss is calling and this arsehole won't get up. Well, let's carry him. On top of it all, the swine weighs a ton. I feel as if my back's broken, the pistol-whipping that I got from Maya must have smashed it. Napoleon would have killed me by now, I'd have been better off in the 1st Precinct, Napo wouldn't have waited so long, he'd have wasted me long ago, I can't take another interrogation like last night's, I ache all over, I can't feel my wrists any more, I think they're going gangrenous, my whole body reeks inside and out. Phew, this prick's heavy, let's take a rest for a minute, meantime you punch him around a bit, you never know, he might get up. Let's see if he responds to a kick in the guts. I feel as if I've got nothing left inside, I reckon when they were beating me last night I vomited my whole inside out, I can't even feel the blows any longer, I think that kick broke my sternum. My muscles won't even respond any more to protect myself, I feel it all going dim, my anal sphincter closing. That bastard kicked me in the guts. I can feel nausea tormenting my body, it absorbs my brain, it makes my flesh creep, nausea seeps into every corner, absorbing everything, dominating everything, my sphincter closes and a bubble of vomit erupts as if I were inebriated, like the first time I got drunk and threw up dramatically, it's rising just like the first time, that was an impressive puke, a spectacular spew, I'd never been drunk before, I was fifteen years old, my grandmother was always admonishing me: you shouldn't drink, drunks are bad sons and bad fathers. And bad pimps too, I'd mutter, 'cos with a skinful they can't get it up. Every Saturday, regularly, my father shut himself firmly in the living room with all his mates for a liquid lunch: they passed round the food calling the bean tacos appetisers. After a while the volume would rise: everyone talking at once: raucous laughter: everyone singing in unison: everyone going out for a slash, one after another. Every time they left the room, their faces altered, growing redder and stupider by the minute. By the end of the evening arguments, brawls, fights, my grandmother desperate: / They've broken my new vase / they've smashed up the fish tank / I'm so dumb, why on earth did I leave it there / Father: shirt tail hanging out, shirt front all open revealing flat, flabby, hairless, breasts, his mouth hanging open, gazing vacantly into space: you can all piss off, I invite you back for a few drinks and you fuck up my house. Granny: go on inside my boy, don't go looking at such a bad example; you, you wastrel, you're setting the boy a bad example: Father, pushing his mother out, get off my back, mother, can't you see those buggers have broken your fish-tank and now on top of this you won't even let me chuck them out on their arses, go to your room boy, what the hell do you care what I do anyway, come on you lot, piss off. Father: face down on his bed, fully dressed, snoring. Okay, we've had a rest, grab his feet and I'll hold him under the arms or if you prefer it you take one hand, I'll take the other and we'll drag him. Okay, but hold him tight because this time he really has passed out. Why did you tell me to kick him? You'd better take a look and see if he's still breathing, it'll be real bad luck if he dies on us 'cos then we'll really be for the high jump, the colonel will be livid and he'll take it out on us, he'll have us arrested and kick us out or have us tossed into jail. We'd better carry him. Feel his heart. Yeah, he's still alive. Better if they'd left it to Napo, he'd have wiped him out by now. Shut up, grab him round the stomach and sit him up so I can lift him by his feet. That bastard, grabbing me round the stomach, the puke's going to go all over him and he'll be mad as hell, here it comes, it's going to be a big one like the first time. The first time was a right rave-up. I was fifteen. After the first drink we were hooked, we didn't turn up at school in the afternoons, we spent them in the bar and in the whorehouse. I had a mistress called Rosa in El Hoyito brothel, a gorgeous, tasty piece of arse from room number one. From the first day she set eyes on me she watched me, she wouldn't leave me alone, I was her son, her doll, her big prick, her handsome boy, her husband, her lover. She spoiled me. She pandered to my whims. She gave me blowjobs. In secret, away from the other girls she served me whiskey / this is just for you, my little longshlong, just because you're so well hung / and, afterwards, she'd give me sex for one, two, three hours, she'd kiss and lick every little bit of my body and finally she'd put two or three quetzals in my trouser pocket, which I'd spend in the bar where we'd meet up after our disorderly flight from the brothel. The first to arrive was always Rat, who boldly hurled back the blinds, shouting / Hi girls, your lovers have arrived / a quart of Indita rum for starters, madame / After three quarts everybody was half cut, Rat would lean on the jukebox and put on the same old song every time: "You passed me by disdainfully. Your eyes did not even turn towards me" he wept, sang along, intoning nasally, "I saw you but you did not notice, I spoke but you did not hear and all my bitterness chokes me." Then more appetisers, chips with mayonnaise, pork scratchings, pork tamales and tripe and another quart of Indita. At seven, we'd leave, holding each other up, emotional, rebellious, insolent, rat-arsed: "It rends my soul to know you forgot me, that I do not even merit your disdain": to crash out on the tennis courts at the Olympic City; there we'd nod off, sober up, throw up. Lords of puking, shouting, shitting and singing our heads off, "and still you live, a part of me and if I live a hundred years, a hundred years, I'll think of you, ta ta tata tata tata ta rararararararara ... rara." Right, lift him up, let's hope he doesn't shit on us because who can stand that stench, there's only the corridor and then the colonel can have him. But don't forget, we've got to take him back to his cell afterwards and, if he shits himself during the interrogation, when we take him back we'll all get plastered in it. Don't think about that. The thought of it makes me want to retch, lift him up in one go. The first time was wild, way out. Nobody (apart from Rat) had drunk before. We were fifteen. Rat, mysterious, garrulous, seductively convincing, the pimp of persuasion, precocious tippler, embryonic inebriate / Right lads, let's go and celebrate the end of the exams / Chink, ever dumb / how about an ice-cream, what do you think? / Skinny Dog, the dreamer: / Or to the pictures / Rat, taking the piss: / Why not hold a mass and invite our mums? / We all eyed each other hesitantly. This dodgy dark bugger was plotting something. Nobody said a thing, zero, zilch. Boozer started spitting and that made me dead jumpy, he could spit right across the street, he was unrivalled. The very first day I saw him he was spitting, it was like a jet, I don't know where all that saliva came from. He said it was because he was nervous. We were sitting in the same row of desks across from each other but with a row between us, so not that close to each other really. He was next to the wall and I was in the middle of the room. It was just the two of us and the teacher that was supervising us who looked hungover. We were re-sitting our tests. Boozer was eight and I was seven. Before he got his crib out, Boozer spat, the ball of spittle sailed over all the desks, flew through the door of the classroom and landed in the courtyard. I was gobsmacked. While the teacher did a visual estimate of the distance the gob had travelled, Boozer nonchalantly took out the small strip of paper with all the answers on that subject on it. With his left hand under the desk, he began to roll the crib, writing down all the answers with his right. He created a heap of saliva beside the desk before he'd finished. Then he rolled up the paper accordion and stood up to hand in his exam paper, totally unfazed / Do you want it? / Yes please / he tossed me the tightly rolled crib, it didn't fly open because it was one of those wrapped around a reel and secured with an elastic band. The teacher played dumb. He knew he was going to get money out of us. For several days we got together to re-sit the papers we'd failed. Boozer had made cribs for every subject. He'd been expelled from Santa Cecilia's School and I'd been chucked out of the Liceo Guatemala. But when I started trying to spit like him, I got jumpy just watching him doing it. He stood in the doorway of the El Cairo store on the corner of 6th Avenue and 9th Street / Watch! From here I can reach the City of Paris store / and that's exactly where the gob landed. He got himself all keyed up, filled his mouth with spittle, rolled it around a bit until it was the right consistency, snorted, hawked, drew up the phlegm by holding his nose, mixed the snot with the saliva, masticated a bit more, arched his body backwards slightly and zoooomm, the gob shot across the street and fell on the largest window of the City of Paris where it began to slide slowly down the glass / Let's see who can do that / he laughed. I tried. I practised at home every afternoon, I used to lean out of the window of my second floor room and spit in the direction of next door's garage. Each day I managed a bit further. I was on the point of reaching my mark when the business with the police occurred. We were going through Central Park when we started spitting at each other, bloody Boozer gobbed straight in my face and hurtled off along the Portal del Comercio, he disappeared up Rubio Alley and plunged into the Biener Store dodging amongst all the counters, then he ran into the entrance to the Panamerican Hotel on 6th Avenue and straight out of the exit on to 9th Street where I lost him. Gasping for breath, with my throat parched, I joined the others who'd been running behind and getting into everything / Let's go to the billiard hall / Yeah okay, who knows where he's vanished to / Maybe he's there already / Okay, let's go then / A ball of spittle hurtled out of the door of the City of Paris and hit me full in the face. I went totally apeshit, I saw red and began to foam at the mouth, like a lunatic. Livid with rage I chased Boozer between all the counters. When we reached the shop door again amidst hysterical cries from all and sundry of / Get those boys out of here / They're from a private school / Well they can't have taught them any manners there / Look what they've done to the shop window / Call a policeman / there he was standing in the doorway. Now I've got him, I thought, I gathered all my spittle until I couldn't produce a drop more, sucked down all the snot from my nose, thick, sticky and green, took careful aim and gobbed. Boozer ducked. On the pavement outside, an elderly gentleman in a hat and spectacles was strolling by. The green gelatinous gob slid down from his hat on to his glasses where it trembled, danced, clinging firmly to both. Boozer, the little sod, was doubled up laughing himself stupid and I was rooted to the spot. The copper was not easy to win over. From that day onwards, I've tried not to spit, but when Boozer starts gobbing, I get decidedly edgy. All that came up was saliva. There's nothing left in my stomach now. The nausea was from the kicking that mother-fucking cop had given me. Right we're here, shall we carry him in or stand him up so he can walk in on his own? What do you think? I think it'd be better if we put him on his feet, otherwise the colonel will think we hurt him more than we did. I just wonder if he can take any more after last night, they beat him non-stop. I reckon he's going to croak without giving away a thing, all this effort will have been in vain. Still, that's not our affair, it's up to the colonel, so hold him under the armpits and I'll take his hands, let's try and stand him up, then you grab one arm I'll grab the other and we'll lift him, that way the colonel will believe he can take a bit more, either way we've got to get him on to a chair inside. I feel as if the floor is coming up, I can't take any more, if they give me another beating like last night I'll snuff it, anything's better than standing these whippings, I feel as if the floor's going to hit me in the face, everything's spinning, the door, the covered windows, the white walls, why are they trying to make me stand? Can't they see I can't do anything any more. If they stand me up, it'll be a lot worse, then I'll keel over completely. I feel so dizzy I can't hear, am I really able to hear? Has last night's beating left me deaf? Or is it just that I can't hear because I'm fainting off continually? If they raise me to my feet they'll beat me harder, if they don't support me, I'll fall. I feel sick like the first time. We were standing on the corner by the school not knowing what to do, irresolute, vacillating, each of us put forward a suggestion, except Rat, we eyed each other, Rat watched us, saw he had us on hot coals, waiting hopefully, uneasily, apprehensively, where do you suggest then? He surveyed us with his small rat eyes, his rat mouth, his rat colour, put his forefinger into the cleft in his chin and pressed the sides with his thumb and middle finger, then he raked his hair down over his forehead nervously / let's go and celebrate in the bar / We were all gobsmacked, the unexpected shock made us gulp. Rat remained totally unfazed. We eyed each other slowly. Chink's slit eyes narrowed even further, he put his hand in his pocket and played with one of his balls; whenever he got nervous he put his hand in his pocket and fingered a bollock. Skinny Dog wasn't that decorous, when he was thinking he'd grab his entire packet and give it a good grope / Way out, but what if we get arrested? / Boozer stopped in mid-gob and watched Rat out of the corner of his eye / Yeah right, lads, it'd be really way out to go to a bar / Rat, impatient, pushing back his quiff: / what a bunch of pansies, why should they arrest us? They can't do anything to you just for drinking / Me, anxious, not knowing whether to go for it or not: / Well, maybe they can if you're underage / Rat, more sure of himself now, put his forefinger in the cleft in his chin and pressed the sides with his thumb and middle finger. Pushing his hair forward into a Tony Curtis quiff, he eyed us scornfully, then he asked Chink: / What do you think? You lot, what do you think? / Way out / what do you think, man? / Me? I don't know, what do you think? / Boozer and I: / great, let's go for it / Three against two. Rat put on the pressure. He'd won. He smiled, mockingly, raked his hair, Tony Curtissing his barnet and pressed harder: / and you two, what's it to be? / Chink and Skinny Dog stared at each other, lowered their gaze, raised it again, Chink's hands began to sweat, he dried them on his trousers, whenever he was afraid they'd sweat like that. Boozer made up his mind for him, he slapped our Asiatic on the back / What's this then slave? I'm the boss round here, stop buggering around or I'll belt you one / Chink looked at him surprised, his hands sweating profusely, he was Boozer's slave and, when the latter was in a bad mood, he'd twist Chink's arm in front of all the class, force him to his knees, humiliate him, then he'd take off his belt and whop him with it. Chink, mind focussed: / Yeah okay, let's do it / Skinny Dog was on his own now: / Okay, let's go / Let's go. Grab his arm, open the door and take him in. They opened the door and dragged him inside, hanging between them. Inside, sitting on a chair at the back of the room smoking a pipe, a fat, shiny colonel with a taut sallow skin was waiting triumphantly. In front of him was a large empty area with a wooden chair in the centre of it. Here was all the space they needed to carry out what they had to do. In the corner, a small radio. Above the solitary chair in the centre of the room hung a set of pulleys with straps stiff with blood. That's where they hung me last night, now I'm beginning to understand what's going on. Can I have slept all night or all morning or all afternoon? What time can it be? Is it day or night? That face. I'll never forget it. Hog. He was the one who beat me all the time I was there. There's the radio that played non-stop in the background at just the right volume to hide my screams. Bloody Hog! When I left my school desk he laid into me for the first time, Moor tried to intervene but Hog landed him a blow that knocked him into the corner. When I attempted to get up, Hog grabbed me by the shirt, lifted me off the ground and floored me again, I lost all awareness of where I was and tried to grab his balls, I aimed at his fly from where I was lying on the floor but all I got was a handful of nothing, then he put the boot in, everybody froze, nobody wanted to get involved because Hog was the bully of the class, the top dog, numero uno; then he lifted me and, with my school bag that was on my desk, hit me twice so hard that my brain rattled in my skull / That's so you'll learn not to fuck me around / but, in spite of this, I managed to lob at him a gob of phlegm that stuck to his shirt, then, before my eyes, he grew visibly fatter, went scarlet with rage, and laid into me, that was the last thing I remembered, except that, as I fell and my eyelids closed, I saw my knife, which I'd lost, lying forgotten beneath my desk. When I came to, Hog was begging me to wake up, throwing water over me from the tap in the rear courtyard / Wake up Lad, don't say anything to the priest / I'm not going to say anything, even if they kill me, even if they tear me apart, I'm not going to tell that mother-fucking brass-hat a thing. He's turned on the radio. Now the torrent of blows will start. Now it begins. They seated him on the solitary chair and lowered the straps by the pulleys, tied his wrists behind the chair with them, and started to raise him. He was held, suspended a centimetre above the chair, his bottom in the air and the chair hanging from his arms through the back slats. The pain was intolerable but the victim was lucid. The colonel approached him laughing / Are you going to tell me where the arms are stored? / I don't know / Where is the printing press? / I've never had anything to do with propaganda / Where are your friends? Do you know this one, and this one, and this one? Where are your friends? / My friends? Yes, where can my friends be? My friends lifted me, picked me up from where Hog had left me beside the water fountain with my nose swollen, pouring blood. Everything was throbbing, I just managed to say to Rat go and get my knife, it's under my desk, my eyes kept clouding over and Boozer and Skinny Dog were throwing water into my face. That day 'the boyze' were born, our secret gang, the clan, the mafia that would impose its own laws. Because together, united, we are stronger than as individuals. When we are united, we must wreak our vengeance. The first we're going to shit on is Hog. We've put up with too much for too long, we're going to spy on him when school's out / My knife / From today onwards, all of us will carry a knife and, if they try anything on with any one of us, they'll have to take on the whole gang / Where would my friends be now? The colonel lifted the man's head, so you won't talk, eh? I'm going to flay you alive you son of a bitch / Hoist him up, men / I feel as if my arms are being dislocated, my back broken. I thought I wouldn't feel anything, that my body was numb. That bloody chair weighs a ton. I think I'm going to faint, if they hoist me up again I'll black out. The worst thing is when I do pass out the grunt throws water in my face from the crapper. When I wake up I'm going to destroy Hog's bag. I'm going to slash it to pieces with my knife / He's gone off again. Take him down boys / The henchmen lowered him and the victim was left sitting on the chair. The colonel began to pace back and forth, he shouldn't black out so often, he thought, I'm not going to get anything out of him this way and the Minister will hold me responsible. The worst possibility is that he might go and die on me. And he's the son of one of my friends, a classmate from the Military Academy. If he finds out I killed his son, he'll want his revenge. But if I don't squeeze anything out of him today, they'll relieve me and the CIA won't waste any time, last night they almost killed him, I had to ask them to be patient and give me more time. I had to ask them to let me have him today to see if I can get something out of him. Anyway, it gets right on my tits those gringos coming here and doing whatever they like. It's a dirty trick, the Minister asking those blond bastards for help. We're perfectly capable of getting rid of these damned communists ourselves. What gives these gringos the right to come and tell us what to do? If I get nothing out of him today, this boy'll be dog-meat for sure in their hands / Haul him up, boys / Excuse me, Colonel, he's still out cold / What are you waiting for then? Throw some water over him / Everything exploded. I felt a wave of cold air emanate from the blast. I was filled with a new sensation. Now I could kill. My hands held the power of life and death over another man. "If you want to write to me, you know where I'll be, if you want to write to me, you know where I'll be, on the Madrid front in the firing

line", was all I could think in the darkness hearing the moans
from the shattered bodies on the floor. I couldn't move, all that
was moving in my head was my power, the new power that
sprang from my arm, from my hand, from my body, and the song
from the Spanish Civil War that I had learned from my
instructor, a Spaniard who had fought in '36 in Madrid. He was
in charge of our group in the guerrilla training camp near
Havana. All day he hummed the song. In the darkness I could
make out the shiny little eyes of Napoleon, the Deputy Chief of
Police, staring at me with intense hatred. The grenade had not
killed all of them. We had a meeting that night in the house they
had surrounded. Little Indian and I were late. It was a poor
house in Zone 6, a place of absolute security, according to our
comrades. We had taken a wounded comrade to a safehouse,
that's why we were late. When our jeep rounded the corner, we
saw all the police team surrounding the house. They had
encircled the house with a double ring that it would be
impossible to break through from within. The first shots had
been fired. Little Indian and I studied the situation rapidly. He
told me, throw the grenade into the middle of the ring where the
command centre is, while I break the weakest link with my
machine gun. When we see our comrades come running out, we'll
climb into the jeep and beat the hell out of here. I was frozen,
rooted to the spot, the Civil War song ringing in my ears and
Napoleon's eyes fixed on me. At that moment everything blew
up, several police ran to help their chief and their spotlight hit
me full in the face, I felt as if my brain were exploding, I was in
mortal danger, Little Indian pulled me by one arm and dragged
me to the jeep, in a hail of bullets and my comrades escaped from
the house firing wildly from the hip. The explosion in my head,
the spotlight, were like a pail of cold water which woke me. He's
come round, chief, shall we go on beating him? The colonel came
up with a sheaf of papers in his hand, brandished them in the
face of the prisoner and signalled to the soldiers to raise his arms
a few centimetres. The man let out a dull moan. The colonel
waved the papers in front of his face and began to read in a
monotone, "The path of the armed struggle is not exclusive to
the developing, backward, semi-colonial countries. The armed

struggle, characterised by guerrilla warfare and long years of selfless revolutionary activity is exclusive to nations like ours, where the peasant population is in the majority and there is a limited working class" / Do you deny that you wrote this? Come on, answer. Answer, you bastard or I'll hang you by your balls / He signalled again and they hoisted the prisoner a bit higher. The colonel lost his patience and punched him in the face with the hand holding the papers, that flew into the air. The prisoner moaned softly / Okay men, let him down and work him over with your fists / The prisoner was lowered again the few centimetres and lay exhausted in the chair. My nerves won't take any more. If they go on beating me I'm going to die. If only they'd hit me hard enough my body would go numb like yesterday. Why on earth did I carry all those papers in my bag? What an idiot, always that obsession with carrying papers around, as if I didn't have it all engraved on my memory, 'we classify our revolutionary war as popular because we shall not be a group, a party or a class', in the middle of the discourse the Spanish instructor would sing softly, "They have raised, have raised the four generals, my love; by Christmas Eve they will be hanged, be hanged." Afterwards, he went on talking as if nothing had happened, 'we cannot overthrow the army by military means, this signifies that our struggle must be of a different nature, it must be prolonged, it cannot be a Putsch or an armed enterprise', that Spanish commandant knew it all off by heart. He should have had everything off by heart too, not be carrying it around on paper. On top of it all, the papers that they found on him in the bar had already been reproduced in the newspapers of the FAR. How could he protest or deny anything? It would be best if they flogged him so hard that he croaked since there was no other way out. When he felt the first rifle butt, he knew it. The grunt with the Mayan face was the first thing that he saw when he recovered from the momentary swoon. The last thing he saw after feeling the searing burn in his leg was Efi taking out his .45 and wasting the three soldiers. He only saw that the one who had shot him in the leg was slipping down the counter on to the floor of the bar to the screams of the whores. He had told Efi, warned him, nagged him, begged him not to go to brothels when they went down to the capital, but he was always so stubborn, let's go to the cathouse, we'll have a fuck and a few drinks and then sod off fast. They were on the lookout for me. My mother had already got a message out warning me that Napoleon had marked my cards. Napo had even distributed my photo. And the son of a bitch was right. The bastard had a reputation as a ladies' man among the servant girls and my grenade sliced through his face. It left a deep scar down his jaw. After Maya, Napoleon fell on me, he began to kick my wound, then I said, this is where it all ends and I gathered all my courage and said / Hi Scarface / When he started to pistol whip me I did the same as I'd done when we moved the first arms to the mountains, I sang the song of the 5th regiment. Why the hell should the instructor come into my mind, the old Spanish instructor from the International Brigades of the Spanish Civil War, who sang all the time in the training camp near Havana? Whenever there was danger, I remembered him. It was the first time and I was heavily loaded, the chief of the supplies network told us that there was an army patrol close by so we had to hurry, to walk fast. A rapid ascent always loosened my bowels, I started to perspire, my legs became stiff and my breathing laboured, I had to do something that would draw on my reserves and I began to sing in my head 'on the 16th of July in the courtyard of a convent, the people of Madrid formed the 5th regiment ... take the machine gun and send Franco packing, send Franco packing: with the first four battalions go the finest of Spain, the reddest flower of the nation ... with the 5th regiment, mother, I'm off to the bridge to defend the town ...' / Bloody hell, he's gone off his trolley, listen to him, he's singing / Bullshit! Just be careful he doesn't fall off the chair and quit hearing crap / No, seriously. Come here. Listen, he's singing / Punch him around a bit and you'll see how much better he can sing / I reckon this sod's going to snuff it, he's gone nuts, if we hit him any harder he may die on us and that brass-hat will blame us for his death / But, if we don't beat him, the brass-hat will have our balls, which do you prefer? Watch it, he's looking at us to see what we're talking about. Hold him for me. I'll start beating him / One of the henchmen seized the prisoner by the shoulders, held him firmly on the chair and asked the colonel to turn up the volume on the radio. The other fitted a brass knuckleduster on to his right hand and smashed his fist into the prisoner's face. His teeth seemed to sink into his jaw and, dulled by the radio, there rose from deep within him a loud scream, an animal scream, a mortal scream, a scream of desperation, a scream of joy as if it were his last / Careful boys, or we might kill him / The colonel went up to check that the prisoner was still alive and returned to his seat / What's this *we*? I don't remember him doing any beating / Shhh! Not so loud, he'll hear and report us. Go on hitting him / When I saw the watchman's face, I stuck the machine gun into his mouth. The man almost fainted and I just pushed open the door. According to our information, two crates of grenades, two floor-mounted 30mm machine guns, several Thompson sub-machine guns and a load of ammunition were stored in this place. The order came directly from Resistance Headquarters. We had to get back those arms. The lackey was dumbfounded when he saw the muzzle of the machine gun in his face; he had no option but to stand aside. I pushed open the door and signalled to the boys with the tip of the gun. Not long after, we were removing everything in sacks. It was the cleanest operation we ever did. When we left, I spoke to the watchman. We'd tied him to a post in the courtyard where he would remain all night, we'd taped his mouth and only his eyes could be seen. As we were wearing stocking masks on our faces, he wouldn't be able to recognise me later, so I went right up to him and looked straight into his eyes. They were filled with terror. During the entire operation I'd had him in my sights and the bloke hadn't said a word. From the moment he'd opened the door he'd never spoken again. Now I know why, that's how I began to recognise terror. His eyes were seared into my brain. For months afterwards in my restless sleep I remembered them staring at me, torturing me, haunting me. Now they are here again, at each blow his eyes bore into me. If you give them any information about us I'll come back and kill you, I told him. The next day, he chucked in the job and went back to his village. I saw it in the newspapers. Now his eyes are my eyes, now I see through them, I feel that my own no longer exist, they are still, they no longer move, they are paralysed, his eyes draw me into a labyrinth, into a deep, dark pit filled with slime, with moss of the kind they use in Nativity cribs at Christmas. From this moss there seeps a viscous liquid like blood, to every leaf cling eyes, thousands of eyes identical to those of the watchman which adhere to my skin and stick to my eyes replacing my own. Someone is pushing me into the tunnel, I shout, sing, fall, kick, moan, I rise again and another blow plunges me deeper and deeper into the slimy mud-filled abyss. The eyes adhere to every pore of my body, I feel that each one of my cells bears a Cyclopean eye in its centre, that my body is composed entirely of eyes, of sightless eyes that are sucked into the black void. The blows don't plunge me into the tunnel, they submerge me in the darkness, in the slime, in the viscous liquid and I cannot retreat, cannot free myself from the clinging mud because, when I try, another blow pushes me under again and I plummet deeper into the black void and, although I have a million open eyes, I can see nothing; now two hands drag me and leave me at the bottom of the hole. My million eyes rest, open, sightless / I reckon he's dead, look, his eyes are open and he doesn't respond / It was the colonel's fault, he let us whip him until we were exhausted / He says the sod's not dead, he's just blacked out with his eyes open / I'm ravenous, all that beating and the effort of dragging him back to his cell has given me an appetite. How about going for something to eat and we'll knock back a couple on the way? / Okay, let's leave this arsehole 'til tomorrow. After all this he still hasn't croaked. Tomorrow we can start again / An increasing demoralisation combined with the proven incapacity of the dictatorship to rid itself of the guerrilla movement, if you want to write to me you know where I'll be, on the Madrid front in the firing line, has compelled the army colonels and their American advisers to employ new anti-guerrilla tactics and the first course on offer is fragmentation grenades to neutralise the prestige that the guerrilla movement won when all this began for me.

8

RAT

1967

Now let's go to the circus and face the beast it's a long way from here to Candelaria Avenue and I'm dead on my feet I'm such a bloody idiot I gave my last fifteen quetzals to Skinny Dog and I've nothing left 'til the end of the month if I take Las Américas Avenue I can go straight down Reforma that way I won't get caught in the traffic anyway there isn't any traffic around at this hour okay so I've turned and now I'm going down Reforma in this infernal contraption when will I ever finish paying off this bloody rust-bucket the moment I do Chayo's going to want me to buy a newer model it's never-ending and then I'll be in hock again for God knows how many more years hell what's up now something's wrong with it I think it's still cold let's see I'll put my foot down until I get to the statue of Bolívar when you look at that statue from the right hand side it looks as if the Liberator's got his dick out but it's actually his sword I'll pick up petrol in that gas station 'cos I'm nearly out the gauge is already on empty that sculptor was a right prat how come he didn't notice it when he added the sword the snag is I haven't got any dough dumb-

fuck that I am I thought Alicia wouldn't charge me for the drinks
but the bitch charged me even though I rabbitted on about the
Lad the fat whore said he was really well-hung but she still
charged me for the drinks she's got a damned good memory she
remembers everything that I do too if I brake too hard I might
spin the car so I'd better take it steady but anyway at this hour
it's unlikely that another vehicle will come along I'd better not
come to a complete halt I'll just brake gradually and keep going
Chayo must be hopping mad I hope she's asleep and I catch her
really zonked out so she doesn't give me any strife because I'm
totally knackered I won't go in to work tomorrow or rather today
she can phone the office and say I was sick in the night the worst
is that if she gets stroppy she'll refuse to phone in and then I'll
be crapped on from a great height I thought I was going to get
my leg over last night at Grace's but at least I haven't gone into
hock to her it's a bloody good thing Skinny Dog didn't insist or
by now I'd be on my way back from a fabulous fuck with a floozy
and well skint then Chayo would want to know what I'd done
with the spondulicks what damned great ruts in this road the
only reason that shitty Ponce Monroy is mayor is so he can be on
the take lousy Chiquimulan thief he's already built himself two
new houses and the streets are like your granny's face full of
potholes I almost ruined the springs on the right wheel it's
always the same one I can't think why it's always the same
wheel that hits the ruts seems like monumental bad luck to me
I forgot to get some petrol why am I such a berk oh well I'll fill
up at the gas station opposite the Obelisk O-bell-isk what a
weird name like that bloke who studied with me at the Uni
Gobbleguts they nicknamed him he was a fat pig who played
football in the major league I don't know how he could run with
that great paunch he had on him mine's like that now it's
dreadful how could I have let my belly get so fat it flops over the
steering wheel and stops me driving properly that's why I have
to go slowly I hate driving slowly but if I don't I might crash the
car I can't control the wheel I'm going to see if I can't do some
exercise it must be the booze that's made my gut swell up like
this I can't even walk properly Chayo's to blame too she only
gives me junk food that makes you put on weight like the devil

maybe I'll start going to Los Arcos and swim or play tennis or basketball or something like that any of that crap is good for getting your waistline down I used to play tennis with Big Bonce and Boozer yonks ago and Los Arcos is the same kind of place Boozer became a communist too but he was a crafty bastard 'cos he didn't stay here for them to get him he took off for Cuba in '62 with a grant and bye-bye buddies not like the Lad who stayed for them to kill him and Skinny Dog who had to flee the other day Big Bonce told me that Boozer the pisshead spent a year in Havana and then took off for Europe where he dropped out of sight of the communists so why can't I do the same then I wouldn't be all gut and putting up with Chayo I can't stand that woman every day making more and more demands and me in hock up to the eyeballs at least if we had a child it would be something but the bitch doesn't want kids sometimes I think she doesn't love me one day when I went out drinking with Boozer and Big Bonce we took a bath in the Obelisk fountain it was a right rave up the fuzz arrived in a patrol car and took us to the 1st Precinct it was great that day we were buggers but that was nothing compared to the time we had the punch up with all the waiters at El Gallito all because of Big Bonce's bloody-mindedness another damned rut and it's the same tyre again what crap was it I was thinking about I spend my entire life thinking crap oh yeah that day Big Bonce was on a high he was intolerable nobody could control him when the drink got hold of him he went totally ape-shit insisted that a chick who was with a bunch of old guys dance with him the bunch of old guys were mad as hell really sorry they'd gone into El Gallito they thought they were the dog's bollocks and there was Big Bonce insisting on taking the girl on to the dance floor Jesus he was pissed out of his skull his body was swaying from side to side like a hammock and his big head seemed like it was balanced on top the punch up started because one of the old blokes thought that Big Bonce was about to keel over so he stood up to hold him up Big Bonce thought the chap was going to hit him and whop he landed the first punch then all hell was let loose the waiters hurled themselves on Big Bonce Boozer took off his glasses and began flailing out right left and centre and we all leapt in behind him Quino the Lad Skinny Dog Crone and me the entire gang was there that night when I heard the police siren I shouted a warning and pulled Skinny Dog out but there was no way of prising Big Bonce loose we all legged it except him what a shlemozzl they got him into the police car by sheer force of blows and not even then did he stop fighting all I could see was the backseat bouncing every time one of the cops whacked him with his truncheon the car was rocking from side to side and the noise was deafening they took him to the 2nd Precinct with us following behind keeping a close watch when they let us in dammit now I've gone past another gas station that's what comes of remembering all this crap I'll end up out of petrol and then I really will be in the shit I won't get home by seven more like eleven and by then Chayo will have kicked up a helluva rumpus she'll have called the hospital and my mother and the sodding mother that spawned her and there'll be a bloody awful row when I go down the hill by the stadium I'll pick up petrol I should have buggered off with Boozer he said to me once let's piss off out of here if I don't manage to get the grant for Italy I'm still off even if it's to Cuba let's bugger off together if I'd listened to him I'd be in Paris now pratarsing about like him I don't know why I was always afraid of travelling I only managed to get as far as Mexico my old woman was always on about you go for it luv go and study in the States or Paris and I always replied no Ma what do I want to go all that way for it's bad enough being screwed here so I stayed Chayo must have been awake all night praying the bloody woman's that damned sanctimonious I don't know why she demands so much from me like I received the President's salary or something or were the owner of some shit-heap like the Biltmore Hotel if Gloria's Ice Cream Parlour was open I'd have a big ice cream my throat's all dry it must be the hangover maybe if the Bamboo's open I'll drop in for a beer we should have stuck with just beer last night but I was so nervous if the cops had grabbed us I'd be in the 4th Precinct right now black and blue all over that's where the Mano's got its main barracks where they break all the guerrillas how can the boys get involved in all that knowing what evil bastards the military are the worst is one's mates are the most deeply committed and

there's no way you can dissuade them only Big Bonce and I
didn't get enmeshed in all that madness and I can't think why
Big Bonce didn't get sucked in 'cos he was a mad bugger he'd
take on anybody he was a complete loony most likely I'd have
forgotten the episode at El Gallito but, when we got to the 2nd
Precinct, Big Bonce the dumb-fuck was up against the wall
surrounded by pigs every one of them wielding a truncheon and
he was hollering come on you bastards try it just try it you
mother fuckers and all the cops leaped on him when we got him
out the next day his head was even bigger than ever because of
the bruises shit look how pitted the road surface is here
considering that Reforma Avenue is a tourist area and a
residential suburb and its here the military have their lair geez
that Alicia's got fat when I left her place it was already daybreak
she talks a load of cobblers that woman I can't think how I
managed to stand her for like five hours if she were a bit tasty I
could have given her a good fuck but she's got a belly on her
worse than mine it was a miracle that Skinny Dog didn't
suffocate by the time I came out I never noticed I'd left the car
locked tight the poor devil was scarlet I thought he was going to
give me hell for locking him in he's a bloody nuisance he's
constantly getting me embroiled by now they must have checked
his passport I wonder if they've grabbed him at Immigration
tomorrow I'll find out from Titina's brother at the Pan Am office
if he managed to catch the plane but anyway if he didn't it won't
be any use checking because by now he'll be dog meat nowadays
they kill them quickly to avoid any protests by the families or the
student associations this situation is getting more and more
hairy anyway Skinny Dog hasn't been a student for quite a while
but nevertheless the boys would kick up a stink if they seized
him at Immigration I'll let his parents know so they can claim
the body it'd be a dumb move for them to kill him but in this
lousy country it's like that Mexican song says life's not worth a
bean not a bean now I've passed the Bamboo and I didn't look to
see if it was open there's a Chevron station up ahead I'll put a
drop of petrol in or I won't get home we spent a load of dosh at
the Bamboo over some ten years or so we went there every
Saturday regular as clockwork like we were going to church and

every Saturday it was the same old hassle that traffic light at the Polytechnic caught me out I had to stop and waste petrol waiting for the lights to change to green then into first I'll put my foot down and see if I can coast on the drop of gas left it's all downhill the accelerator's flat down I can feel she's not pulling the tank must be empty and who's around to give me a push to the gas station at this hour I'll have to wait for the boys from the Guatemala High School to come by on their way to school to give me a push between them it's about two and a half blocks Sadist studied at that lousy school Porker Zelina used to tell a good story he said he'd seen Brother Mario put his hand on Sadist's arse and begin to stroke his buttocks he always tormented the poor guy but Sadist would only hang his head it was well known that the Marist brothers buggered the pupils even the Lad teased Sadist even though he was the smallest in the class he said he'd followed them one day and that Brother Mario took Sadist to his room but the brother was impatient and couldn't wait he was already taking down his trouser braces before he reached the door that time he told it Sadist had a massive punch up with him but he only took him on because the Lad was small he never said a thing to deny these stories until years later when we forced him to go to the cathouse with us and even had to pay for his fuck then he didn't hang his head instead he laughed maliciously right I've reached the Chevron without any mishap I'll ask for half a gallon

that damned old fart didn't hurry himself like a bloke's got all day to wait about to be served by him Chayo must have been up all bloody night and this old so and so moves like he's crapping himself a turd at a time or something I nearly swore at the old sod this car over-revs in second I hope the gearbox isn't packing up on me I should have told that old wrinkly to check the oil but anyway I haven't got any dosh even if I'd needed some I couldn't have paid for it Chayo won't lend me even a few cents 'til the end of the month she'll ask what I do with my brass what the devil I spend it on and she'll start on at me about you ought to be more careful with money that's all the bloody woman cares about money's for spending not for keeping that's what I say if

the Bamboo had been open I'd have scoffed a ceviche the ones
they serve there are out of this world they always served us
ceviche and chilli with our beers it used to make our mouths
swell but we could always stuff down one more that must be
fifteen years ago now how quickly time passes the same waiters
have been working here all these years the owner died we
nicknamed him the Yeti or the Snowman I think it was Boozer
who dubbed him that Boozer used to come up with some terrific
nicknames he was the one who nicknamed me Rat that little sod
screwed me up for the rest of my life all on account of a Richard
Widmark movie we went to see at the Palace it was there he
stuck me with Rat even back home they call me that he gave
Skinny Dog his nickname too it caused him a lot of suffering the
kids in primary even invented a whistle that sounded like the
name and Skinny Dog spent every break-time chasing half the
kids in the school to thump them because they kept whistling it
nobody was afraid of him they all made fun of him I could turn
right here and go along 12th Avenue maybe that'd be quicker
when I leave the Stadium I'll take a right and head up 13th
Avenue but it all amounts to the same thing anyway because
once I'm on 12th I have to go back to 11th Avenue so either way
it's the same shit I'll go this way and then I'll turn on to 11th so
I won't have to turn back a cigarette wouldn't go amiss or a good
drink to take away the hangover that's beginning to do my head
in if I get a real headache it'll be a bugger having to stand the
volley that I'll get from Chayo with that piercing voice of hers
that bores right into your skull and her endless nagging, nagging
and her non-stop whinging one of these days I'll give her a good
hard backhander to shut her trap once and for all I said last
night I shouldn't drink beer it always makes me ill the following
day and its not only the headache I get the shits afterwards beer
always gives me the trots and I'm stupid when it comes to beer
let's hope that Carvi rum I knocked back at Alicia's will settle
my stomach 'cos otherwise I'll not get a wink of sleep it'll be
endless running to the loo and Chayo shouting after me I told
you so I'm glad that's what you get for being a drunk that's why
you shouldn't go out boozing you're too old for all that worse if
she finds out I was with Skinny Dog she hates him when I had

him at our place she nearly had a nervous breakdown especially when he brought in the arms and he of course didn't give a toss if I had a few cents I'd drop into the Antorcha bar for a quick one that bloody bar brings back some memories whenever I pass it I recall a song by Pedro Infante that I used to sing when I was half cut when I felt totally befuddled with drink I'd sit by the jukebox and listen to it how did it go you passed me indifferent your eyes not glancing once towards me I watched you without you even noticing I spoke to you without you hearing afterwards completely bollocksed we'd leave and crash out over there behind the Olympic swimming pool what a life we led in those days let's see if I can get up the slope by the Stadium in fourth I won't change down just to see if this rust-bucket can make it I was mad about Lilywhite in those days and it was our song and I was always rat-arsed and crooning it rends my soul to know that you forgot me to think I merit not even your disdain the car couldn't make it in fourth so I've had to change down to third dammit I'll go up the hill a bit faster anyway I've got petrol now I'll put her into second to go under the railway bridge fast I don't much like going that way 'cos all those coming down from 2nd Avenue take that bend under the bridge going like the devil and it's hard to control the car because when she pulls out of the curve she jumps it's happened to me coming downhill there before let's hope I don't meet any oncoming vehicles as I go under the bridge we went to the Antorcha for about five years running need a light Antorcha matches see you right shouted Paddle's pa through the loudspeakers of his van who knows what Paddle's up to now it's years since I've set eyes on him who I have seen is his old man still driving the van with those loudspeakers blasting your eardrums he's got the voice of a boring little old git I remember when we were in high school Paddle had a brother who was a gangster who whenever he had an accident would draw his gun and shoot his way out I wonder what happened to Paddle need a light Antorcha matches see you right it'll be terrible if my mother turns up at the house today then I'll be in deep shit Chayo will sulk and won't speak my mother will start asking her a load of stupid questions just to stir it up she'll ask why I'm sleeping or shouldn't she go into the bedroom

and wake me it'll be worse if she notices a whiff of alcohol on me
she'll wake me up and start hassling me I hope to God she
doesn't turn up because afterwards Chayo's always as mad as
hell and she'll start nagging and nagging where's mammy's
darling little boy you ought to be a little man and tell your
mammy not to come here telling you off in front of your wife that
stupid bastard's not looking where he's driving he'd have hit my
bumper if I didn't have such well-honed reflexes even though I
haven't slept all night I'm going to pass him to show him that his
old crate's not a patch on mine it must be a fifty-six model and
he's swanking around in it the wanker won't pull over and he
can hear my horn when I overtake him I'll give him a mouthful
damn it all I passed so quickly that I didn't see if La Vieja garage
is open yet the owner sells cars now and drinks like a fish
everybody in this shit-hole of a country drinks like a fish if my
mother comes over I'd better get up fast and go to work even if I
get in late she's bound to shout to wake me up why can't I tell
her to go to hell once and for all everybody pushes me around
they all do just what they like with me my mother Chayo the
head of the office that I have to invite home to dinner once a
week to fill his face if I don't invite him he turns nasty for the
rest of the week and Chayo demands that I invite him as if it
were obligatory even Skinny Dog has always done whatever he
likes with me he's landed me with some huge problems there go
the girls from the Belén Academy off to classes about what time
is it then bloody hell its ten to seven the first ones start at seven
I wonder if that story's true about the Belén girls masturbating
at school with Coca Cola bottles they say that one of them
pushed it in and out so many times she sucked her inside out
that song roses in the sea is great the girl that sings it is Spanish
they say she never bathes but you can't put any credence in what
lads say they said they had to take out the girl's womb to get the
bottle out that girl over there has got a fabulous arse I ought to
say to her look here mother I'm a married man now why don't
you go back to making Dad's life a misery and leave me alone
but I don't have the nerve I'm sorry for her she's half round the
bend semi-neurotic it was her that forced Chayo on to me and
kept on at me to get married and now she calls me at the office

every day just to run my wife down when are you going to have
a baby I want a little grandchild what the hell's it got to do with
her when I have a kid so what did you get married for then as if
that was the reason I got married I did it so I wouldn't have to
put up with her any more and to have sex for free I was sick of
prostitutes they were getting on my nerves when's your wife
going to get pregnant take her to the doctor because she's the
one at fault not you how could a son of mine not be able I can
imagine my father with a skinful fucking her she must instruct
him how to put it in and take it out of her now go and wash it
with Lux Lux Lux for fucks that chick over there is a great piece
of crumpet she's from the Belgian school when I get to the
Children's Park I'll get a cup of coffee or a Coca Cola I'm dying
of thirst my throat's so dry I can scarcely swallow my own saliva
I've got a tongue like sandpaper I can get one from the Spaniard
at the little café opposite the park I used to go there for a coffee
with Blondie when she worked in the Recinos bakery or if not
there I'll get one at the Recinos Cafetería the coffee's the same
crap either way ah but the Recinos is most likely shut at this
hour and the Spaniards do a breakfast so I'd better park over
there opposite I've got hardly any cash left still I ought to have
enough for a soft drink there's a parking space over there as long
as I don't get hassle from some taxi driver or other Crone used
to call them all arseholes and he should know his old man was
a cabdriver life's weird if I go forward there's just enough room
provided that I don't hit the bumper that would really be the
perfect end to this lousy night I've spent with Skinny Dog it's
like I was a queer spending the night with blokes lovely darling
this clutch is a bit worn this bloody car's an endless open drain
I hope to God the clutch isn't packing up I should never have
lent it to Chayo not content with screwing up my life she's
screwed up my car too the clutch sort of grinds when I go slowly
like this here comes a drunk to hassle me with his keep an eye
on your car sir like hell they keep an eye on it they do sod all
and if you say you don't want them to and tell them to bugger off
they steal your hubcaps themselves this drunk's like me he
hasn't slept all night he looks like an inveterate wino I'm going
to tell him to go to hell but what if later he buggers up my aerial

according to him he's showing me how to back the car in I'll tell him to keep an eye on it hang on I haven't got any money and I can back it in perfectly well on my own what am I short of an arm or something here comes a taxi driver to tell me only cabs can park here they think the square belongs to them I'd better park fast get out and lock it after that they can suck my dick this clutch is almost knackered it's grinding I'd better put on the handbrake 'cos these cabdrivers are crafty sods they might manage to bump my car out since there's a gang of them my eyes are all red from not getting a wink of sleep the lock must be rusted I can't get the key in next time I'm going to buy a Volkswagen those don't bug you as much as these damned American cars that are supposedly so luxurious oh good the key's gone in at last I'll ignore him if I turn my head to see what he wants he's going to tell me to remove my car I'd best play dumb I'll cross the road quickly and nip into the café this coffee's like dishwater it's so weak more like gnat's piss I would have done better to order a Coca Cola but I got really cold getting out of the car Blondie and I sat at this very table she thought I didn't know that the Lad was shagging her and she was flirting with me and Boozer had already told me he was giving her the occasional bonk or two and Little Dick was her official boyfriend she was a right little goer was Blondie I was the only one who knew the whole scene because they all told me about their affairs and then I'd come and sit with her here and tell her everything to see how much of it was true the worst thing was that the Lad was her cousin and he almost got her pregnant that's why he stopped fucking her in those days he went round scared shitless because Blondie's period didn't start and the Lad thought he'd put her in the club and the baby would turn out to be an idiot with a big head as if he'd been given a potion of sow's milk the worst thing was both their families were living together in the same house what a load of trouble that would have been every sip of this coffee is worse that taxi driver's spying on me the sod he thinks I'm going to let him say something if he tries to intimidate me I'll give him a mouthful he thinks he's got some right to rail at me but I'll soon tell him where to get off nobody's going to try it on with me wow I've got an erection every time I have a hangover after a night on the tiles I get a massive hard-on or maybe it's because of this heat according to these Spaniards they brought over the style of the Madrid inns to Guate with their little alcoves and all those bits and pieces like the rustic wooden tables and the little curtains that's what Blondie's friend said that little Spanish girl who made my prick stand up every time I looked at her arse she had big legs like baseball bats with plump calves but she had a luscious tight pair of buttocks each time I looked at them I wondered what it would be like to stick my dick between those buttocks and then sit on a chair with her on top squeezing me the cockteaser she laughed at me every time she saw me because the priest told me off once in front of her they lived on the second floor of the school and I used to sit at the bottom of the stairs and watch her go upstairs I'd sit on the first stair and watch her arse as she went up Sonja she was called like the ice skater that time the priest caught me spying and gave me a tongue lashing when I looked up there she was laughing at me but the best thing was when Tribilín, the Lad and Boozer got in through the school roof at night and pinched the end-of-year exam papers this coffee's so bad I could throw it in the bloody Spaniard's face its weak as my pee and really cold totally undrinkable I'm getting hungry I should order a pastry but I don't know if I've got enough for one I've only got coins and I'd better not take them out of my pocket it's such a hassle counting out the cents to see if I've got enough I'll put my hand in my pocket and try and find out how much I've got by feel that's a five these two coins are a problem they could be a ten or a one cent if they are only a one I haven't even got enough to pay for this lousy coffee why didn't I realise I was so skint outside I'm absolutely broke Chayo's going to kick up one almighty stink more because of the money than for not coming home all night this is a ten because it's got a milled edge so that means I've got fifteen cents that's enough for the coffee and if this other one is a ten I can afford a pastry I think it's a one while I was taking my break Blondie used to call me and ask me to go and have a coffee with her since I worked just round that corner in the courthouse in the Americas Building I'd feel really macho and accept but then she started to take advantage of me she'd order an empanada or a rum baba or a pastry and when it was time to pay she'd play dumb and I'd have to put my hand in my pocket she'd watch my face the wicked little devil I was in love with her for years and she didn't even give me a look she said I was a drunkard and too dark skinned she was a racist the wild creature what a lousy night I've had going round and round in the car for hours on end my hands are numb from so much driving I've held the wheel so long I'm going to have a massive pain in my shoulders tomorrow I used up a tankful of petrol it was a rough night and all for nothing I ended up paying like twenty quetzals and saw fuck all for it Alicia is old and fat with a big belly and wrinkles she's got crow's feet that reach to her ears I think she's even a bit doddery not only did she soak me for money but I had to put up with her endless spiel all night long and her belly's so revolting it hangs on her in spite of her girdle I couldn't get close to her the rolls of fat hang out over the top of it a woman with a big belly is repulsive when Chayo's lying on her side her spare tyre droops when I take her from behind I put my dick in between her buttocks and run my hands over her belly and I can feel her fat flopping on to the sheets why doesn't she want to have kids blasted woman finally after all those drinks Alicia got randy and started rubbing herself up against me but I wouldn't give her one even if I were pissed out of my skull it must be like dipping your wick in mushy porridge God knows how many men have been through her cunt must be so sloppy and loose you could dive in without touching the sides and get lost up the tunnel I didn't order the pastry and now I've almost finished my coffee and I've got no money for another one I'd better not order anything but get going straight away I'm sitting here thinking rubbish and Chayo must be as mad as a rattlesnake these Spaniards have taken on a waitress when they came from Spain they had a big fat daughter built like a barrel and on top of that full of bullshit she thought she was really something she looked down on all of us considered us all Indians she only associated with people from the Spanish circle the bitch and she was dead ugly too the useless tub of lard when they first came here they waited tables themselves what a set up now they've got a waitress and the Spaniard must be shagging her because that wife of his is not up to much now I wonder why Spanish women get so fat when she came from Spain that Virginia had a great arse we'd bunk off classes to go and watch her at the Euzkadi café Isaías used to get furious and call the priest and we'd be watching Virginia all morning I saw her the other day she looked like a prize porker ready for market all Spanish women get like barrels as soon as they're pushing thirty that little serving girl is quite tasty Indian girls are like that they don't get fat they always stay slender that's why when the missus gets past it the Spangos start to shag Indian girls and take on waitresses so they can poke them too the Chinese are the same the owner of the Fu Lu Sho changes waitresses every six months he bonks the lot of them and then gets in new ones practically all of them end up on the game and screw up the boys that bird Rosemary gave Big Bonce a dose of the clap and she was a virgin so she says but more men had flown her than United Airlines let's see if that little Indian corn grinder notices I'm calling her to bring me the bill ten cents for the coffee I'd better go and pay at the till and leave her five cents for the tip the poor thing probably starts work at six in the morning bloody hell that's practically the day before and she wouldn't finish much before eight at night they're exploiters these useless bastards I don't know why this rotten country's like it is all these no good foreigners come here and take advantage and we're always the ones who get screwed they arrive here without a bean to their name and in three years they've got a shop or a cathouse or a restaurant or some other goldmine and in a little while the bastards are rolling in it that little corngrinder's blind I'd better go and pay at the till I didn't want to see the Spango's mush but this Indian pussy doesn't notice a thing

bloody hell there's that taxi driver still waiting for me just to tell me I shouldn't park here the twat I'll play dumb and not answer him or it'll be worse this key's still trying my patience hell it's nearly seven already and its a bit cold it must be the lack of sleep that's making me feel chilled because its warm and sunny I left the car facing directly into the sun so it must be like an oven I spent like about twenty minutes slumped in front of one cup of

coffee what a berk no wonder the Spango was watching me as if
I were pinching something I'm going to get this lock oiled or else
one of these days the key'll break off and then I'll be right up the
creek those taxi blokes are full of bullshit that chap spent twenty
minutes waiting for me and then didn't dare say a thing I
wonder what he read on my face that made him back off and just
look at me askance now he's the one playing dumb he can kiss
my arse does he own the place I'll park where the hell I like and
only the cops can tell me otherwise and not even them because
if they give me a fine I'll take it to a mate and he'll make it
disappear let's try the clutch without pulling away yes it's got a
very strange noise a kind of grating Chayo must have knackered
it what possesses me to let her have the car to learn to drive in
she justs experiments with it and buggers it up and afterwards
it's me that has to pay and she complains that the money doesn't
go anywhere it'd be better if I paid for her to have driving lessons
at the Sandoval Aquino School see nothing happened here there
wasn't a fight I got it right it's weird how my words come out in
rhyme like that without me trying to do it strange how they
mean something quite different if you just change the order
around a bit I'd better concentrate or I might get a bump in the
rear if I pull out without taking care all the juggernauts and
articulated trucks heading for the Atlantic highway come along
here I'd better keep my wits about me if one of those hits me
there'll be nothing left of the rear end imagine the stink my
mother would kick up then okay I've got out without anything
happening zilch what a bore to have to see Chayo's mug she'll
sulk all week I can't stand her any longer I ought to take a
mistress and not be always following the same old routine going
straight home from work if I go for a couple of beers with my
mates she sulks and then she's all buddy-buddy with my mother
she rings her and tells her I haven't come home and who knows
what's happened to me it's gone seven and I must be out boozing
and the next day my mother the old troublemaker won't let me
work she calls all day long and nags me I've got Chayo sulking
and the old bat nagging I ought to get a mistress then there'd be
something to row about what a boring life I lead from home to
work and back again getting drunk on Saturday suffering my

143

mother's endless tirades and Chayo's sulks on Sunday then back to the same old shit on Monday lying in front of the telly every night of the week the next day the same both of them giving me strife I should get a mistress and fuck her regularly maybe she'd give me a child and things would look up if it weren't for my mother kicking up such a stink I'd probably go out drinking every night but all hell's let loose every time I get a skinful the old crone must think I'm still her little darling that she can nag to death but I'm the twat for not standing up to her and telling her to go to hell still not even my father could manage that there he is the poor old sod all cowed prematurely aged his head hanging he never could raise it my mother must have told him when he could have a drink when he had to go to bed when he had to fuck her I nearly ran over that dog thinking all this crap a bloody dog would really have done in my bumper especially since the cars nowadays are like tin the slightest bump dents them right in and only half a block from a police station he was a big dog he'd have made mincemeat of me if I'd hit him there'd have been ructions I'd have had a whole bunch of cops from the 2nd Precinct on top of me in a split second it's just as well I had to turn at La Merced Church and they couldn't see me any more because I had to jam on my brakes hard scared shitless only the cop who's always hanging around on the corner of 4th and 11th turned to look but he turned a blind eye when he saw it was a dog once I hit one by the cemetery and my bumper was a complete write-off the whole thing caved in and it was no joke it cost me about eighty smackers and the sodding dog just limped off howling bloody dogs all that din they make I can't stand them that Sonja the Spanish bird had one and the time when that lot broke in over the school roof to steal the tests the lousy mutt began howling like something demented and screwed the whole thing up they had to jump down into the courtyard of the house next door what a caper the fat woman who lived there called the fuzz because in the hassle Tribilín dropped the bolt he was carrying and it went rolling down hitting every tile in turn 'til it fell into the courtyard the family next door was sitting having dinner when that lot came hurtling through the middle of their dining room the Lad nonchalant as ever raised his hat and went evenin' all as he whizzed past them mad buggers I'd been waiting on the corner watching out for the old bill and when I saw them legging it from the house next door I nearly wet myself laughing and all because of a dog I'm nearly there now my nerves are all on edge why should I get nervous they can go to hell the lot of them I can't do whatever I like nowadays I'm always on edge expecting a row when I lived with my old folks and I went out on the razzle I had to get a right skinful before I got home so I wouldn't think wouldn't hear wouldn't give a toss I couldn't even hear what my mother said to me I just laughed at the sound of her voice from afar from far far away in my alcoholic stupor I could make out her muttering that wretched drunken boy my father just stared at me in spite of my inebriated state I could see his little eyes dancing with glee behind his glasses the poor old chap enjoyed my piss-ups as much as if they were his own he must have thought that if he couldn't do it himself it was great that I could I was never able to rebel completely if I had been maybe I'd be with the others in exile or dead or up to my neck in something or other but I never had the balls to do anything that went against my s'mother just drink and when the old crow cried because I was boozing I'd laugh like a drain on the inside and insult her the old hypocrite she lived in the church why do I go on putting up with her Chayo can't stomach her either but she uses her against me why didn't I go off with that lot at the time of the Liberation when the cadets fired on the liberationists in the Roosevelt Hospital on the second of August all the boys joined the liberationists to fight against the military and the only thing I did was put notes under the door of their houses to let their families know that they'd gone to Zacapa and I stood by the truck thinking about my mother and the ear-bashing she'd give me if I went with them they sang as they left that was their first adventure what an escapade and within five years all of them were communists the Lad was even killed poor old Lad if I'd had any guts I'd have gone with them and not be still here with my life all screwed up putting up with my bloody s'mother Skinny Dog's exiled in Mexico Boozer never came back again he's living in Paris I wonder what Paris is like the priest buggered off too he couldn't

take Guate any more this country does you in there's sod all to
do no parks no good films the censorship won't permit anything
just a load of bars this is a city of bars and churches oh shit that
was my sodding mother coming out of San José church and the
old bitch can recognise this car from a mile away I'd better burn
the gas and pass quickly in case after mass she intends to go and
stick her nose in at my place I was under the impression that
they'd given us the house as a wedding present but she calls me
and tells me its mortgaged how generous what a bargain but she
goes chucking money around in all directions so much for Father
so and so, so much for the parish priest bastards the lot of them
they're like octopuses the sons of bitches they consume you bit
by bit curse every bloody one of them if my mother found out
that I don't go to mass any more she'd make my life hell one
more block and I'm home I wonder why I'm so on edge what can
Chayo do to me the most she can do is scream and sulk all week
maybe if I give her a fuck right now she'll calm down but the
snag is in the morning she smells vile her breath stinks she
reeks of sweat her hair sticks up on end and her mouth's like a
sewer when you kiss her you wonder where her tongue's been
her cunt has the stench of urine and on top of all this she won't
let me do it she hurls at you Oh God no not now she's always full
of I'm too tired my something or other hurts I'm ill it's one of
those days the hypocrite can never say I've got my period but
maybe if I shag her now she won't bug me so much and if my
mother comes she won't say anything but how could I think she
wouldn't tell her that's how she gets her revenge I don't know
what it is she wants revenge for she's always looking at me with
hatred in her eyes I can't imagine why 'cos I give her all my
salary I come home early I buy her whatever she wants she's got
me up to my eyeballs in debt she brings back a heap of receipts
she's signed for every time she goes out to the shops she signs for
everything sign sign sign and she can't imagine how much in
hock I am I take her to the pictures at least once a week I buy
her the ham she likes I fuck her at least once a week or a
fortnight I mustn't let her see that I'm nervous or she'll want to
know where I've been 'cos I've got a guilty look about me God
what a boring life I've never been able to do whatever I fancied

when I fucked her for the first time she kicked up a huge fuss she made a big scene on the wedding night and right from the beginning she started complaining the woman next door's a bit of alright and she gives me the come-on if she's not careful I'll put it in her freshly bathed pink arse the nicest thing about her is she hasn't got a big belly and she's got luscious legs she gives me some real come hither looks if she's not very careful I'm going to grab her and give her one the snag is its very near to home I'll have to pull up very slowly so Chayo won't hear the car otherwise she'll come out all dishevelled in one of those ridiculous nightdresses she wears it makes her look a real old frump okay now I've got to open the door my little neighbour looks like a girlfriend I used to like once how come I didn't notice that before I'm always rushing in and out so I'd scarcely noticed I reckon it's this life of fruitless running around that makes me ill always stuffing crap up my arse for my irritable bowel Fibogel or Nivea Cream or some such stuff Chayo says it's because I go everywhere by car but the doctor says it's nerves all this rushing around will be the death of me and I hope it'll be soon I'd never really looked at her carefully because of all this belting about when I leave home I'm really hard pressed and when I get back it's late and Chayo's got her knickers in a twist and then there are the phone calls all day long the secretary's already hopping mad 'cos it's at least five times a day it's your wife on the line sir she's always watching always checking up on me she can't see that no woman's going to look at me with this great paunch she ought to get a job the lazy bitch then she wouldn't have time for all this spying I'm sick of all this surveillance if I were a womaniser that spent all his time chatting up birds she wouldn't even notice because that's life when a bloke's a skirt-chaser the wife doesn't even realise they're such stupid bitches now to open the door the darned great thing creaks like the devil it'll be like a horror movie where you open the creaking door and there's the witch in a long nightshirt down to her ankles toothless rheumy dishevelled foul-smelling with yawns that belch fetid fumes in your face arms crossed deathly deadly pale as a corpse if she's like that now I'll scream just to make her mad anyway she couldn't get any angrier well what a surprise the door didn't make any noise but when I drive the car in the bloody woman will get up and come out to kick up a stink I'll drive it in in first with just one press on the accelerator so I won't have to let the engine thrum inside once I'm in I'll switch off straight away and not leave the engine going 'cos it echoes all through the house the only thing is that the noise of the brakes may be worse well let's see what happens oh God if a bus comes by now as I'm crossing the avenue it'll make mincemeat of me it'll toss me at least half a block but it's only a minute while I position the car to go in why is the garage on such a slope it makes it much harder to get the car in anyway she already knows I didn't come home all night so what the hell does it matter if she knows that I'm back it went right in with just one movement and the brakes didn't even make a squeak now for a spot of shut-eye what if I wash my face and wake her up and tell her I've just got up no she's not that stupid that only works in jokes if only I'd had a good fuck with a whore but to have to put up with an ear-bashing for nothing is dead unfair Skinny Dog should be arriving in Mexico now no the BAC one eleven jet takes about an hour and twenty minutes so right now it'll be just about reaching the frontier I wonder if I'll remember that I've got to find out tomorrow if he got away alright or if the police caught him that door has buggered everything up I was closing it quietly and the damned thing got stuck and let the cat out of the bag now to face the monster what a life bloody awful a real drag and dead tedious if it weren't for these exciting moments really what else would there be to make it worth living and now I'm left alone without my only friend even if he is a guerrilla I wonder if I should get myself a mistress because now life's going to be more boring than ever

9

BOOZER

1964

How was I supposed to love you or desire you or keep you? I couldn't love any other way. I watch your face, your eyes are closed; you seem to be suffering, whilst I "perform the infinite between your thighs". You close your eyes, you moan, it seems as if you're about to cry, I go more slowly, I'm alarmed, am I hurting you? I thrust and thrust, you moan and close your eyes. I loved you as much as I could, the only way I was able. But, perhaps the truth was I didn't really know how to love you or possess you or keep you. You perspire, you dig your nails into my back, you shudder and let out a little cry. I'm frightened again, you flush, I don't know what to do any more, whether to go on or stop, I'm easily alarmed. It wasn't all my fault, I did everything I could. How should I have acted? By adapting my words, my actions, the facts, so that you would go on loving me and I go on loving you? Do you think I knew everything there was to know about you? Do you think you did all the right things so I'd go on loving you? You shudder, you start, you moan again, I stop, I imagine that I'm causing you pain. Is it possible that I'm your first? Can that really be blood on the sheet? / cliché / You didn't want to remove your clothes, I even wrote a poem about the first time it happened. You undressed without me telling you, without me asking you to / even your clothing lying inert, abandoned on the tiles, was red with shame / Your thin body was defenceless and you blushed from head to foot / you asked why we like to make love in the nude / it certainly could have been the first time, how could I have known? But now I'm sure of it. Were you so certain that I couldn't stop loving you? Was that why you adopted that sensual, tragic pose that evening on the Malecón in Havana with your silhouette framed by the red orb of the setting sun / cliché / Did you already know it then? Your hands, your feet, flutter, they cling to me, to my hands, to my feet, you tremble all over, you thrust upwards lifting me violently, I'm alarmed again, can I be hurting you? You weep, your body threshes, I try to withdraw, you pull me back into you violently and cry out, I'm embarrassed, I'm not ready to climax yet, I can't concentrate, you open your eyes, I close them immediately, your legs grip my body, my back aches. It was a year ago and I'm still wondering. When I left the airport I could feel your eyes riveted on my back, I felt shame, panic, a desire to turn round and go back, but that's the way I am. How should I have loved you to make sure of keeping you? I gave you everything I had except my security, why did I leave you? Not even I myself know that / I creep along, someone is moaning in Pepa's room, the corridor is long and dark. The last time that I got up to pee, I felt a hand grabbing my shoulder in the darkness, I screamed and then everything went black, when I awoke I was in my mother's room, they were giving me warm water and rubbing alcohol on my forehead. I never learn. Why did they have to put my room near the garage? Whenever I want to pee at night I go to the maid's loo, it's much nearer. Pepa really is moaning, but she's laughing too, she lets out little cries, she must be dreaming. Should I go into her room and wake her up? Mama says that it's bad to have nightmares. I ought to go and wake her. It's very late and she's got the light on, she's moaning, I can hear her moving around a lot, I think I'll go in. But what if it's locked? I get down on my hands and knees to look under the door, the bed creaks, she's crying. Maybe somebody's trying to kill her. I think I'll go in. I open the door. Pepa's on her back with her legs wide open and she's putting a huge candle into her hole. She didn't even hear me come in. But if it hurts her and makes her cry, why is she putting it in? I stand silent, her body jerks and she cries softly, she whimpers and moves faster, she closes her eyes and seems to be dying. I'm terror-stricken. Afterwards, they're going to say I killed her. Why did I have to come in here? Pepa emits a deep, hoarse moan and relaxes her body completely, she stretches her legs and lies as if she were dead. They're going to say I killed her. I scream and faint / I'm not going to come yet, whenever I move I think a load of rubbish. You are off in a world of your own. How hard it is for you to come. But you enjoy each moment as though it were unique. If only I could feel the same. Why must I always be thinking? I loved you. I really did. My briefcase was heavy and the plane was standing on the runway far, far off. Your eyes remained fixed on the window of the waiting room. They burned into my back. I loved you in the way I love: without loving. It's been a year and I'm still thinking about you. Maybe I think about you today because I received a letter from your sister attacking me: "It's best if I simply tell you that, since your departure, Tatiana has felt that you deceived her. Possibly she felt it long before then. I contributed to this state of mind before you left because I saw that you were contradicting yourself on many matters and because you lied with impunity right from the start." You pull me towards you, you're perspiring, your brow glistens with clusters of pearls / cliché / there's foam on your lips, you scream and pull my hair, I abandon all control, I feel a swell surging from within me, your legs gripping my back relax, you lie panting, you open your eyes look at me and smile, you are like a little girl thanking me for a present, I love you, I love you, you say, I laugh and close my eyes. You move away and turn me on to my back, you climb on me, you mount me, you take my hands to support yourself and close your eyes to "perform the infinite between my thighs". When I reached the airport you were already there, you seemed impatient, you said only the essential, your eyes were red but you were very calm. You went with me to check my passport (*What foolishness. If she only interests you as a memory, why are you reliving everything that happened? Don't you realise you're harming yourself. What is this obsession with remembering? But don't you realise that it's not me who's remembering. I'm being made to remember. Someone is recalling me and remembering through me and through you. We no longer exist, we are past, we are just a memory. Someone revives us because his past won't leave him in peace, because we are his memories. Isn't that an excuse on your part? I think that we invented him, and he lives again through us and that he couldn't write if we didn't exist, that he is our present whilst we are his past. He lives, relives his past and our past and everyone else's past. The worst of it is that it's causing us pain. That's why I repeat that, if she no longer interests you other than as a memory, it's best to leave her alone, because you may wake her and you'll hurt her deeply. Drink your wine and leave us in peace, go and walk through Saint Michel and throw yourself into the Seine. Perhaps that way you'll leave yourself in peace and us too, because if you are a masochist we certainly aren't. We aren't. We are dead. Let us sleep. You want to waken us and it's so cold. Can't you see that mist? Can't you see it's night time and you're drunk, you've had several bottles of wine. Do you have the money to pay? It's getting late for you. Remember that you have to take the underground from the Luxembourg Station, you have to descend those endless steps and, when you arrive, it'll be after one and it'll be too late to catch the last train and you'll have to go back up all those endless steps and stand like an idiot on the corner of Rue Gay Lussac and you'll have no other alternative than to stand looking at the Luxembourg gardens like a fool and you'll start to bring us out again into all this cold, here at least there's a little warmth and there's wine, but out there in the street, when you begin to walk through Saint Michel towards Port Royal and you reach the corner of Montparnasse stiff with cold we'll be hanging frozen from your empty head. Leave us in peace now. Forget us. Don't think about us any more, you're hurting us.)* Then I looked into your eyes, they were damp, red, sad. I caressed them with infinite sadness. I caressed them as I caressed your buttocks when you were lying naked, face down on the bed in my hotel room, when you lay still with your face in my pillow and I began to explore your body with my hand. I twisted your fine hair through my fingers and you moaned softly. As I ran my finger tips down your back, spasms of frenzy seemed to shatter your fragile spine. I descended lower and lower until I reached your tiny exquisite buttocks where my hand paused and I caressed, probed and kissed your two creamy orbs that were white as milk, no as marble, as alabaster (cliché, be careful with memories, they become honeyed and cling). I felt them, I explored your most secret parts, my erection grew hard, I penetrated you from behind where it hurt you most, where you seemed to split open, where you felt no pleasure but only moaned with pain, yet still did not refuse me. That's why I did it, to see to what degree you belonged to me. How far my power over you extended. At that moment I could have made you a prostitute or a medium into whom I could stick pins without you feeling a thing and that power made me strong, dominant. But then I withdrew and I kissed your buttocks tenderly, with love, because you have to know that I did love you. "She never said anything to you. She's not like me. She never says anything that might offend. Tatiana was totally disillusioned by you and, believe me, she has forgotten you in spite of the fact that we do occasionally speak about you. But, almost always when you crop up in our conversation, it's because we're talking about literature, never about love." (*And still you go on harming yourself. That letter from Tania served to hurt your pride, to take the lid off your conscience, to awaken us and destroy our peace, you're incredibly vain, whilst you were sure that she continued to love you you never thought about it at all, but now that you've received that letter you think about her all day long, you awaken us and don't let us rest in peace. You're like all writers, a vain wretch.*) You must always know that I loved you, you must know that I love you and that you love me, because that's how it has to be, because when I wiped away the first tear that you shed when you accompanied me to the window to check my passport you looked at me and your face told me, it told me as your lips had never done, because it was not until then that I realised that I was making a mistake. You must tell me that Tania is wrong, that when you talk about me, even though it may be about literature, you're telling yourself, I love him, I love him, I love him. It's all that I have left now, your eyes fixed on my back and me with the feeling of mistake, of defeat. I'm no revolutionary I didn't leave for that reason. I left because you made me a revolutionary. Because your idealism made me a revolutionary who had to return to his country to bring about the revolution. I never thought properly about it, but now I realise that the only thing that interested me was you. I left just to please you, so as not to let you down, and here I am sitting in a café on the Boulevard Saint Michel drinking wine and remembering you. I'm a deserter. I don't want to return to my country, I love you, because now you are my impossible. I cannot die for you, I cannot get to be for you pure literature, because for me you are the best thing that ever happened in my life. I knew it when you gave me your hand and said so you're leaving, then I felt a gripe in my stomach and I remembered that I hadn't defecated that morning as I usually did and that it was a real drag to have to go to the airport toilet because it wouldn't be long before the plane took off, but then I had a second stomach cramp so I gave you my briefcase, the briefcase that while I was in the loo you filled with all my memories, with the photos that I'd given you, with the bracelet that I'd given you, with the ring that I'd given you. It wasn't until I reached Prague, when I went to the toilet in Prague airport and took out papers from the briefcase that I found all my memories piled there. Why did you do it? How was I supposed to love you or desire you or keep you? Why that last act of revenge that would make your memory eternal? At that moment I knew it, as I sat on the loo feeling the heat of my faeces flow slowly between my buttocks, I knew, I knew with absolute conviction that I was wrong. I recognised my mistake. I can't believe that my memory is dying now. "It's like your poem says 'I shall die like an old memory that loses it's significance with the years.' What a good poet you are, what a good friend and what a bad lover!" You mount me, straddle me, impaled on my member, you take my hands to keep your balance and you move, rocking back and forth on top of me "performing the infinite between my thighs". You moan, you close your eyes, you flush, you're no longer like a little girl but a mare on her stallion, possessing him, dominating him, you fill me, you're the perfect man for my size, I feel that I'm complete inside and outside, you say, you utter incoherences whilst you gallop me, you ride me, you cover me, you hold me by the reins, you are the perfect man for my fire, and you are the perfect woman for my penis. You begin to perspire again you are incandescent, you glow, your whiteness blazes like fire, my erection grows, I arch my back thrusting up my buttocks to ram it into you up to the hilt, amidst your gasps, sighs, moans you thank me, I never thought that it would be like this, my love, my love, my love, and you fall on top of me exhausted, hungry for me, biting and kissing me all over. It was then that I asked you. Before I left I washed my hands carefully. I knew that I was going to take your face in my hands and ask you, did you ever really love me? Why is it always the same old hackneyed stuff, the same words for the same situations? (*Can it be that, even if we haven't read Corín Tellado romances,*[7] *we all bear something of them within us. These clichés are atrocious, when one's off-guard words get together in such a format that they seem to have come straight out of a soap opera. Their meaning is the same and their form too and, this is the worst part, it's the same here in our brains as in the brain of the soap writer. They make us into a living cliché a photo charged with words.*) So, not to get disillusioned, I sit drinking in Paris, it's the most serious thing that you can do whilst remembering, whilst analysing your past actions with a pitiless letter in your hand, a sheet of paper loaded with resentment. Jealousy travels through the ether, it clings to the paper, it's within you, it's everywhere. Then I took your face in my hands and I asked you, I wanted you to be honest, truthful at that last moment, I gave you the chance to be so at that last instant of our life together. "But you weren't honest, comrade. Tatiana is a young woman who is mentally strong. That's why I don't understand why you deceived her for a whole year. I say deceived because that in reality is what you did. Maybe you don't care for that word but it's the best one that comes to mind and I'm not one who minces her words. Deceived because you were lying and because she believed those lies for a while. That is deceit. In the dictionary it says 'To deceive: to mislead: delude: cheat'." I waited but you didn't give me an answer. I took your face in my hands and kissed your sad eyes. I kissed your eyes madly, I drew you towards me, you were already biting my neck, moving again with greater fury, revitalised, ferocious, insatiable, with your hands on my shoulders, your legs tight around my thighs sweating with desire, your moans seared into the depths of my brain, I was coming but I had to hold back, I couldn't disappoint you now when you were about to climax, I had to think about something else, "So many years have passed since that yesterday. They left in their grey wake a thousand disappointments," the coloured trio sang close to the microphone to make their voices sound softer, so they didn't need to shout, you took my hand and pulled me, you led me into that little bar, the El Dorado in the Havana Riviera, it was our first Saturday together since I'd kissed you angrily at Río Cristal in the miniature castle the day that your blonde girlfriend got married. "But when I want to remember our past I feel like ivy clinging to you. And so for all eternity I'll follow you. I'm bound to you more closely than ivy." The coloured singers opened their mouths wide as they intoned the pop song, you pulled me to a table and ordered two cuba libres. It was the same song, the song they were playing the first day I arrived in Havana. It was impossible to hold back, I had to come, come with me, I'm coming with you, wait for me, it would be best if you write to me and I organise my papers because today it's impossible and if you miss the plane who knows when you'll be able to leave Havana. If at that moment you had asked me to stay I would have done so, I swear it. That's how I make my decisions, with no complications, I'm not complex or mercurial. When I make a decision, it's final. "Tatiana is not mercurial, Tatiana is a woman who needs a permanent relationship, she needs to have a home and children, to be both companion and lover, wife and mother, sister and friend. It's as if I were trifling with the affections of a man full of dreams. As if I told him that I can be that woman for him. You did something like that to my sister. Something like that, comrade. You gave the impression that you were a normal man but you're quite the opposite, you're a complex complicated character. God only knows what you're looking for but you can't find it, you never will. You're trying to find yourself and when you do you'll be absolutely horrified to see what you're really like because you're not a man of peace, with stable loves and a calm life free of psychological complications. That's why you spend your life fleeing." Then I left, I went off towards the airport exit, I turned to look at you one more time, you were motionless, standing like a statue facing the immense window which separated the runway and the building. You remained engraved on my brain. Fixed in time. When I came you came too. Then you fell upon me, your breasts lay on my chest, soft, still, somnolent and your sweat began to flow, to slide between my legs, over my belly, my shoulders, you were still kissing me, I had dug my nails into your back, I had taken you at the last moment when you said to me in your last frenzied gasp, come with me! But you didn't say it, I left you standing facing the window, waiting for you to say it to me but you didn't. You only gave me the briefcase, handed me the briefcase that you had filled with the presents that I had given you; instead of retaining me, you sent me away avenged. Then I gave you one last kiss. I took your face in my hands and you kissed me, your body was weightless your eyes were open and you looked at me tenderly, you laughed, you smiled mischievously, you had taken me, you had possessed me, I was yours, you had hope. If only you had said it to me, told me, but you always stayed silent. Perspiring, exhausted you slid down beside me and lay on your back with your legs wide apart, thinking, gazing at the ceiling of the hotel bedroom. I went to the bathroom, as I urinated I began to realise that I was tying myself down. You were tying me and I had to break free. I hadn't come to Cuba to stay, to be tied down again. I'd fled from my mother, from my mother's intolerable love. I'd broken the bonds and I couldn't go back to my chains. I had to be free. You represented children, home, house, family, fixed income, revolution prepared, seasoned, spoon-fed into my mouth. That wasn't what I wanted for myself. I had to choose. I had to leave as quickly as possible or stay forever. For me you represented settling down. As I shook my member, I decided. The Party rep also thought like you, he wanted to enlist me into a cadre school so I'd graduate as a Marxist. How ridiculous. "I believe that when you come through these mental traumas you will be a good Marxist. Not before. The Marxist is an individual free of complexes and traumas, of absurd unjustifiable suffering, of lies. The Marxist is a person who lives reality and does not live in fantasies or climb into the clouds to say I love you. Do you want to know who has the makings of a good Marxist? Tatiana. Do you want to know another? Certainly the child that she'll have when she marries." I had to leave or stay. I had to go away or marry you. And I loved you. But I loved my freedom more. It's really cold. When I reach Denfert-Rochereau, I'll be half way home. I've been sitting in that café thinking rubbish all this time. The metro's closed and I've got no money. Now I'll have to walk to the University City. It's a long trek and it's already nearly two in the morning, it'll be about three by the time I get there and I'll be knackered. (*You're really kidding yourself. What made you leave was your fear of staying or fear of yourself. Why do you come out with so much inane rubbish now when it's all so simple? You didn't love her. You never loved her. It was all just to have another mother. Now you're alone, stupidly alone. Your only contact with the outside world is a few letters that arrive from time to time. Is this freedom? Is this what you've fought for all these years? Wouldn't you be better off living peacefully in an apartment in Marianao or El Vedado, not having all these pangs of conscience you carry around? And especially not taking us out to dance in this terrible cold. We don't want to take part in the dance, leave us here thrown away, abandoned, on René Coty Avenue, frozen forever. We're tired of coming out to perform every time you fancy it. We are words, just words, toss us out and leave us, don't conjure us up any more because we're tired of meaning, of justifying things that we don't understand. Go and live in isolation, disappear.*) And what if Tania was right? That letter upset me a bit. I've spent the money that I was going to use for next week's food. Now I'm going to have to wait for them to send me the next fortnight's allowance. What am I going to do now? I don't know where to go? How long will I be in Prague? What am I going to Prague for? When I get on the plane, it will be impossible to return. Then I'll be beyond you once and for all, even now there's still time. Your eyes were calm. Did you love me? I think you did. Then why didn't she say, stay with me? Then why didn't I tell her that, at that moment, I had taken the decision? She was on my bed in the hotel room, her legs apart, resting. The sweat was running over your chest, over your legs, over your brow, and your sex was wide open, red, throbbing. Then I forgot everything. I forgot what I'd decided. Not yet, you said, but I couldn't hear you any more, I was once more like I always was, like I was before, like I was after, on top of you, "performing the infinite between your thighs". I looked at you for a long time, your mouth was saying no but your eyes were calling to me, I waited for a moment, a single instant to watch what you were doing as you refused me, you thought that I was going to do just what you wanted me to, that I was hesitating, and you pulled me towards you, you raised your buttocks to reach me, to sink me into you, you pulled my waist, drawing me towards you. Then it was I who said not yet, with a smile on my lips, with all the cruelty of my throbbing prick, then you begged for it and I let myself fall, I fell upon you, as I always did, as I had before, as never before, whilst I sank my head into your hair. Then you moved away for a moment, you abandoned my head that had just sunk into your hair that smelt of the sea breeze, of perfume, of you, and you looked at me. I remained sitting on the wall of the Malecón watching you, I asked you why you were moving away and you told me it's better if we don't go on seeing each other, there's no point, sooner or later you'll go away, you'll leave me, you'll go back to your country. I looked at you for a long time whilst the waves beat on the stones at the foot of the Malecón, then I gazed at the sea whilst I sat thinking, it was like a desert, like an endless blue cloth, like a silver disc that stretched between us and separated us forever; only its borders betrayed it, proving it vulnerable, movable; it disintegrated among the rocks which had lain at the foot of the Malecón unchanged throughout the centuries, black, glistening, polished smooth, weary now of so many caresses, of so much salt water that lapped them daily. The sea was calm, there was no wind and the spray shattered into myriad droplets that flowed back to the sea which remained motionless in the distance, alone, like a silver disc, seamless, flawless, leaden, blue-tinted, timeless, never leaving, never returning, static, eternal. Then I said what I didn't feel, I said what I shouldn't have said. I built the miniature castle that would collapse now that you stand facing the window, not knowing what to do or say. Words, only words did all of that, created all that which trapped us. What made me speak? How should I have loved you or desired you or kept you? Why didn't I stay silent at that moment and let you go? You would have said, do you agree? And I would simply have nodded. Everything would have ended there. You would have given me a kiss or perhaps you wouldn't have, it made no difference, you would have left, at that moment night would not have fallen, it was just starting to grow dark and you would have walked away along the edge of the Malecón without turning to look back, you would have reached the Avenida de Los Presidentes where you would have taken the 72 bus that would have dropped you near your house in Santos Suárez on the corner of Juan Delgado and Acosta Avenue and you'd have greeted your mother as usual, perhaps you'd have thought or cried a little, but everything would have ended right there with no tragedy. As it is ending now, with no tragedy. But then I spoke, I lied, I made it possible for me to be holding now in my hands this letter which makes me think about all these things, which won't leave me in peace as I walk along the edge of Montsouris Park, in Paris in the early hours, cold, chilled to the bone, burdened with all that garbage which my memories constitute. Memories are like old fabrics that are stored in the attic of a house which is also old, or like stinking sores that never dry up, that's why I don't like to remember. (*Now I'm destroying them, I'm changing them into words and words are worthless, they're like trash, like scrap that should be put into a crusher and be smashed to pieces. Changing you into words is now my last act of expiation. From now onwards, you're dead once and for all. I'm killing you. You survived in Prague, in Paris, everywhere, because I needed you for this, to change you into words. Because you were a story, a tragic story. My wife doesn't understand why I keep so many of your things, nor do I feel disposed to explain it to her, but it's for this, to reinvent you and kill you, now once and for all, whilst I listen to Beethoven's 7th and drink a glass of Johnny Walker.*) I ought to tear up this letter, and throw the pieces into a bush in the Montsouris Park, but I put it away again, I show myself no mercy. Then I carry on walking, I'm not going to look back because I don't want you to see me crying, my briefcase weighs a ton, like when I left my mother's house carrying a suitcase loaded with marimba records that I abandoned in a hotel in Mexico City, it's the same briefcase, the suitcase which is also the same one, is already stowed in the belly of the plane. And now I love you, yes, I love you, I didn't want to go, just a word, a gesture from you would have been enough and the suitcase would have stayed in the belly of the plane, forgotten, abandoned forever. But your face remained impassive, you didn't make that gesture that you should have and I left. But I didn't go down completely, I kept moving with just the tip of it in, it didn't matter that I'd come because I wasn't going limp yet, I was sufficiently excited to keep going, I didn't even tell you that I had come, beneath me pinned by the weight of my chest, you continue to smoulder with lust, your legs move, you thrust your belly up and down, then, pierced, you writhe rolling your buttocks, you moan and sob, you push me up, my penis is still erect, stiff, firm, I hold you by the neck forcing your head into the pillow letting my mind wander. I'm going to try to think so I won't come too soon. I need to think because I don't like to be mindless, like an animal, like a sexual machine. It's always the same; you move and move and then, after it's over, lie still, inert, shapeless. The wind that blows here is colder because there are no streets or houses to break its force, a park is always an open, empty, cold place where one can think better. Why do they make parks in cities? Can it be for the old to sit in and the children to play? But none of them go on forever. Even Central Park in New York and Hyde Park where Jack the Ripper committed his murders have an end. All parks end. This one, Montsouris Park is coming to an end too. There's not far to go now, my feet are tired, they're like lead, it's been a long way, the briefcase weighs a ton, when I took it out of the hotel I didn't think it was so heavy. Memories weigh like that too, "I'd like to love you less, not even see you any more, save myself from this fire that I can't resist. I don't want this love, that gives me no rest, for I suffer if

I'm with you, and far from you I can't exist. I'd like to love you less, for this is no way to exist, my life is ruined from loving you so much, I don't know if I need to love you or lose you, I know that I have loved you more than I was able, I'd like to love you less, to try to forget you, yet instead of loving you less, I love you even more." My mother sang that song all day long and at night she cried. She did the same thing for years and years until she dried up inside and out, she wasted away and only lived for us. The only thing she had left were her memories, waltzes and tangos, all day she sang and bugged us with her don't do this, don't do that, and we always did exactly what we fancied anyway. Whenever I remember something, I recall it with the music of a tango or a waltz. The mist begins to cover everything. But I've arrived. Words are like mist, they cover everything, now one can't see with clarity, everything becomes diffuse, images pass distorted, blurred, shapeless, defying the deductive reasoning of common sense, mist shrouds the mind, only movements and incoherent words remain, like those of an animal, moans, soft weeping and movement, you can't think any more, because if you don't think then you don't feel, I place my two hands under your buttocks and I drive it deep into you, you throb, quiver, vibrate, I recreate you now in words, in deeds, in thoughts, the words become deeds, objects, pillows, nipples, hair, glances that no longer exist, the mist becomes thicker when I get to Jourdain Boulevard, now I'm home, I'll sleep only to wake again, always the same cycle, but tomorrow won't be today and you'll have vanished, I'm going to put away the letter and, in many years' time, I'll read it again, and then you'll live again but without the pain of this moment when the memories are fresh, now it's only a year ago, by then two or even ten years will have passed and then the letter will only provoke deeds, objects, thoughts that will have died many years before and by then no longer exist, they will only be signs, meanings, I reckon the winter will arrive soon, earlier than in other years and then it will snow, the steps of the Belgian Foundation will be deep in snow that will crackle under my feet, then I'll recall other things, other eyes, other caresses, other vibrations that are not yours, perhaps yours never really existed and I invented them, perhaps right now I'm inventing you, if it weren't for that damned letter I'd think that all this is invented and that I'm walking up the steps of the Belgian Foundation inventing objects, thoughts, words, I'll ask the receptionist if there's any mail for me and the letter that he hands me will start me off again, I'll invent new situations in which you aren't present, in which my mother will appear, or another woman, or a man, a comrade, a friend, and if the receptionist doesn't have another letter for me, I'll continue with this one, in which you'll be throbbing, vibrating, moving like you did in El Sotano that Havana nightclub on 23rd Street in La Rampa, where we used to go to dance in the dim light, and I'd feel your waist dissolving in my hands to the rhythm of the cha-cha-cha of César Portillo de la Luz "if loving you is a sin I want to be a sinner, how sweet is the sin that is born of love", and you'd dance close or sway to the beat of the cha-cha-cha and then we'd go to El Gato Negro opposite the Malecón near the Hotel Nacional to listen to José Antonio Méndez with his guitar until one in the morning when we'd take the last bus, then everything will return to oblivion, my hands will play with other things, with the typewriter, with other breasts, with the cold. When I boarded the aircraft I wanted to turn my head, to make you out, to forget you quickly, but I couldn't, I had a lump in my throat, my eyes hurt, I had another cramp in my stomach, the briefcase weighed as heavily as my feet, the stewardess smiled at me and greeted me in Czech, I didn't understand a word, I just followed her, put the case under the seat and sat down, I opened the curtains at the cabin window and tried to find you but you were no longer there. Did you leave before the plane took off or did you move to another place? I'll never know. Then your face began to change, to blur, to dissolve, to become another, from that moment I started to forget your gestures, your moans, your gasps, your movements that were violent despite your fragile body, then I knelt on the bed again because my back began to ache, the sounds were distant, my head was spinning, I'd slept for two days consecutively, a car was waiting for me at Prague airport and I was taken directly to the International Hotel, I woke hungry, with your face in my hands, with your warmth on my skin, I peered out of the window and everything was white, covered in snow, my mouth was dry and my mind confused, I lay back on the bed again and took one of your hands, the evening had passed quickly, you were sleeping gently now, naked, white as the snow, your breasts rested peacefully, your nipples were no longer erect but soft, calm, satisfied, your legs were open and relaxed, I went to the bathroom once more and took the decision, I couldn't go on seeing you like that, loving you without loving you, because I did love you but I was going to leave one way or another. I had to be fair to you, it was the only thing left to me "to write one has to love and you have the necessary capacity to love and be loved. But please, when you come across another Tatiana, leave her alone, don't hurt her", I had to leave you so as not to hurt you, so as not to go farther into the tangle that we'd woven together, when I went out a piece of ice hit me straight in the face, the tram that went down to the centre of Prague had its terminal opposite the hotel, it was a number seven, I had to remember it because if I forgot it I wouldn't be able to return, if I didn't forget you at that moment I wouldn't be able to return. I had to tell you there and then, afterwards it would be too late, night was falling, when I left you were already dressed, you drew close to me and kissed my forehead, then I forgot everything again, but the following day I began to arrange my departure, it was then that I tried not to see you, I didn't answer the phone, I didn't go back to the hotel, it was that Sunday that I saw you from my room, I had left a message at the desk that they should say that I wasn't in Havana, that I'd gone into the interior of the country, I saw you from the ninth floor, standing on the corner of G and 7th all day, looking upwards, I wanted to go out and tell you, tell you everything, but you wouldn't have understood or I'd have changed my mind at the last minute, a week later I left Havana. If I get on the tram I have to observe very carefully where I get off so that I can return, everything's covered in snow and everywhere in Prague looks the same, white, like the snow. That's all that I have left of you now, your whiteness. A mist envelopes all of Paris now that I have arrived, drunk, ready to fall into bed. Memories, words, images, mist, darkness, your face, everything, everything is the same now: a memory. (*I told you to leave us in peace. When we're awakened, we get angry and then we attack. Everything's fine as long as it doesn't corrode, but we are like rust, we destroy. It would have been better if you'd tossed us into the Seine or thrown us out in Saint Michel or in Prague, but you insisted on keeping us for your pleasure, for your pointless masochism. The past is past, you said that to her once when you were standing on the Malecón and you wanted to keep her because you couldn't stand the fact that she'd realised before you did that it was all pointless. Your narcissism, your bloody vanity messed it all up. Now put up with it. You told her that her past was going to destroy her eternally but the roles have been reversed. Now it's you who have no future, nor present, nor past, you're a barrel of words, of images that you'll never be able to erase, that will pursue you forever. Well, that's the way you wanted it, you've always insisted on hearing, and feeling the emotions of others just to keep them as trophies, like a junk collector. That's what she put in your briefcase so that the circle would be complete, junk. Now see if you can throw it out once and for all, because we're staying, we're not going on with you. We're tired of your pointless game. That's it, we're quits. Beethoven's 7th is coming to the end and you too, forever. The fragile link between us is finally coming apart. The notes are fading, now only the bare sounds remain, no more your voice, no more your laughter, no more your tears. The Johnny Walker is coming to an end too. All that's left is the ice in the bottom of the glass).*

10

THE LAD

1966

When did all this begin for me? People were milling around a void. The mass moved, came and went, coalesced and separated, merged and dispersed, ran and stopped, shouted and fell silent. The noise slowly increased and suddenly ceased. In the centre of the street arose an eddy that gently expired at the edge of the pavements. The cars sounded their horns, hooters, beepers, and dispersed the groups, dissolving them in spray. The tide ebbed and flowed amidst isolated cries, muffled, dull, sotto voce / Death to Ubico / Down with the tyrant / Blood poured from my mouth and mingled with the urine that bathed the cell and images flickered through my mind like a kaleidoscope. Fear and bravery merged in faces exhausted by so many years of terror. The eddy brought the cars to a halt and forced them to form endless queues of throbbing sound. A solitary policeman appeared with a whistle in his mouth, spreading his authority amongst the small groups that formed and dispersed. The metallic thread fell silent for a moment and then began to advance, zigzagging between the crowds. Less timorous, more resolute voices began directing the masses. Demonstration! My mother held me tightly by the hand. We were standing on the corner of 12th Street and 6th Avenue. We were going to the eleven o'clock mass at San Francisco Church, it was Sunday. My mother was radiant, dressed in purple, wearing lipstick and rouge. She held my hand firmly. I could feel her skin against mine. Nervously I turned to break free, the rank stench of urine held me in its grip. I inhaled through my mouth and exhaled through my nose; after a while my mouth became dry, I was forced to breathe through my nose again and the pungent odour penetrated deep into my lungs and stomach and my pain intensified; no part of my body remained intact. The cop with the knuckleduster had done a perfect job on me, had made no mistakes, left no part of me undamaged. Then I went back to inhaling through my mouth and I had more conscious control over my breathing. After a while my throat was dry once more and I began to feel frightened. The eddy was taking on form, the voices became clearer, men and women in black appeared along 12th Street, coming from 15th Avenue, and dragged us towards San Francisco, my mother began to loosen her grip on my hand, I saw fear growing on her face and her lips start to tremble; as she gradually released her grip, I pressed ever closer to her. Finally the crowd took shape, the men who were pulling us along with them reached the door of San Francisco and one of them, no longer afraid, began shouting / Demonstration / Human Rights / Fourteen years of tyranny / When the tide started to form waves, the tension between my mother's hand and mine reached its maximum, the shouts had assumed the booming of the sea and panic once more spread across the eddy which splintered and reformed, someone screamed / the cavalry / I felt as if an electric current issued from my mother's body and the strain became overwhelming / Son / was the last thing I heard, then her hand had gone and I was alone, abandoned. Solitude, silence filled my eardrums, my skin, my eyes, my tongue. My mouth was silent and one single sequence of thoughts pounded in my brain. I think every dying man has this film developing within him. Last night they took me out again. They've been torturing me for three days non-stop now, punching me with knuckledusters, beating the soles of my feet with batons, hanging me by my arms with a gas-hood over my head, slowly suffocating. I'm rotting alive. The wound on my leg stinks. I'm broken, alone, abandoned, deaf, mute, blind, but I think, therefore I am. Or as Otto René used to say when we knew each other in Germany / Get with it man, get on the ball, it's I AM THEREFORE I THINK / OKAY, I am therefore I think. Matter is first. Thought is the first thing that starts to die, the roll of film is erased in reverse sequence to how it was rolled except at a fantastic speed because now there is no more life left for it to pass slowly. That's why the figures pass like images from the silent movies, fragmented, fleeting, at times invisible, leaving only their scent, their aura, their silhouette in daguerrotype. Some vibrate more than others. They have fixed their volume, their colour, their stature forcibly on the mind which dilutes them, fragmenting them into smaller smells, colours and sizes. I don't think I can survive another day. My mind is almost blank, just a few horses galloping through it. When I was least aware of it, the tidal wave engulfed me, I felt that I was drowning, I could see only shadows, legs, skirts, the whirlpool had finally swallowed me, it carried me away, devoured me, drowned me, dismembered me, shattered me into pieces, I ran forward and was drawn back at the same rhythm as the wave that rises and falls on the sand. The whirlpool nebulised leaving clearings through which I could see the horizon. Men in light brown uniforms rode up on horseback with immense sabres in their hands. A column of soldiers in battle dress advanced up 6th Avenue on both sides of the street. The horses advanced more quickly than the soldiers, the tidal wave was retreating and dragging me towards the porch of San Francisco, towards the cloisters which were tree-lined and protected by a high stone wall, now the voices were not those of panic but of decision / Cut down branches from the trees / Let's confront them / A group of women approached the door of the porch which opened on to the street / Come on, they won't ride over us, we're women / The first to jump over the wall was an immense horse bearing an immense soldier with an immense sabre who began to slash out at the women, the men, the priests, (*they're not men, they're a kind of bastardised hybrid species*), the children, the trees, the flowers, immense bloody slashes. The door which opened on to 6th and 13th was forced, torn from its hinges and through it poured the tornado, horses, soldiers (they're the same thing) horse-men, foot-soldiers, weapons, huge swords: then the tide fled towards the other doors, the group that attempted to escape through the central door met the sword-wielding centaurs face to face and there the first screams of the dying rang out. I left, ejected, projected, blown, expelled through the other door, borne by the tidal wave, dragged by the undertow towards Concordia Park, the sea was rough and the waves were breaking over the Malecón, the Spanish instructor was telling us, it's El Norte, the north wind which lashes these Cuban shores in the months of January and February, when the breakers wash over the Malecón flooding it, one daren't go along it in case the surge washes you out to sea drowning you, the water reaches up to five blocks into the city. The roar could be heard from as far off as 18th Street, the tidal wave respected nothing, it was a flight, a mass exodus, a stampede with me caught in its midst, in the epicentre of the church, the eye of the typhoon which plucked me up from the floor; there in the centre held aloft, with a void beneath my feet was / I. The screams, the noises had destroyed my eardrums. I could no longer hear my own screams, only the radio that muffled them. The colonel was the one in charge of the radio because on the second day he shit himself, he didn't have the balls to go on whipping me and he set his sickos, his morons, his cretinous henchmen to break my body whilst he sat back and enjoyed it, escaping all responsibility. He threatened me, shouted, begged, told me that the gringos from the CIA were going to take over and then there would be no hope for me. I knew that there was no salvation for me anyway. From the moment I found myself face to face with Napo, I knew I was a goner. The gutless mother-fucking brass-hat told me last night that the gringos would arrive today, so today's the great day, today is the last great binge because today is Easter Saturday and the Jalapa fiesta is being held at the club, today we're going to it together for the first time since she's been my girl. When I felt her skin next to my member I held her tight to me, I felt that the bonds that had constrained me all my life were breaking and I held her close, I pressed my penis against her dress and began to move myself against her and she in turn rubbed against me, kissing my neck, licking me, wetting me with her saliva. I was thinking about the fact that she was my cousin, that I wanted to fuck her but she was my cousin and it was a sin, our children would turn out like pigs, idiots with huge heads, so, when I was coming, I pulled away from her, she looked at me, furious with frustration, then I hid my head between my legs but I raised it immediately because the stench of the urine cleared my mind, when I lifted my neck the pain was intense. The gringos will be in charge of the last party. There will be music and screams and cudgels and electric cattle-prods and all that the mother-fucking bastards can dream up. I'm going to go deaf from all this shouting. My feet were back on the ground again, my legs were too small to follow the tide and I was getting left behind, alone in the middle of the street, the whirlwind began to disappear from around me and arise within me, the bouts of nausea became more and more frequent, matter is disintegrating, soon the machine will cease to function, thought and matter are coming apart simultaneously, rapidly, the inner pump no longer operates on full power, the heart, the kidneys, the lungs are pressurising the brain, ordering it to stop; the latter sends out orders to continue the task, the film is still almost intact. However quickly it unwound, there was no way to empty the reel and the images superimposed, juxtaposed, imposed, changed place, colour and taste whilst the spells of nausea increased in frequency and intensity; I leaned against the wall to prevent myself from falling face down into the urine. Then came another period of nausea, everything was engulfing me sucking me down into the pit, an immense tranquillity began to sweep through me leaving me numb, I felt nothing any more, I only heard the horses that were pursuing me, I couldn't feel my legs, they were heavy, they refused to walk, to run, to flee, I abandoned myself, yielded to whatever might happen, I ceased to think, to ponder, to run the reel of film, it was then that I felt the tug, the slap across my face as if I were the one to blame / Come here you little beast, what are you doing running off from me, can't you see you're going to get yourself killed? / and the shooting and the murmurs began. Feeling safer in La Concordia Park the people began to re-form into groups, they assembled and dispersed, they separated and came together, assumed different forms, the murmurs rose and fell, they spoke loudly then softly, indignantly, everyone was outraged, eager to protest, the gringos had invaded Cuba via the Bay of Pigs, we had to protest. We left the Law Faculty after the call to hold a demo and a public meeting. When we passed the Sagrario Church on 8th Street, Skinny Dog crossed himself automatically in a sort of reflex action, I laughed and asked him why he'd done it, he said he hadn't realised he had but he had bad vibes about it all, he was worried. After leaving the Law Faculty, we'd gone over to the offices of 'El Estudiante' opposite the Instituto Nacional for a while. There we chatted a minute or two with Toad and the other newspaper editors. When we reached Central Park, the big groups were still scattered around but a more compact main corps was beginning to form, someone hauled a loudspeaker up on to the top of the Portal del Comercio and from there lowered a microphone, I grabbed it and began to shout / Comrades, unite, we must protest / the whistling and the raucous laughter increased in volume, by now all the corners of 6th Avenue and 8th Street were thick with people and they kept on arriving in ever increasing numbers / Hi mate, what a caper, eh? / Afterwards, we're going over to stone the American Embassy / Maybe the police will show up and there'll be a punch up / Let's start the meeting or else it'll get dark / Yeah lads, let's start now / But the leaders of the Law Association haven't arrived / Never mind that, get on with it / I did, I shouted, gave orders, incited them to demonstrate, invited them to join the demo, the crowd moved a few centimetres and returned to its place. My gums are smashed and I can't stop the trembling in my limbs, I don't think this will go on much longer and, if the gringos come to interrogate me, it'll be even shorter, those blond bastards don't waste any time and they'll soon finish me off. If only my back didn't hurt so much, I feel as if it were broken, that's where they were kicking me and Maya's blows have wreaked havoc on me. If only I could sit up, but I can't move my injured leg, I can't even feel it any more, I can only smell the rank stench of my rotting flesh, it doesn't even hurt now. Every time I get near it vomit rises into my throat and stays there, I retch but I haven't eaten for three or four days and nothing comes up any more, I've almost lost track of time, my head is throbbing and I'm losing control, I can't see very well, I'd better climb up on that mound of earth so I can keep an eye on the people who are farthest off, I pulled on the microphone wire and it gave way, now in control of the entire throng I continued my harangue, The crowd reached as far as the Peladero in Centenario Park and up 6th Avenue to 9th Street, on the Portal side the multitude stretched over half a block, someone began singing "Cuba, how lovely is Cuba and socialist Cuba is even lovelier, my beautiful Cuba", and everywhere people improvised revolutionary themes / Yankees go home / Death to the gringos / Demo at the Embassy / and the leaders still hadn't appeared. The crowd began to grow impatient, they dispersed, leaders arose spontaneously, I shouted through the microphone that we were going to start the meeting, on one side leaflets appeared passing from hand to hand, the Humanities Association had printed them off, they were poems by Boozer dedicated to Cuba, I gave them a quick look over, a rapid dekko, a swift shuffty, I saw the short-sighted face of Boozer who zoomed past distributing the papers, we shared a laugh, Skinny Dog said I'm going to give him a hand and vanished into the crowd, the heat was intensifying and the shadows falling when the meeting started / Comrades, at this moment when the first free territory in the Americas is under attack from the imperialist Yankees, we, the committed revolutionaries of Guatemala must stand ready to fight to defend the sovereignty of the first socialist country of the Americas / The speeches followed, one hot on the other, I began to lose the thread in the heat of all the shouting / Viva Cubaaaaah / Cuba will overcome aaaaall / Cuba will overcome / Cuba Cuba Cubaaaaah / Comrades, the Cuban revolutionary army is at this moment fending off the imperialist aggression, according to our latest reports the mercenary traitors are fleeing in disarray-ay-ay / Cuba will overcome, Cubaaaah / The heat was restricting my throat, making breathing difficult, nausea overwhelms me, maybe it's the smell of urine which makes me want to black out all the time, my feet are swollen and I can't stand because of my wounded leg, I can't stand or sit or lie because the urine sears my back and my chest, I have to lie on my side, supported on my right hip, my elbow taking all the weight of my chest, I have to stay like this all day or all night, who knows what time it is even, if it's day or night, I suppose that it's day at the moment because it's at night that they take me out and torture me; when they take me I feel the silence clinging to me, at night they drag me along the passageway to the white, dry, lonely room, devoid of all furnishings but for the chair in its centre and the pulley suspended above it. Silence clings to me, weighs upon me, accompanies me. It warns me to keep it, to remain silent because, come what may, they are going to kill me, whether I speak or not, whether I break it or not; so I close my mouth and open it only to scream when the agony is more than I can bear, when a stab of red-hot pain penetrates to the depths of my brain and my mouth opens involuntarily and there is a scream, I hear a scream from a voice I cannot recognise which is not mine, which emerges from who knows where, from what forgotten millennia, from what time immemorial, it is a feral cry beyond my control which scales the walls and ceiling of this inhuman room, this lonely, white, cruel, humiliating, naked, terrible room; when the light strikes my face and the rod strikes my feet I tell myself I can stand it, and I do, but against all my will there emerges this cry learned who knows where, who knows from whom, this cry that pierces my eardrums, this cry from a stranger who is not me and which exasperates my torturers, the colonel covers his ears. When my eyes have drifted nowhere, anywhere, I've glimpsed him, from the mists emerges his stocky libidinous figure, I see like in cinemascope, like a kaleidoscope, his form, which flickers for an instant, and he covers his ears, turns to the white wall and, there, dissolves, fades, merges with the wall becoming part of it, then I am alone with my scream, with my wild, animal howl that I learned who knows where and which bores through my eardrums to my brain together with that monstrous pain that leaves me empty, wiped of all thought. Silence pervades my body to my last pore, I'll never speak, I'll never speak, my word on it, I'll never speak, if it's a case of shouting something or other that's fine, but giving a speech, that's quite another matter, I only took the microphone because you lot didn't come, making a speech is something else entirely, I'm no good at it, I'll cock it all up completely and say all the wrong things, it'd be better if someone else spoke, oh alright then since you insist but if you see I'm getting stuck or getting off the point, grab the microphone from me. When I climbed up on the mound of earth my hands were trembling, the microphone had suddenly grown bigger, it wouldn't fit into my hands, it weighed a ton, then the crowd became a sea, a headless monster, a flat, black, smooth slate over which one could walk, a lake, a black pond that might swallow me up at any moment, my hands were sweating and I didn't know how to start the speech, the murmur was rising in tone and isolated shouts could be heard / Get him off / Let somebody else speak / Yankees go home / I'm the best / Fuck off / If I stayed there, things were going to degenerate into a massive free-for-all, so I passed the microphone to the president of the association. At that moment I saw them, it was a second, a second which lasted from the moment when I bent to hand over the mike, raised my head and climbed down from the mound, a column was approaching with linked arms, behind them came a small crowd, not as big as our own, in the centre of the first row they were carrying a banner and, at the sides of the group, came the police wearing gas masks with rifles at the ready, then I snatched back the mike and shouted / Liberationists / THAT WAS WHEN THE TERROR AND THE VIOLENCE BEGAN. The faces of the people reflected their reactions, first disbelief, then belief, the colour drained from them, they were struck dumb, grew red with rage, became terrified, excited, enraged, they shouted, fell silent. Someone cried / Let's give it to them / break off branches from the trees / let's make a run for it / run yourself you coward / let's cut down branches so they won't catch us with our pants down / they've got the cops with them / they're sure to be armed / let's arm ourselves too / The groups dispersed to find weapons, the first began to slip away, the rest ran around in turmoil, in disarray, in an attack, aimed at the trees, the most agile, the swiftest, the most determined of them climbed the ones in Centenario Park and began to tear off the branches handing them down to the more demanding groups; I hadn't moved, I remained rooted to the spot, calm, fascinated, watching the enemy mass approach step by step singing the national anthem, in their hands they wielded clubs, huge swords with which they lashed out at the crowd, the horses destroyed the gardens, the flower beds of Concordia Park, my mother clasped my hand tightly, pulled me and we climbed underneath a slide, the horses leaped between the hedges, the swings, the see-saws, the soldiers with their chinstraps tightly buckled closed their eyes and slashed out to right and left, occasionally a shriek of pain rang out, I closed my eyes, the groups were falling back into 8th Street to take refuge at El Peladero, others hid behind the pillars of the Portal del Comercio, when the two groups were just fifty metres from a head-on confrontation the liberationists stopped, the first row dropped their linked arms stance and drew their pistols, my teeth began to chatter, it's all that I've heard for several hours now, before that I could hear nothing, I was deaf, blind, mute, but now the sound of my teeth keeps me company, breaks the silence, my head is hollow, if the police catch me there'll be all hell to play with my father, he's in the military and, here I am, involved in armed skirmishes, he'll send me back to live with my mother and if I don't get down from here pretty damned pronto it'll be me that gets the first bullet, I'm the perfect target up on this pile of earth. We've got to get away, it doesn't matter in which direction, the essential thing is to get away. My mother stood up, pulled me out and began to run towards 5th Avenue, all I could see was the skirt of her purple silk dress, the one she wore to mass on Sundays, the one that reached her ankles, we went up 15th Street to 4th Avenue and waited for the carriage that came trotting up loaded with people, the buses had vanished, the sound of the horses' hooves echoed in my head, at the first shot I started wildly and fell on to a soft mass of arms which supported me and prevented me from falling, shouts devastated Central Park / Let's get the hell out of here, the police are firing too / No, let's hide and when they're close we'll fall on them / We can't do a thing anyway, they're so well armed / the shots began to ricochet off the pillars of the Portal del Comercio, I stopped running and concealed myself behind them, out of the corner of my eye I saw the door of the Elma building standing half open and I ran towards it to take refuge there, just as I reached it the caretaker banged it shut and left me pounding on the glass, between El Portal del Comercio and the liberationists there was nothing, just an empty space, only the bullets crossed and ricocheted on the cement or penetrated the flesh, everyone was fleeing, they fell over each other in their panic, screamed, swore, ran up the steps, it was dark, it was five o'clock in the morning and the Cubans had arranged to arrive at five-thirty, that was when the flight began. Some grabbed their blankets, others left them, some said they'd go, others refused. Some prayed to God and others didn't. Talking about it was great but committing oneself to the armed fight in the mountains was something else. Signing on was deadly serious. We had to hide somewhere in the building. We had to go into hiding because we hadn't come to Havana to train as guerrillas, we'd come to study for technical careers. That was what they told us in Guatemala. Now we're up to our ears in it. We let ourselves get involved. Like idiots we put up with the haranguing from the Party representative. The bastard gave us this sentimental, emotionally charged speech and like fools we fell for it / The Guatemalan revolution bla bla bla, the comrades fighting in the streets of Guatemala against the tyranny of Ydígoras[8] bla bla bla, the dates in March and April bla, bla, bla / the old sod started bullshitting us, he spun us a yarn and got us involved. Afterwards he, the biggest traitor of the lot, went and committed us. What moral right did he have to talk to us about revolution? By '54 he'd buggered off, when he was the highest Party leader he behaved like a coward, like a shit-bag and, after betraying the Party, he sought political asylum. At the end of that bloody meeting he reminded us that all we scholarship holders had to undergo military training to lay the foundations of the guerrilla movement. What a load of crap! At five in the morning I saw Malanga and Pepito go by, all pale and sleepless running towards the basement of the building in which we scholarship holders were housed. These two were the ones who had said the most the day before, the theorists of the group, the ones who sucked up to the Cubans to get extra leave permits, olive green jackets and new boots. Malanga was the rep of the Base Youth Committee and all that bullshit. Now they were scuttling off like frightened rats with a blanket to hide from the Cubans who were coming to take us to the training camp. Onion ran by next and then the majority of our group, they were heading upstairs. At that hour you couldn't get out of the building because they had a soldier on the door to prevent it. Otherwise I probably would have pissed off myself. You couldn't get out via the dining room because they'd locked it. I sat in my rocking chair on the balcony of our floor and began to sway back and forth looking down into the street below, about ten blocks away the sun was starting to rise from the sea, the burnished blood-red disc the size of a gigantic plate was emerging slowly, gently, voluptuously, from the depths of the ocean pouring forth shards of shimmering light reflected, transformed and diluted by the indigo blue of the sea. From the 14th floor it was easy to see it; we were on 27th Street and G, so the only tall building that lay within my field of vision looking seaward was the Presidente Hotel which had only 10 floors. The ocean was in the centre of my gaze, in the midst of my horizon Havana was blooming, we were at the beginning of April, I had to come to a decision on whether to hide or go and train. If my choice was to train then I could forget all else forever: studies, home, family, social life, recognition, glory, everything, absolutely everything. There was no going back, not even to push you forward, declared Fidel. The sun seeped insidiously through the streets of the Vedado. My decision would have to be definitive, it was for life. It was now no longer a question of talking and theorising but a matter of life and death, killing or dying, with no alternative, no remorse. The revolution had to be made in the shadows, in secret, we were the faceless, the nameless ones, without family, without age, without reward, without memories of the past, who would live with anguish, with danger, with fear and with death. And the most certain of all these was death. The sun crept forward, grew paler on the outskirts of the Vedado, stealing into the bars, the dime stores, the cinemas, the hotels, the houses, the trees that gave the

Vedado its verdant aspect. My chair swayed, cooling me whilst the sun, breaking from its last bonds, weighed anchor for the great voyage of the day, for this day which would be the decisive one when I would abandon everything, when I would find everything. After this there would be no going back, only death in some place. And life, because I've always wanted to live and wanted others to live and be happy, perhaps that's why I'm here amidst the urine, amidst the foul odours of this dark cell. My wrists are ulcerating, I had to break the ropes by force so I could move, that was several days ago now, who knows how many, it's always dark so I've lost all sense of time, a viscous liquid is seeping from my wrists and from the wound in my leg, it must be pus. There's a vile stench, yes it's pus, a stench, I'm rotting alive, a stench, it's piss, a stench, it's my own shit, after the second day of beatings I shit myself, when I fell off the chair the henchmen no longer helped me to stand; the colonel / Get him out of here, he's shit himself / he ordered them to take me back to the cell and they just dragged me by the arms, I left faeces smeared all along the passageway, there's a nice smell at this hour, they're making bread in the bakeries, the buses are the only things that break the silence, within half an hour the building will be like an anthill, meanwhile, the boys hide, flee, take refuge in other people's rooms, the Cubans are coming for all the Guatemalan Scholarship students to take them to a guerrilla training camp. I should hide. But I won't move from here. I won't be able to retreat, all escape, all evasion will stop forever and I'll have to give up my life to the revolution. Will it be worth it? Why don't I get up from this seat and go and hide? This fleeing is always madness. Enough of running away, if I don't stop running I'll never be able to live with myself and I'm going to live with myself, I have to, I have to come to a decision, I must run, if I stop they'll ride over me, each one of us tries to save himself, it's a case of look out for number one, he who runs fastest, he who has the greatest stamina, I'll go into Aycinena Alley and come out on 9th Street, before running into the alley I jumped over Boozer who was on his hands and knees collecting up the leaflets he was distributing, he was looking for his glasses. I should have stopped to help him but the shooting is getting close, the police are flooding the alleyway with tear gas, they're going to hunt us down like rats here, I should stop, face what's coming now. Afterwards it'll be too late. Beanpole is right, he's got asthma so he can't be a guerrilla but I've been healthy all my life, when I was a kid I could run and run without ever getting tired whereas my mother began to turn the colour of her dress, the carriage didn't want to stop because Ubico's cavalry had surrounded Concordia Park and was coming up 14th Street, the crowd spread like a river breaking its banks, shouting, insulting, begging, weeping, agonising, my mother was running and I was practically flying along beside her, then I went up the stairs, the gas couldn't rise to the second floor so quickly and the exits from the alley were blocked off so my last resort was to get into one of the apartments, any one that would open its door. Groping in the darkness I reached a door and pounded on it, it was opened by a woman / Come in, young man, before they see you / shots rang out down Aycinena Alley as if they'd been fired into a tunnel and continued reverberating like a bell with a dull, harsh, poc, poc, poc, my time had come, from 14th Street I heard an army truck pulling up, poc, poc, poc, they were coming for us, I still had time to hide, whilst they were entering and coming up in the lift I could go and stay in the Colombian's room until the danger had passed, he didn't agree with mercenary armies, but I did not move from my seat, I remained there taking the cool air, whilst the sounds of the city became more audible new sounds constantly swelling the volume of the old, the sun began to rise, to diminish in size, any minute now they would arrive, this was the last decision I could make on my own and the first. It was the most important decision in my life and the only one made by me: my mother, my father, the priests, the teachers, the professors at the University, the Party leaders, all of them, all of them had made my decisions for me. Maybe that's why I remained there sitting, waiting. It was my decision. I was a revolutionary. I couldn't betray myself at the key moment of truth. If I had not stayed waiting, they could have spat in my face, it would be like it is now, covered in spit, when the torturers, tired of hitting me with their knuckledusters, of hanging me and beating me with sticks, spat on me, covered me in saliva, in their vile slime that stank of tobacco, booze and cheap rancid food; the colonel was growing impatient and they were tired, so they spat on me contemptuously / Bloody communist, we're going to kill you, do you hear? / I didn't care, I was exhausted, whatever they did they wouldn't get a word out of me, if I'd talked all the leaders of the Central Resistance would have fallen, but they would get nothing out of me. They shouted, gesticulated, sought, pried but they never got a thing, just when I was feeling a bit safer they knocked on the door, the woman, frightened, opened it and the torturers, the police, the instructors came in and seized me / I rose from the chair and said / I'm ready comrades / they grabbed my arms and dragged me from the woman's flat. She averted her gaze, it wasn't her fault, if she hadn't opened the door they'd have broken it down with their rifle butts. That was the first time they caught me. I followed them, when we reached the lobby of the student house there were only twelve comrades there carrying their possessions, willing to train, willing to die; the Cuban instructor was mad as hell, abusive / What's the matter with your comrades, man, there are thirty of you and only thirteen comrades willing, where is your revolutionary conscience? / Did you look for them, men? / They've buggered off comrade / I did a rapid eye count, there was Little Indian, Pig, Baldy, Blackboard, Richard, Boat, Cat, Monkey, a few I don't remember and me, thirteen, unlucky number, the complete squad of volunteers. The door opened and the torturers came in, I couldn't move, I wanted to scream at them, to hurl abuse, but I couldn't move a centimetre. Ready. When they entered, the prisoner was still in the same position as he'd been in twenty-four hours before, lying or rather leaning on one hip with all the weight of his body supported on one elbow. It was as though he were carved from stone, marmoreal, static, dead, stiff. The thugs moved him, pushed him with their feet, taking no precautions, there was no further reason to / I reckon he's snuffed it / Go and see if his heart's still beating / Oh yeah, lost the use of your arms and legs, have you? Why don't you do it? He stinks like a dead dog, when I get close it makes me puke / Hold your nose and feel his chest, man / Anyway, we've still got to carry him so what does it matter? Right, grab one arm and pull / You're right, if he's dead the gringos won't be able to kill him a second time. I hope he is because those blond arseholes are going to crucify him, poor devil / I can't feel my body any longer, I'm sure they're dragging me, but I can't feel anything, I can't see anything, I can't hear anything. They're taking me back to the white room with the white light with its one single, lonely black chair in the centre. They're going to torture me again. I shan't come out of this one alive. Why am I still able to think? The worst thing is I'm still lucid, the skein of memories is still intact, the film still running, although, perhaps, in reverse. When the whole film has been shown then it's kaput, closing time, bucket kicked, last count, final curtain. Better that way. Much better. I'm tired of this scene. I feel as if I've been going from the cell to the white room and back for years. One more beating and the flame will be snuffed forever. There's the light searing my eyes. The torturers set the prisoner on the black chair in the centre of the room, tied his arms behind the chair, this time to hold him up, to prevent him from falling, then they withdrew silently, their nausea reflected in their faces. Two hefty blond men were sitting on seats that had been set facing the prisoner, between them was the colonel / oh my, colonel, you've really worked him over / that's not good, not good at all, you've left nothing for us / My mother stopped on 17th Street, another carriage was coming along 4th Avenue, the noise of the horse's hooves was slightly muffled, people became calmer, they began to talk amongst themselves, groups formed hastily and then separated, gathered and dispersed, amidst whispers, sobs, spasms of fear, protests / They killed a school teacher at the door of San Francisco Church / There are loads of wounded / It's an atrocity, an outrage / Things have gone too far / We'll meet at the cemetery tomorrow for the burials / They say there are about a hundred dead / My mother wouldn't listen, she would have preferred to be deaf, her ears covered forever. She was ashen, wild-eyed, her features contorted by a primeval terror, when the carriage stopped, we climbed in, they pushed me in, they opened the door of the squad car and hauled me in. Before the door closed, I saw a corpse lying on the corner outside the Electric Company, smashed, hurled by the impact of the shot against the iron shutters of the main door of the building which opens on to 6th and 8th; after striking the metal, the victim had bounced and fallen face down on the pavement, tear gas was spreading through the air, the wail of ambulance sirens was growing nearer, I was hauled into the squad car and fell on to a seat, inside the truck there were only wooden benches on either side, it was a Cuban army truck, we sat facing each other, it was too capacious for only thirteen men, so there were lots of empty spaces, the sun began to scale the first buildings on the edge of the Malecón, the Cuban in charge climbed into the cabin and a soldier sat on the tailgate, confidently leaving his rifle inside and holding on tightly so he wouldn't fall out, the truck started up, we looked at each other, we were pale, slowly realising the enormity of our decision, Boat began to tremble, Cat laughed as he always did, but behind his blue eyes his nervousness and uncertainty showed, I thought aloud / Now we've really done it, boys / Then I opened my eyes, the light fell directly on to me and I had to close them immediately, a jet of cold water forced me to move my body, I ached all over from head to foot. When the water drained from my face I could open my eyes, two gringos were sitting opposite me smoking and laughing. Now I really am dog meat, I must put my thoughts in order to last out until the very last moment. One of the blond men got up slowly, calmly, very sure of himself, took from his pocket a piece of yellow paper, the sort used for printing telegrams, unfolded it deliberately and walked slowly towards the prisoner, when he was near he covered his nostrils and held the paper before the victim's eyes. What does this gringo think, that I can still read? Even if it's the very last thing I do, I'm going to spit on this mother-fucking shit-head. The blond individual withdrew his hand with disgust and threw the paper on to the floor; taking out his handkerchief, he wiped his hand and returned to his seat where he took down a lead-lined rubber cosh and went back to the prisoner's side, held his nose with one hand and, with the other, began to beat him on the head, the face, the legs, the chest, the chair, the bonds, the balls, the feet. The prisoner merely lowered his head, he seemed to be thinking. He was a little girl who wanted to catch a tiny bird and, as she couldn't reach it, she put in her batteries and flew and flew, once there was a little girl called Red Riding Hood, her mammy told her to go and tell her granny she had some biscuits for her, then she went to the woods and she met the wolf and the wolf asked her where are you going Little Red Riding Hood, to see my granny and give her these biscuits, then she ran off, who's there, it's me, Little Red Riding Hood, but it was the wolf, so then she gave her the biscuits, but it was really the wolf who was in bed waiting for her, so then Little Red Riding Hood started to pick flowers and she struck a match and put it between her teeth and began to dance, she painted her lips and her eyes with face-paint, then she painted her teeth, but she had died, then she cried out and the wolf cried and granny cried and they died too, so then they put on masks, then they woke up 'cos they'd only been sleeping and they knocked everybody's teeth out and all the wolves came out and gobbled everybody up, they threw away their ears and their teeth and their eyebrows, just imagine, afterwards they howled over the river, they put on the baby chick costumes and started to sing and afterwards they dug up Little Red Riding Hood and put her into the tunnel and she wanted and wanted to get out and she turned into Tom Thumb and she put on his boots and took off her red hood and put on his boots and was very, very brave because she was a man he went into the tunnel and began to walk in his seven league boots and the more he walked the darker the tunnel became and he couldn't see he couldn't see anything any more and everything was growing darker and darker and now he couldn't walk either the seven league boots didn't respond and now he felt nothing simply that the reel of film had reached the end and he wanted to weep but now he couldn't he wanted to speak but now he couldn't he wanted to think but now he couldn't and finally he knew that he was dead.

11

BOOZER

1969

The waves began to beat against the side of the boat in the darkness, their lashing drowning all other sound, splash, plash, splash, plash. The ferry was nearing the English coast. Five minutes before sighting Dover, the sea had turned rough. The passengers were sleeping in armchairs in the big lounge that had once been a dining room. Now, on the Dunkirk-Dover crossing, all the passengers lay as they had fallen in this immense lounge that was once a dining room and had huge, green, overstuffed, leather armchairs. When this ferry-launch-ancient-tub started her engines and pulled away from the Dunkirk jetty everyone looked for a place to settle. The first thing the passengers did was buy cigarettes at cut-price from the duty-free. They formed a queue and bought a carton apiece and then retreated to their seats where they curled up. The tables on which food had once been served held their hand luggage or their feet or were used to rest their heads on whilst they slept face down on their folded arms. They were an odd bunch of people. In one corner a group of people from India squatted, huddled close together, with terror in their yellowish pupils, the colour of nicotine, as if they smoked with their eyes, the bags beneath them pronounced as if they spent all day and all night shagging, their sallow skin the hue of dried cow-dung, like parchment, ravished by hunger. At each lurch of the boat the group became more compact, united, seeking mutual protection. They knew that in Dover it would be hard to convince the British authorities to let them in. It was almost certain that some would have to return by the same boat and now they had no money, the pilgrimage to London had been long. The terror in their eyes did not fade. In another corner a group of English hippy girls slept, one on top of the other, it was an undifferentiated, shapeless, formless, aformal, informal, deformed, sexless, headless group. Their hands vanished between legs or into pubes, not always their own. Their blond hair fell on the green leather of the chairs like sunlight on grass on warm sunny afternoons. One of them, accompanying the radio which dangled from her big toe, was humming a song in the rhythm of a blues: Yesterday, taralaralara la la lay, mmmm mmmm, oh yesterday. The Beatles accompanied the traveller who rolled her eyes and stroked her companion's hair. Possessions were tied and untied in every corner of the lounge which swayed to the beat of Yesterday, the ferry's engines wheezed – fut fut, fut, fut, tired, old, bored with the same daily crossing. It was as if it were protesting at having to travel over the same route every day: its belly filled with vehicles: its lounge with poor hippies who hadn't enough bread to travel by air. The train from Paris released its load at Dunkirk station and, from there, the strange file of people sank into the bowels of the ferry that bore the name Saint Germain and belonged to Les Navires Transmanches. Before it reached Dover, the boat began to sway dangerously, the sea became choppy and, bored by the calm, decided to make everyone's life misery. In a corner of the lounge, at the last table, was an uneasy traveller. Even before the sea started its tossing, he would stand up, take a few steps back and forth, sit down, light a cigarette dragging on it desperately, crush a letter in his fist and then smooth it out on the table top, read it again, stand once more and put it away in his trouser pocket. He was oddly attired. Although it was night-time, his eyes were concealed behind dark glasses. He wore boots and black jeans and sported a small pointed Lenin-style beard. On the table lay his rucksack, it was all the luggage he had. He was about thirty and prematurely bald and his back was beginning to curve. When the boat began to lurch, just before it reached Dover, the traveller, who had a Latin look about him, regained his composure, removed the leather wineskin that hung from his shoulder and took a swig, wiped his mouth with the sleeve of the leather jacket he was wearing and pulled back the little curtain covering the porthole, lit a cigarette and held on to the rail so as not to sway to the movement of the sea. A ship's officer came into the lounge and informed them in French that there was no problem / pas de problème / that the boat was not in any danger and they would soon be arriving, they should keep calm and collect up their luggage as the journey was almost over. It was a matter of ten to fifteen minutes. And, moreover, in the name of the crew of the Saint Germain he thanked them for travelling with them. As if there had been any choice. The traveller at the porthole, rested his bald forehead on the glass and surveyed the darkness calmly. At last we're arriving, the same darned lights everywhere you go. It'd be better if this tub were to sink, that way I could stop thinking. That way I could stop running away. This letter has destroyed all my peace of mind. I'm tired of going over and over it. What am I doing here? I decided on this awful journey from Madrid just to go farther and farther, to put water, sea, salt, oblivion, distance between the man I am and the man I was, or rather the man I never was. I went through the revolution in the air, in a vacuum. For five years I lived, fleeing, hiding, changing houses, name, faculties. When my grandmother died, the last thing she begged me was not to get mixed up in subversive political activities, she said she was taking this worry to her grave. When she squeezed my hand, closed her eyes and never opened them again, I swore that I would do what she wanted. But only two months later the comrades were demanding that I organise things for them. I had to do it. I'm a revolutionary. I was a revolutionary. You can't make a revolution by remote control from Paris or Madrid. The revolution is made with arms, with organisation, with propaganda. But my nerves were shattered. That's why I asked for a scholarship to Havana – I'd have made a good technician but for the Cubans' idiotic insistence on involving everyone in the armed conflict. They've got me going backwards and forwards like a dog's tail, with no direction. And one by one all the comrades have died. The one I never thought that they could kill was Efi, I always thought that bugger was immortal. He always came out of everything without a scratch. From his first action in Cuba, when Basher got a load of people involved and Parrot screwed it up and they had to flee with the entire police force in hot pursuit blazing away at them. He was a real tearaway, I'll never forget the time when he caused a helluva shindig in the Tropicana, what a performance that was, he'd become the lover of the daughter of Julião the Brazilian peasant leader. Anataylde, I think the girl was called. Strange how indelibly everything remains engraved on your memory, it was six years ago and it's as clear as if it were yesterday. That night we got dressed up to the nines and went off to the binge at the School of Medicine. Memory is a sod. Things should happen one day and be forgotten the next. It's painful to bear all these memories constantly. Man is an animal of memories or vice versa, I don't even know what to think any more, somebody said that once or maybe I'm making it up myself right now, who knows? Anyway, it really doesn't matter much. Every day one reinvents words. It looks bloody cold out there. When the boat docks I'll get my poncho out of the rucksack or I'll freeze to death. The port lights seem to be moving. You can't get any true perspective of things on a boat. Your brain tells you it's the boat that's moving but, visually, you perceive that what's moving are the lights of the coast. If this lurching had occurred in the middle of the English Channel I reckon I'd have been scared shitless but now you can make out the coast. The Party rep wanted to force me into all this too, he wanted to enlist me in a cadre school. I reckon all of it was pressure from the Cubans. But I got away from them. Nobody's going to tell me what to do with my life. That wasn't the only reason I pissed off, if I'd stayed I'd have got hitched to that girl, what was her name? The coast's not as misty as I'd imagined. The London fog is still a long way off, or is all that guff about London fogs just a wind up? I reckon it's just a load of hooey that they've made up for the dumb-arsed tourists. All that about Dr Jekyll and Jack the Ripper and Hyde Park. I bet the English made it all up for tourist consumption. In past centuries the propaganda was for the consumption of tourists from the Continent or petty African Kings, nowadays all that guff is invented for the cretinous gringos or Latin American playboys. Bastards. The bloke who came to calm us down looked like a lobster, red all over. The colour of Europeans gets right on my tits. They look like Californian apples. That's why I left the French bird I had in Paris. I couldn't stand looking at her skin after we'd fucked. She went red all over, as if her blood were going to pop out through her pores, as if she were going to burst. I only had to stroke her arse for it to go bright red, like the shell of a lobster. The colour of the skin of these bastards makes me puke. How could they kill Efi? That night of the party he was really chuffed because Anataylde had been elected Queen of the Faculty of Medicine. He was crazy about her, and so proud. He was all togged up and he'd slapped on the perfume. He looked kind of weird in a suit. The first blow was when the girl told him she was going to dance with everyone that asked her. Efi accepted it much against his will because he was as jealous as hell. Then we went to the bar and ordered a Titanic of Bacardi. When only the dregs remained in the bottle, Efi let out a strange groan, rose to his feet, mad as the devil, headed for the Tropicana's dance floor and began to look for her. I followed, trying to calm him down, but he told me to sod off. He was really steamed up. When he located her he went straight up to her knocking over everyone in his way and grabbed her by the arm / Let's dance / Wait until the end of the dance / No fucking way, I'm telling you we're going to dance right now / Then he smacked her across the face and all hell was let loose. The girl's sister and her boyfriend wanted to intervene but he decked them too. He was a dab hand at landing punches was Efi. After that, five Cubans and I fell on him. There was one helluva ruckus. The party came to an abrupt end, the orchestra threw themselves into the fray, Efi punched and kicked out in all directions. The very first wallop knocked me clean out of the fun. When I came round Efi was in the middle of the dance floor of the Tropicana in his shirt sleeves and there wasn't a bloke left standing who could land a punch anywhere near him. The sea's choppy. If we don't land soon I'm going to be panic stricken. The snag is the bar's closed or I'd knock back a couple of snifters to steady my nerves. Still, this boat's pretty wide and can take all this rocking, but if I'd had the cash and I'd known I'd have flown. Rhymes again. I'm a poet and I don't know it. But all this rolling around from side to side would break even the best of us. The worst of all this is that Ma won't cough up with the readies any more. I've been fartarsing about for five years and the old girl's got cheesed off. This journey's really been exhausting. But, after that sodding letter, I couldn't stand Madrid any longer. Yeah, everything started when that sodding letter arrived. Up 'til then, I didn't have a care in the world.

When he awoke, he rubbed his eyes to remove the sleep from them. He put on his glasses repeating a ceremony that he'd been performing daily for fourteen years, from the day when the ophthalmologist had told him you're short-sighted you have to wear glasses. From then onwards, it was always the same routine: he opened his eyes, rubbed them, wiped away the sleep and automatically grabbed his glasses from the bedside table, or the floor. He put them on and lit the gas stove, his heater. It was cold and the wind that sneaked through the crack in the window struck his feet. He opened the wooden shutters covering the windowpanes that, at night, kept out the light from the streetlamp on the corner, and the pale grey light of the Madrid winter penetrated into the farthest corner of the boarding house where he lived. The now ex-sleeper gazed at length at the trees in the Plaza de Oriente. Between the tall, thick trees one could make out glimpses of an equestrian statue. He'd been living in Madrid for a year and a half now and it had never occurred to him to find out whose statue it was. He hardly ever went through the Plaza de Oriente. It wasn't on his route to and from the house. Or, more accurately, during all this time he had never crossed the centre of the square. He always returned either along Bailén from the Plaza de España or walked behind the

Opera House coming from the underground station. He had no reason to cross the Plaza de Oriente to reach his room. He took off his glasses and rubbed his eyes again. The gas heater was crackling now and began to heat the room. The cold had woken him early; it was 8 a.m. The now ex-sleeper pulled a face when he looked at his watch. He wasn't in the habit of getting up until ten. Then he sat on the chair at the table where he usually wrote facing the window, facing the Plaza de Oriente, on the third floor of an old house in Pavia. He put his hands together and rubbed them with pleasure. The cold was retreating. He pulled the heater alongside the table and stuck his feet close to warm them. Then he saw the letter. The housekeeper was in the habit of leaving the mail propped up against his books or against the pot on the table where he kept his pencils. The ugly ex-sleeper picked up the envelope that he hadn't seen the night before because he'd come home in the early hours half cut and had immediately switched on the lamp on the bedside table, taken off his trousers in the semi-darkness and slipped between the sheets. Hence he hadn't noticed the envelope. Slowly, listlessly, he tore off the end of the envelope, rolled the strip of paper he'd cut into a small ball and aimed it at the windowpane. The ball bounced and fell back on to the table. He picked it up and dropped it into the empty ashtray. He drew out the letter and surveyed the envelope to see if it bore the name of the sender. There was no return address. So then he knew that it was from the comrades and hastily he smoothed it out on the table top to read it more easily. When he read the opening words he knew what it was about. It was the reply to a letter that he had written two months before. At that time he had been desperate, going through a tremendous crisis of conscience. He had asked to return to the fighting. He read the letter rapidly two or three times, then he crushed it into a ball and threw it furiously at the window. He began to dress quickly, his anger swelling to rage. He didn't bathe as he normally did. He kicked the heater aside and pulled on his boots. He dressed entirely in black and then, on top, put a rubberised black windcheater with a hood to protect him from the cold. When he was ready, he pulled out his gloves from the chest, took his passport from a drawer and a bankbook from the breast pocket of his overcoat. Finally, he picked up the letter and put it away in his trouser pocket. He left without a word to anyone, banging the street door behind him. Walking rapidly, he turned right at the first corner, went along Calle de la Bola, in three minutes reached Plaza de Santo Domingo and two minutes later was in the Gran Vía. He was red-faced and panting, his breath forming a mist in the cold air. He orientated himself, walked two or three blocks and went into the Atlántico Bank. He withdrew all his money, took off rapidly down the Gran Vía to Plaza España, on down Onésimo Redondo practically at a run and, ten minutes later, was in the Estación del Norte. At one of the windows he bought a rail ticket for London in a sleeping compartment. He paid for it and left the station. Now breathing calmly, he began to walk slowly up the street.

I haven't been able to sleep at all during the crossing. It was scheduled to take five hours but we did it in less. Perhaps the lousy boat has been making up time. It left Dunkirk late. There was no way we could leave port before. We'd been waiting since 11 p.m. and it didn't sail until one. I'd imagined I was going to be able to sleep but I didn't get a wink. What's the matter with me now? Not even I can understand myself. So what is it that I'm so worried about? What do I care if everything's been shot to hell? If the comrades came to grief, well they asked for it. Don't look for trouble, it'll always find you, my granny used to say to me. I told them so, right at the start. I always thought that scene was madness. And, being a dumb-fuck, here I am beating my breast and crying *mea culpa*. What in the hell possessed me to send him that letter? But I was going through a bloody awful crisis. Afterwards I forgot completely about it. I *am* surprised to hear the news about Skinny Dog though. He stuck the fighting for about ten years. I just don't understand it. But then I don't understand practically anything any more. That girl sitting in the corner, opposite me, couldn't sleep either. I've been watching her all the time. She looks French but not one of those red ones, she'd be about twenty-five I guess, I should chat her up but I'm not in a mood for shooting a line to a dolly bird, it'd be a dumb move, no fun at all. The news about Efi hit me hard. They could never catch him, not even on the day they blew away his brother. So how could they have managed to kill him? On that occasion they surrounded him in a bar on 12th Avenue and 9th and Efi shot the copper in the face point blank. It was there they killed his brother. But he managed to get away over the roof of the buildings. The army arrived and stretched a cordon around it, but he blasted his way out. Man, he had balls. I heard all about the 17th Avenue exploit from a comrade on his way through Paris. I always thought that Efi would get to be one of the top leaders. The Cubans took him and gave him special training because they said he was a born fighter, that he had the same qualities as Camilo Cienfuegos. They had him in La Cabaña, isolated from the other Guatemalans, preparing him specially. After that, they had him at the Hotel Presidente for about eight months, resting, held in reserve, whilst the first members of his group were back putting their arses on the line. That's where I met him when I was on holiday pissarsing about in Havana. Back then the poor bloke used to wake me up at 6 a.m. to make me walk eighteen kilometres a day to Cubanacán beach. God I'm a right prat when it comes to walking. I didn't give a toss about all that shit. What a mad bugger he was. He must have died fighting. Well, what other way would there have been for him? It was his life. I think we've arrived. The boat's entering the inner harbour. I think it's going to dock.

The ferry rocked towards the jetty of Dover harbour. The pilot manoeuvred skilfully and brought the hull up against the concrete wall where it was to dock. The engines gradually faded and stopped. The boat began to bump against the rubber fenders that protected the jetty. The fog horn blared out, harsh and mournful, buuuuu buuuuu buuuuu. Ropes flew from the deck and men ran to catch them and tie the vessel to the bollards embedded in the concrete pier. The boat stopped rocking a little when they dropped anchor and the stevedores secured the cables to the bollards with bowline knots. At last the boat was made fast. The passengers began to stretch, yawn, shake the sleep from their eyes, light cigarettes and feel the calm returning to their bodies. The traveller who had remained with his face pressed to the glass of the porthole took from his pocket a ball of paper, opened the porthole and threw it into the sea. The paper, carried by the waves, hit against the jetty and then, buoyed by the water, began to unfold and spread out like a blanket on the surface of the sea. Then one could read

"Boozer of Junksville:

You've been fartarsing about playing the hippy for six years. Now it's time you got a few things clear. Come back and die fighting or die totally spaced out on the ultimate trip but quit bugging us with these whingeing letters that you do us the favour of sending. As if it were a bed of roses here, as that Mexican Indian arsehole said. Trashy poet. Here we have death by the truckload. Now the shit has hit the fan and death is everywhere, spreading and clinging like weeds. There are very few of us comrades left. They killed Efi. They wasted him last year on the 7th September. At the time, I didn't know where to write to you. Things have got very hairy here. We're pulling out fast, fleeing for our lives. They could wipe us out at any minute. The break finally came, the FAR and the Party fell out and fought each other, everything's gone to the dogs. Those most to blame are those old turds who lead the Party because, right from the start, they let the armed boys do just what they liked and wouldn't bust their balls to grasp the nettle and sort them out. They held on and let all the fighting boys die so they could go on sharing out the cake the way they wanted it. Then, when they saw that everything was screwed up, they let it happen so that they could go on running their 'travel agency'. It's all coming apart. The order of the day is 'Every man for himself'. So as Capulina says, 'Forget it old boy'. You keep calm. Hang loose! What's all this crap about you planning to come back and join up again? What's the point of you coming back here just to get blown away? Forget it! Stay there in Madrid, screw all those big smelly white Spanish birds, sow some good seed in that old clapped out continent and leave off beating your breast in anguish. Nothing here is like it was any more. This isn't an order or said to upset you. I won't be leaving here unless it's feet first. I'm not going to give those gringo bastards the pleasure of taking me alive so they can beat my balls to a pulp. So this may be the very last letter I write to you (now I sound like Ufemia's

husband, that Mexican bloke in the ranchera song, 'When you receive this unexpected letter'). But that's the way it is. I chose my life and now I choose my death. Nothing more complex than that. It's all completely clear to me. Since we got into the movement, I've done what I had to. And I'm not blaming anyone if they have been less resolute than me. You were never totally convinced, I always told you that. So forget the whole business, don't dwell on this letter, do your own thing. Stop all this crap about pretending to be a revolutionary and get writing, for a writer is the only thing you are, you're a jungle monkey, as the Popul Vuh says. Stop pretending to be anything else. Leave the fighting, the violent death and the armed struggle to us. Die of old age, or chronic cirrhosis, Boozer of the Junkyard, you daft bugger, inveterate weaver of dreams. But take this in, get it into your noddle, fix it firmly in that bald bonce you must have by now and understand it once and for all, the revolution is no dream. The revolution is struggle and death not words or illusions. Only the man who is totally committed to the action can serve the cause. You are not. Accept this now once and for all. If you really are such a good writer finish that novel that you say you're writing. When we bring about the revolution we'll send for you. Rest assured of that. As an extra bit of interest, I'll add the fact that Skinny Dog has scarpered, done a runner, absconded to Mexico with the Section funds. The organisation has condemned him to death for theft and desertion. I'm telling you this so you can see that not everyone shows courage when facing reality and it's not all simple and straightforward. So, take care, you old bugger. Travel, screw, booze, throw your conscience to the wind, for here we are dying so that you can write, so that everyone can learn to write and read and eat well and have a home and work and lead a happy life free from fear. May God protect you, but as he doesn't exist, look after yourself and stay the happy carouser you've always been.
THE COMRADES"

12

SKINNY DOG

1967

The Sons of Bitches
1967
I realised it wasn't going to work right from the start. I phoned him and the first thing he demanded to know was who had given me his number and who I was. I gave him all he asked. He set up a meet in Parque México on a bench on the east side and instructed me not to speak to him until he gave me a signal. He started to bugger me around right from the beginning. That afternoon, I spent three hours sitting waiting for him. I had to sort out my immigration problems, I had to know what to do, where I stood. I cursed him the whole time I was waiting. Son of a bitch. What does he think? That I'm going to wait here for him all day? Stuck-up bastard with his airs and graces. Pretentious prick with persecution mania, a Mercedes Benz and tortoise-shell shades. I had no money. I'd been in Mexico for a week and I didn't know what to do. I went back and forth, I walked from Ángel del Campo to the Alameda, I went to the post office to send news to everybody, as if anybody gave a damn where I was or what I was

doing. I tried to locate him for a week, at his house they said he wasn't in, they gave me another number to ring but he was never there either. I didn't know where to get hold of him. I didn't manage to locate him until today and I don't reckon he's going to show, the lousy bastard. I started to get nervous. What if they really were following him? I knew it wasn't true. The news of his bullshitting and his dodgy activities had reached us in Guate. A bit different from Víctor. When I passed through Havana he was the Party rep. He answered the phone straight away and came to the hotel immediately. He was always helpful and obliging. He asked if you had money, if everything was okay, how did you get on with your papers comrade, be careful if you go to such a place, there are always Federal Police in that restaurant, watch your back with the owner of that hotel, if you need anything let me know. But this son of a bitch is never going to turn up. I've got cramp in my arse from sitting so long. The snag is that, if I move from here, he could come and, if he doesn't find me, he'll take off and I won't get hold of him again for another fortnight. I've got to settle my situation 'cos my cash is running out, even though I go without nosh and travel all these massive distances on foot the brass doesn't go anywhere. I had to pay a month's rent in advance and I've got to keep back enough for another month 'cos who knows what'll happen, you never know what's going to turn up. Especially with that sodding rep, you don't know where you stand. On top of all this, my shoes are going home fast, I hoof it for about ten kilometres a day and I'm wearing a hole in the sole. But I can't take being shut in alone, I get desperate, it gives me claustrophobia, I get nervous and mad as hell, so every afternoon I amble down to the centre, stand around in Immigration, then on to the Post Office, why in the devil do I waste money on letters? It's bloody stupid. Then I sit in the Alameda to rest for a bit, buy an ice-cream and turn around and plod back again. In the evening, when the sun pisses off for the night and the old bat goes off to church, I have a shag with Totoneca (nostalgically) and afterwards she gives me a coffee. Totoneca is terrific, she washes my clothes, she supplies the soap so I don't have to spend my money on it. I fuck her, she washes my clothes and gives me coffee. But I can't go on like this because she can't pay my rent or food, and that bloody rep still hasn't shown up. He'll have to find me an opening pretty damned fast before he receives the report that I scarpered with the Party funds. Well, what was left of them anyway. There was only a hundred quetzals and with that I paid the airfare and bought a suitcase, which left me just thirty-five dollars. If he finds out about this, he'll tell me to go to hell. But a report takes a month or more to arrive so I've still got a chance for several weeks yet. If Rat hadn't come up with some mazuma, I'd have really been up the creek. But he came up trumps. He's a great bloke. His fat lump of a wife must have given him hell. I can imagine the right bollocking he got coming home at God knows what hour of the morning without a cent. The bloody woman's so jealous I bet she thought he spent the night at a cathouse. Anyway she needs to keep an eye on him 'cos he really is a lecherous arse-chasing sod. This bastard hasn't come and there's a really nasty wind getting up. This jacket's so thin it lets in all the cold air. Ah, here he comes, about time too. He's all wrapped up in a big overcoat so he doesn't give a monkey's if you're freezing your balls off waiting. Bloody hell, look at the gear on that flash git. He's got rid of his beard. When he was in the Law Faculty he was known as "Whiskers". He was always full of crap, mediocre but with pretensions, thought himself a real cool dude. What a poser! Now he's the rep because he's well in with the Ruskies. They're all a load of shites so he fits in perfectly, he spends the whole week boozing at receptions and drinks parties with crap bureaucrats in their lousy embassy. Why is it the Soviets get on my tits so much? They're exactly the same as the gringos, in Havana they have the same attitude as the gringo tourists in any Latin American country, they think they're the new conquistadors. Russian arseholes. In Immigration I met China and she told me all the tales about this bastard. Well, as long as this dumb-fuck comes up with the goods I couldn't care less about all that crap, I'm safely out of it and I don't give a toss about anything else. Now what the fuck's he up to? Why doesn't he come straight over? Is he lost? I'm sure it was on this bench he told me to wait. Let's have a look, I wrote it down here, yes this is it. So why has the stupid bugger gone the other way? I'll catch him up. I'll signal to him. He knows me so why is he playing dumb? But if I signal to him he might get mad and then it'll be worse. I'd better wait calmly and see what he does. I can see him clearly from here so if I see that he's going to leg it I can reach him fast. If I see that he's going to get into his Mercedes, I'll run like hell. I got it wrong. Why do I always think the worst of people? He's turned round and now he's coming this way. He thinks that by turning like that he's shaken off anybody who was following him. Dumbcluck! These comrades have lost all feel for the field-craft needed in situations like this. They think the revolution is like a James Bond movie. Like that bloke I brought into the Party who thought that going undercover was just a matter of putting on dark glasses. I've got to tell him to get me a job and give me a hand to get my papers sorted with Immigration. He must have contacts, know the right people. Let him get on with it, then. I'll have to be convincing so he doesn't smell a rat. If he asks for a letter or a message, I'll tell him they didn't give me anything so as not to compromise me. He's right near. I feel a bit nervous. Yep, he's recognised me, he's coming this way. Hi! He's just signalled to me to follow him. What the hell's he playing at? I'm following him like a bloody idiot. I feel like tripping the bugger up, that way at least he'll get a damned good thump on the head. I'm behaving like a berk. I can't hear what he's saying. Speak up comrade.

"I can't talk to you today, I'm being followed. Call me in a week's time."

Saigon City
1968
When you opened your eyes you saw the pyramids of Teotihuacán. On the bus radio Manzanero was singing "this afternoon I watched the rain, saw people running, but you weren't here". You sat up and looked out of the window. It's just as well I got a window seat or I wouldn't have seen them, you said. Your back hurt. On the last stretch of Insurgentes Avenue, you'd fallen asleep. You were tired, exhausted. You hadn't managed to find a permanent position all year.[9] "With you I learned, to recognise a new world of illusions". On Thursday, Whip said: Let's go to

Sahagún City this Saturday. It's an industrial complex so you stand a chance of finding work. That's where the Renault factory is located, they make the carriages for the railway and there's a lot of other factories too. There are four Guatemalans working there and perhaps they'll give you a helping hand. You made up your mind to give it a try. What was there to lose? Maybe there you could get back on the rails. "Don't watch the sunset, it's the saddest thing and that's how I feel about you, only you". That Manzanero's an arsehole, he's only got one theme, depressing stuff. What's the purpose of this heap of stones, one on top of the other? The Aztecs were shitty slave owners, however many people must have died carrying stone after stone up on their backs? You sat up straight because you were only going to get a fleeting glimpse, the bus climbed quickly pushing its wheels forward as if eager to leave the State of Mexico for Hidalgo, so you craned your neck and stared at the mountain of stones which, placed one on top of the other year after year, decade after decade, century after century, back after back, bone after bone, had grown into a pyramid. The Pyramid of the Sun. Then you turned away, tired, you moved in your seat and thought what the hell do I care. You tried to go back to sleep. Whip shook your shoulder and told you that's the Pyramid of the Moon. You closed your eyes thinking they can both sod off. "No, even if you swear that everything has changed, for me it's all over between us." When you woke again it was wall-to-wall maguey cactus, anteroom to a pulque bar. Whip smacked his lips, mulling over the prospect. We're arriving, he informed you. You thought, if he doesn't get a glass of pulque soon he's going to start getting cantankerous. Wake up. I'm going to show you Saigon City. Then you stopped thinking and came awake with a jolt. As soon as the bus passed the monument that guards the city you leaned against the window squashing your nose against the glass (like some antediluvian monster) and managed to make out the Dominican Friar Sahagún raising his protective hand in blessing over the second-class bus which you'd taken in the Villa de Guadalupe. What a joke, the city of vice protected by the statue of a friar, you thought: that kind of thought will scorch your brain. The industrial area opened up before you in all its layers. You classified it as lower middle class.

Comfortably off proletariat. Bought, controlled, identical. Poor, unpainted. On the outskirts of the city were the executive houses. Bigger, in different styles, distinguishable one from another, classifiable. At three in the afternoon, a pale weak light bathed the wide empty streets. Everybody's drinking at this time of day, remarked Whip in explanation. We have to get off as the bus doesn't go right to the centre. It doesn't remain here either but carries on to Apán. When you alighted, Manzanero was still frigging your patience not now from the bus radio but from the radio of the Saigon City Social Club: "Forgive me for destroying all the good that you have done me". Worker must be in there drinking with Pig, observed Whip "if at last I pay for all my mistakes with interest". The club had been built to prevent the workers from blowing their entire week's wages on hard liquor every Saturday night but, as the building was filthy and neglected and nobody came, they decided to sell beer on Saturdays instead. Worker rose to his feet when he saw Whip. The atmosphere hit you in the gut, shouts, roars of laughter, how's it going mate, what'll you have? A beer? Come on Whip, sit here. I want you to meet a fellow countryman of ours, Whip presented me and a group of workmen stood up and shook hands, pleased, delighted in fact, to meet me. Pig came up to where the group was standing and said to you I know you and he embraced you, they used to call you Skinny Dog, and as he hugged you he said softly in your ear and you're from the Party, right? Worker looked at you jealously out of the corner of his eye, his gaze clouded by the pulque he'd drunk. At length he opened his mouth and said slowly:

"Another little bourgeois prick, eh?"

You looked at him and were amused. He was about forty-five. A born worker, tough as nails on the inside and dirty and smelly on the outside. Whip blinked and said he's a comrade, Worker. Worker grudgingly proffered his hand; rough, hard, calloused. He gripped your hand squeezing until the pain shot up your arm but you made out that you couldn't feel a thing and squeezed back. Worker grinned from ear to ear and said to you:

"Pleased to meet you, comrade, so you're another Guatemalan. Let's get stuck into the pulque, shall we?"

Yes, let's do that you said, although you hated the stuff. When you were walking towards the table where Worker and Pig were sitting, you noticed the flagon of pulque under the chess table which was now used to hold the beers, and you thought I won't get any work here it'll just be one massive piss-up and a bloody awful hangover. You sat down and took the glass that Worker handed you. Cheers comrade, you knocked back the dirty sticky milk, harsh on the palate, and swallowed, "that man who wished us happiness told me that perhaps tomorrow you'll return", the tears trickled between your half closed eyelids. When you awoke you were in an Apán cathouse. A vision that defied belief, scalded, burned, seared, bored into your paralytic, hungover skull. You were sure you'd died and gone straight down to hell. A vile dive, a rough bawdyhouse, the underworld, inferno, death. The dive wouldn't hold a single body more and still they kept pouring in. It reeked of sweat, sex, shared bodily fluids, pulque, cigarettes, tequila, farts. You couldn't see a foot in front of you. In the centre, several couples were dancing close, gland to gland, rubbing their sexual organs against each other lubriciously, deliciously. Everybody was pissed out of their skulls shouting "Cheers! Mud in your eye! Cheers baby!" when the group playing stopped killing Manzanero you saw Whip, Pig, Worker and The Stranger coming towards you, each with a whore in tow, having a helluva good time. So you've woken up at last, they said. Worker came right up close, grabbed you by the arm, forced you to your feet and said:

"This is the foreman, mate. You've got a job at the Renault factory."

El Hoyito
1953

It became a habit with us to spend the afternoons with the whores at El Hoyito. Just before two we disperse and spread out through the park to wait for Crone. He goes for the car. Some of us head over to fat Carmen's shop, 'The Rosary', for a quick one, others squat on the pavement behind the parked cars, the rest hide in the flowerbeds in front of the Town Hall. Everybody's keeping an eye open for the priest. At two minutes to two, a cassock appears around the corner with him inside. He's reading. He's always reading some bullshit or other, so he never knows what's going on. Just after two, Crone's big Lincoln appears. It's a flash '49 job, big enough to hold the entire gang. On the corner of the cathedral, Chink and Big Bonce climb in. In front of the lardarse's shop, Rat, Boozer, Quino, the Lad and I pour in. All the 'Boyze'. Then we do a gangsters' take off that leaves the tyres imprinted on the tarmac. The priest reading in the school doorway isn't aware of a thing.

/ The boys are here / shout the happy hippy horny whores sashaying over.

At that hour of the day there are no punters so they're sewing, knitting, mending, cooking, doing their hair or taking a nap. The stagnant air is heavy with heat, lethargy and farts. In the first room, which is the best one and looks on to the street, is Rosita, also the best one. She's the Lad's lady / Come on, my little Long Shlong / She laughs as she propels him into her room, so young but so well hung / In the second room of the house on the right (à la drwat, as they say) Black Beauty, Rat's quarrelsome, contentious bit of arse is ready waiting for him with a kiss. I reckon that supercharged strumpet's got a sentimental side. Right inside up the top of the passage (that's where we're all hoping to get), near the kitchen, is Berta's room. She's the oldest of them, (already pushing twenty-six) has a big mole on one cheek and fucks like a goddess. She's Boozer's tart. The other girls only drink and flirt with us, but won't let us screw them 'cos they've all got their own special bloke. We sweep in invading on all fronts, establish ourselves, take possession of the house, bar the doors. The striptease party starts. Berta always has a hipflask of Polano rum: she's generous, salacious, dumb. We lie, sit, stretch out in the parlour, glass in hand: red lights, curtains closed, and a good measure of the best hooch. The madame comes out and gives us the same performance as she does every other day.

/ If you're not going to use the rooms you can just sod off. You only come to play with the girls and touch them up. You don't even bring any money with you. So young and such pimps /

The girls, anxious, cooling fast, on the defensive, protective / Oh Miss Mary, let the boys stay. After all, there aren't even any clients right now /

Rosita, Black Beauty and Berta spring up, (one, two, three, what great little movers) / Anyway this is my fellah /
They embrace their respective loves, feeling, fondling, inflaming them. These, of course, are smirking like a dog with two dicks.
The boozing starts but, as for snacks, fat chance. There's a bunch of us and not a lot to drink so you grab what you can and hang on to it. One each for starters. When there's a big bottle there's enough for two measures per head, but two drinks have no effect at all, they just whet your appetite. The dancing starts. We dance, swaying, entwined like pythons, holding each other up. The whores with lovers come out to join in.
/ Just dancing, have you got that? Don't go getting randy 'cos you're not getting anything /
That's the rule, it's understood and accepted. Anyway you have to pay attention to the dancing, otherwise there's no fun at all. We stand, sit, get turned on, get turned off, sleep a while. We even read if it gets to be a drag. We chat / How long have you been here, I haven't seen you before. Wouldn't you like to be my girl? / Oh yeah? So you can get a free fuck, right? / No, I really like you / Better not, my bloke'd knife you and he'd slash my face / About four o'clock those with a mistress go up the passage for a bonk.
/ Don't take long boys. Just one fuck /
They go off smugly, wrapped around each other, lusting, rutting, the semen already spurting, touching each other up openly for all the poor to see (the poor in spirit that is).
/ Let's go and watch a fuck, boys / I invite the bunch of voyeurs who are left red-eyed and frustrated (like me). Everybody agrees. We invite the girls with lovers to the room.
/ Bugger off, boys / stubborn, randy, heated by the liquor, they'd like to stay but don't dare. They mill around but don't dare to remain. Their fellah might arrive and play merry hell / We'd better go / They head off for their respective rooms (They're like mares on heat). They start to sew, to do their make up, masturbate (that's something at least), its nearly four and their big white chiefs may arrive at any minute.
The most accessible room on which to peep, spy, get a good

butchers is that of Rat and Black Beauty Incorporated. They get their gear off and then it's endless chat. Rat's got his fads. He's into psychoanalysis / Well, into anal-ysis anyway. Black Beauty is affectionate but an endless talker. There's ten minutes of earbending. Total waste of time. Bullshitting. Like / Why are you here? You've never had a decent job / My mother left me when I was very young and my father deflowered me one day when he came home drunk / I needed the money / It's always the same, him in his underpants and the tart in her bra and knickers / I needed the brass / where are your parents? / have you loved many men? / lots / and do you love me? / yes daddy, I adore you / (incestuous piece). She is the more shameless and starts the big bang going, she goes straight to home-base, she grabs his prick, Rat gets shy, inhibited, flushes, and shuts his eyes. Very soon he gets an erection, then its pants down and she's syphoning the python. Flat on his back, Rat soon forgets all about psychoanalysis. Face down, she psychoanalyses him with a blowjob.

Thick-lipped Black Beauty. This is real good stuff. The boys in a frenzy of wanking. The one in front, squashed, half stifled / Stop pushing, it only makes it worse / Can't you see the wood's going to break? / We're going to fall on top of them / Stop pissarsing about boys / Get your hands off my arse / he who touches arse wants to screw / Screw your mother /

These guys never learn. The same thing happened when Chink lost his cherry. They never learn. That day, by pure chance, Chink had fifty cents on him. He showed us on the way. Look you've got to pay. You'll have to put in whatever you've got or you won't get anything. The cathouse was really far from the school on 19th Street and the railway line. In the back of beyond. That day Crone didn't bring the Lincoln. The snag was that the brothel was right by Crone's house so we had to make a long detour so that Crone's old man wouldn't see us and cock up the defloration of our skinny, grotty Asiatic (he never took a bath even when you cast aspersions on his mother's virtue). According to Rat, only schoolgirls who lived in the posh Zone 10 went to this brothel. There was only one room. In the centre, a folding screen. On one side: matron, cashier madame, her desk, old wicker armchairs, the old sod's cat, waiting room. On the other side: the bed.

/ Bloody hell, so many lads / (procession of pricks): old witch, stripper of innocent young girls, owner of a hovel / The cops are going to raid me and close me down because of you lot. Only the one who's going to fuck her can go in / We can't allow that. He's a virgin. You might pull a fast one on him / Some of us have to take care of him / Chink is pale and silent. We hawkers, traders, guardians of innocent boys, procurers, pimps, buddies / oh, alright then. Three of you can stay.

We draw to see who'll watch. Odds or evens. Heads or tails. Boozer, Rat and I stay. We were the negotiators. The ones who handled the business so there could be no abuse.

/ How much are you going to charge? / celestial chorus.

/ The girl is new, decent. She's only been here three times / Old witch, suspicious, lying, ex-prostitute / Take a look at her, peep in, there she is sitting on the bed.

The girl, pale, scrawny, scraggy, undernourished, wild-eyed, nervous, needy. She smiles at us timidly. We close the curtains.

/ She's hideous lads /

/ Well what do you expect for a first fuck? Stop complaining / Chink pricks up an ear but doesn't hear a thing.

/ Get in there Chink /

Backing out doesn't count. Chink tries it, his look reveals his fervent desire to make a run for it, he's unsure, in a cold sweat, he implores them, his hands trembling. No way, either you go in or we'll bash you up. But she's as ugly as sin. I'll come back another day. Let's have the cash up front, warns the old bag. Chink, triumphant, me only have half dollal. Never mind, we'll pay the rest. Between the three of us we put up the other fifty cents. Chink's defeated. The old battleaxe grabs the dosh and, eying us distrustfully, stuffs it into her pocket in double quick time. Chink pulls back the curtain. He's over the border, crapped in the Rubicon. Chink and the vestal virgin face to face. The girl's uglier than the madame, than the old bat who's watching us. I've fucked both and there's not a lot to choose between them. This bag of bones spun me the yarn that she had a house with a pool in Zone 10 and she only screwed for kicks. More like gave arse for brass, I thought. I'm a spiteful Skinny Dog. Now she's probably spinning the same tale to the Chink. We stand on the wicker chair, ready for an eyeful, willing to support the cause with a sympathetic wank. Our hands sweat nervously, ready for action. On tiptoe, only our eyes peek over the top of the screen. Chink has no idea. Chink "velly wollied" definitely not "leady for loggeling". Chink not suspect. Chink stand "ligid", eyes "livetted" on young "plostitute".

/ Sit down, young man / she initiates the proceedings.

/ Thank you velly much, Ma'am / Oriental arselicker.

/ You've never been here before.

/ Go othel place / lying bugger, what a load of shite! The dude's trembling all over.

/ Do you want me to put off the light?

No! – shout all the voyeurs in silence.

/ No / Chink timidly.

/ Shall I take off my dress or do you want to do it?

Who gives a flying fuck! Boozer, vulgar, foulmouthed. Who gives a gnat's arse: Skinny Dog equally crude. Everyone stays silent. Our hands are sweating and nothing has started, zippo (her zip still closed). I'm dying for a smoke. Chink makes a move (It's worse than trying to climb the Great Wall of China). He perks up. He strokes her hair (he must think she's his mother, yellow whore). She becomes bolder, she strokes his balls. Chink sits so you can't see he's got a stiffy, modest, callow, half-cocked, not yet fired. She takes off her dress (at heart she's a tart). When she's finished, Chink is in his underpants, on his back, erect. I'll put off the light. I told you not to: hoarse, commanding, a real macho man. He pulls her by the arm, draws her to him, makes her lie at his side, he caresses her, fondles her, tears off her brassiere. Oh, you've torn my bra. I'll buy you another one. The lying bastard, he did have more money and he conned us. When he finishes, he can pay us the fifty cents we paid for his deflowering. He sucks her tits. Oh daddy darling. He puts his hand inside her panties and sinks his finger into her crack like with his virgin girlfriend in the cinema, stroking her oozing cunt. She starts to pull down his underpants with her foot: experienced: there are lubricious developments. He starts to masturbate her, pushing his finger in and out (later on he'll expect to shake our hands with that hand impregnated with the marine odour of her cunt). She takes off her panties. Both are now bollock naked and ambidextrous. No, not in your mouth, says Chink fastidious, prudish. He only kisses her on the cheek. He mounts her, frantic, fevered, frenzied, inflamed, looking, groping, feeling inexpertly for the target: virgin. She takes him, controls him, masters him, possesses him, sets him on the right road, takes his stick and puts him inside. Inside!!! A sigh of relief comes from our panting breasts: pure Mills and Boon, lovely darling. One more ex-virgin. Signed, sealed and delivered. We could swear to it on the Bible. The rest was just the usual decorous procedure, cold skinny arse slapping up and down. Load of hassle all of it. Breathing more slowly and rhythmically now we reclined against the screen which proceeded to topple over on top of Chink and the horny harlot who were shagging like stoats. The witch on her broomstick kicked us, ejected us, exorcised us from the squalid dive. We legged it fast with Chink bringing up the rear his weapon cocked but still unfired, his load undelivered with a pain in the bollocks, the new ex-virgin.

But they never learn and keep pushing / don't put that near me / get yourself some money or a mistress / Rat is still enjoying his blowjob, on his back, supine, his mush scarlet, almost purple, his teeth clenched, his buttocks too probably, just about to come, to go stiff all over, to shoot his load, to be quiet, exhausted, groggy / he's going to come / stop pushing / cut it out / Blackie sucking his cock, Rat on his back, gripping the sheets frenetically, his legs up on her shoulders: good pose. A scream from another room paralyses us, tears us from the wall, run, run, Blackie leaps up, Rat, left breathing heavily, grabs his tonker and masturbates fast. We rush to see what's happened (as if we couldn't guess). A tart in her slip with a pair of scissors in her hand is pursuing Big Bonce. She's one of the ones with a lover.

/ You little bastard, I've got a fellah. Did you think you were going to come here for a free shag with anyone that takes your fancy. I'm going to slit your face, you little swine. Go and grab your mother's tits / Armed and dangerous, the hefty foulmouthed whore chases him all up 7th Avenue in just her slip, bare-breasted, brandishing her weapon. We, like a pack of hounds, follow behind in hot pursuit and bringing up the rear.

Rat, pale and frightened shitless, runs belt in hand, clutching his fly.

The madame (the same as every other day).

/ If you come back here I'll have you put inside /

We meet up in the usual place.

Half a block up the street.

Lets see how much cash we've got. Booted out of El Hoyito we head straight for the Antorcha bar. "Need a light, Antorcha matches see you right". (Paleta's dad: the advertising bloke with the loudspeaker: the Spaniard). Now we're down to grubbing for cents: all we have between us.

You can't get anything on credit here.

The waitresses are dead ugly. Hookers with the clap.

The first in is always Rat. He's also the one who orders the drinks. Always the same. Right from the very first time.

The Idiots

1969

I'll put the record player in the corner. Or on this table. The flat looks a bit empty without furniture. But it's better like that. That way it'll be the right atmosphere for The Venturas and The Sound of Silence. If I pull the armchair that I bought at the pawnbrokers up this way a bit and I put the table in the centre we'll be able to dance. Or maybe it would be better the other way round. Tomorrow I'll go to the Lagunilla market and buy a knotted carpet. It'll cost me some ninety pesos or more. Perhaps it would be best if I wait for her to come with me so we can decide on it together. That's how we make decisions. Everything has to be by mutual agreement. This flat's pretty and very centrally located. It's hard to get one like this just round the corner from Parque Mexico and only two blocks from Parque España. The only snag is the buses. All those that go by here finish in Chapultepec. None of them go to the Centre. To get there you have to walk to Insurgentes and it's not that close or take a taxi from the rank on the corner. Now that really is a bit inconvenient. But, anyway, it's not that bad. Dustin Hoffman was great in The Graduate. That afternoon, after the film, we went and bought the record player and the Venturas version of "The Sound of Silence". Lovely name. Silent sounds. I think that I'm at peace at last. Maybe the joints she passes me help me a bit. We've been together for nearly five months. I've been in exile now for two years. I think I'm going to stay here for the rest of my life. She spoils me, indulges my every whim, gives me grass, takes me to the movies, talks to me about Bob Dylan, John Lennon, Paul MacWhatshisname, Neil Diamond, takes me to Las Musas and the Zorro Plateado, introduces me to her friends from the Colegio de México with a childish pride, she's a little girl who lives with an ex-guerrilla, it makes her proud, her friends come to the flat just to see me, I'm about twelve years older than her, she's like a toy that will disintegrate in my hands, I can't make my own decisions any more, I'm always waiting to see what she says, if we're going to the Movie Club or to the Comonfort or the Hidalgo Theatre or to listen to jazz, I really don't understand much about that, move your body, move your head, your waist, twist at the waist, go on like that, and she moves me, I twist and clap my hands, twist, clap, twist clap, and I move my head like an idiot, if the comrades could only see me doing this, all those that come to see me are bearded, but bearded because they're filthy, not like we were down there when there wasn't even time to shave, twist, twist, I move my head and my torso and click my fingers, I'm getting into the mood, she nods with pleasure and draws close to me, the record ends and begins again, I'd like to dance close to her, to feel her body next to mine, to feel she's really mine, I don't manage to feel this, even when we go to bed and she, raunchy as she is, possesses me, takes me, puts me into her like a doll, I'd like to dance cheek to cheek, like we do in Guatemala, Never My Love starts up, that's slow, I try to get close to her but she pulls away and threshes about contorting her body with a grace that makes me laugh, she looks as if she's coming, having great orgasmic spasms, she closes her eyes and her face twitches convulsively, whereas when she really climaxes she doesn't even writhe, she comes quietly, that's when she seems more like a marionette than a woman, not like those females who, when they come, moan and cling to you going oh darling give it to me harder, right up inside, no, when she comes she looks like a defenceless little bird and when she dances she looks as if she's having a mind-blowing orgasm, she's a paradox, no way does she seem to be mine, not in any way, I'm her toy, I can't possess her but I'm at peace in my showcase, I don't work, she has a grant from the Colegio de México, five thousand pesos as a researcher into some crap or other and the two of us live peacefully, I couldn't stand it in Ciudad Sahagún any more, I was exhausted by the factory when she appeared, oh Delilah, my oh my Delilah, I'm going to hold her close, dance cheek to cheek, even if she gets mad, even if she makes a scene, let go of me, don't be such a pain, get in the groove, no way, this flat in Nuevo León is better than the other, I'll put in the record player, her fundamental part, her sexual equipment, her climax maker, her orgasmiser, it and the Beatles, and me, I'm her doll who carries out the normal functions of sex, one night one of those that she brings here told me that it would be exciting 'exciting' he said if we both . . . I was really high but I understood, I punched him so hard he flew through the air and landed on the record player, she leapt on me like a tiger, the little bird disappeared, I knackered the record player.

Well, anyway, it's got to go some place. Preferably not in the middle of the room, because that's where they dance. It'll be alright on this table. I'll have to move my arse 'cos she'll be here soon and she gets mad if she doesn't find it tidy. I never thought I'd come to this, living off a hippy. She's even made me grow my hair long. If the comrades could see me. All her friends come and look at me with admiration, and they talk about the Revolution. Then I remember the Lad and Efi and all the dead comrades and I smoke this shit in desperation, I cry inside whilst I rock myself, Hey Jude, clap, clap go the hands, she introduces me proudly and the Beatles finish, these people are like cardboard cut-outs, I feel that a deep weeping comes over me whilst she comes to the Beatles. How different from the true whores. They're real flesh and blood women, oh what a wicked prick, it's so huge, they grasp it, fondle it, suck your balls. These rich whores won't even touch your cock, it's as if they're made of glass, they come in silence. One of these days I'll give her a bloody good beating and bugger off. The worst part is when they talk about the Revolution whilst they're smoking grass and singing, they sway like idiots, swing their heads and try to be the centre of attention with Che Guevara said this and Fidel said the other on his podium. They can kiss my arse, all of them. Then I'm overcome by an overwhelming urge to weep or to sink into the sound of silence.

Bestiary
1967

Skinny Dog:
Thin famished dog with big sad eyes and a droopy double chin. Long-bodied, but narrow. He tells stories that not even he believes. He left his master's house because the latter wanted to waste him and is still looking for him to make him into dog soup. Sometimes he howls, especially at night, especially when very tired. In spite of all that has happened, when he is weary, in the evenings, in the rain, wherever he may be, he starts to remember these stories.

The Bear:
He escaped from a circus with his mate and his small daughter. His mate was heavily pregnant but that couldn't be helped because the owner of the circus wanted to kill him. Fleeing, he crossed the fence of his master's property. The owner of the neighbouring farm reluctantly gave him refuge but drew the Bear's teeth before letting him cross into his territory. Now the little Bear lives by selling medicines door to door in a place where, according to rumour, there exists a tree called "The Sad Night". Every night The Bear comes to weep a little at its side. Then he goes off to Tacuba to sleep next to his two cubs. He swears he will never return to the circus. He is small of body, chubby, with a flirtatious moustache that twitches when he is drunk. In the circus he had a very special position: he was the chauffeur for the head of propaganda.

The Whip:
Indian chief with a strong physique but soft heart. He left his tribe because it was perpetually at war and he was a born pacifist. He pitched his tent next to Coyoacán and there he swears every day that one of these days he's going to lose his cool and pick up the tomahawk, put on the warpaint and take an active part in the killing. However, he knows that there is nothing certain about this. Every day he gets farther away from the war, because he studies assiduously the philosophy of the Greeks: sybarites, bachanalians, bingers, onanists, pacifists, queers. Then he sits at the door of his tent and smokes a little marijuana in his peace pipe.

The Pig:
He left his sty up to his neck in shit. Oddly, outside of the sty he started to think. He stopped eating shit mixed with maize and began to drink pulque. Of the best brand. The pink kind. He is not a vegetarian so he doesn't smoke material. He left his first sow wallowing in the mud and found another. He did the right thing because this sow is quiet, she doesn't mate with the leaders of the sty just because they are the leaders. She only mates with him. He is at peace and gets fatter by the day. Pulque is like meat. It has the same vitamins or more. The only thing that does not let him sleep peacefully is that one day his photo was taken with the commandant and this photo went round the world. Sometimes he dreams that in the place where he lives, just round the corner from the Chilpancingo roundabout, they come looking for him because of this photo, in which, despite his eyes being covered, the CIA managed to recognise him. In spite of it all, he lives peacefully. Growing fat.

The Monkey:
He always swung around and shouted more than anyone else. He has a red arse and a white face. He's a red-arsed fair-haired simian: blond. That's what he's known as now: the blond monkey. Because of the volume of his shouting, they always paid attention to him, gave him the best journeys, the best dinners,

the best scholarships. Nevertheless, he knew that he was deceiving everyone and lived in a state of anxiety. He was an intellectual and, according to him, a fighting monkey until one day he grew tired of the farce and entwining his tail in the first tree that he saw went leaping from one to another until he left the forest in which he had spent all his life. As he was not stupid, he soon found another forest where he could go on deceiving people with his haranguing. Afterwards, he sent for his sisters. His friends always considered him a traitor, because they insisted he had betrayed them all his life. So why the fuck did they elect him to the Central Committee of the monkeys, then? At the instigation of Efi he was condemned to death. The Monkey married a little black simian of a different race but, despite everything, they live peacefully in the forest of Chimalistac.

The Macaw:
Macaw with a big beak and pale colours. This latter factor due, possibly to his constant and progressive malnutrition. When he was born, the Macaw fairy sprinkled salt on him. He's a witty Parrot who comes off badly whenever he gets involved. He has a very sad look and a string of tiny macaws, including a pair of twins. Nevertheless, he takes care of them and loves and protects them with the last few feathers he's got left. When he can't stand the sadness he gets drunk and goes out at night to walk barefoot and alone to Hundido Park. He's a learned parrot, with a law degree. When he smoked marijuana for the first time he almost went crazy. He's a Macaw who has travelled and suffered a lot. He goes from place to place, and flat to flat. He can find no job because nostalgia prevents him from getting a life.

The Lynx:
Hot blooded wild beast with blue eyes. She slept with one of the big animals from the Zoo and bore him a son. Afterwards she fled. She laughs all day at their tales and at her own. She roars and roars with laughter. She was quick with the gun. But at night she doesn't sleep, she can't close her eyes until the early hours because her nightmares won't let her rest. She always

dreams the same thing. She dreams that when she escaped from the cage the two comrades that helped her to escape gave her a machine gun and told her to wait for them. She couldn't because she was scared to death and they killed them and buried them in the trunk of a tree. At night in her dreams Juan's eyes open and she screams in desperation. At night she relives her remorse. Despite everything she yoked up with an animal of a different species and they had an offspring. The Lynx spends the whole day carrying him around San Jerónimo de Lídice and wondering if perhaps it would have been preferable to die with her comrades.

The Watusi:
Pure blooded African. Yellow from so much hash. He escaped from Africa because they were going to cut his throat for getting into something that was none of his concern. His tribe sends him a wad from time to time but they have disowned him since he became a hippy. He's the guru of his community but in his heart he doesn't believe all that crap, he keeps it going to be able to live without working. His frizzy curls hang to his waist, he wears faded blue jeans and walks barefoot through the Zona Rosa. Sometimes he thinks about his old masters, of the time when they made him dance in the public square without asking him if he wanted to or not, then he seeks them out and gets drunk with them and, totally pissed out of his skull, he fights and screams like a madman. He never forgets the jungle he came from. Nor Tarzan. Then he tries to imitate him by howling.

The Fox:
He has black, sunken eyes. Clever and cunning. He has many scalps on his belt. He went hunting with Chinese Yon.[10] He was one of his pack. When he gets drunk, his instinct comes to the fore and he begins to swear and threaten to kill, his lean body tenses, stretches and he slavers at the mouth. The Great Chicken grabs him and then he calms down because this Fox, once he had tasted human flesh, ceased to like the flesh of chickens. For that reason, he calms down. He lowers his head, fingers his balls and drops his eyes to the earth. He thinks about

his great escape and begins to purr. After the fourth bottle, he stops being a pain in the neck and crashes out. Then he stops bothering his fellow man.

The Great Chicken (Gallus gallus maximus): His breast is already very tough. He's very old. That's the reason why they decided not to kill him, his flesh would be of no use. He began to study like mad and became a lawyer. He abandoned all that he had and went to pontificate in a foreign hen-coop. After some years, he realised that he could tell what he knew and he couldn't stop talking. Now he has the appearance of a typical Mexican. He even speaks like a Mexican. But at heart he is an Indian chicken from Cuilapa. The only thing that he doesn't forget every night after talking and talking all day is to eat his tortillas and beans. Then he shuts himself away to read so he can continue talking. He doesn't understand a bloody word of it, but no matter, he talks and talks and reads and reads. On Saturdays he drinks Castillo rum. Only that brand because all others disagree with him. As he doesn't like whiskey because it cracks his tongue and in Altillo University there's no Indita hooch, he's into Castillo rum that he drinks with Macaw. Shit-faced, the two birds talk for hours on end. There's no way Gallus ditto maximus will cough up any cash, sometimes he takes out a knotted handkerchief, undoes it and says I'll put in one peso, then, afterwards, he makes a great fuss about it. When he's alone he becomes honest with himself, nostalgic for his old hen-coop he plays Luna de Xelajú, dresses like an Indian with a cloth on his head and starts to dance to the beat of the Guatemalan Son. Then he goes out like a light.

Blackboard:
A piece of black furniture which can be placed anywhere you fancy, is full of chalk, is written on and then erased. Nothing has happened on it, nothing has remained. Except for a white mark about which he puts on airs: two bullets in the shoulder, two white scars that he'll show when it suits him. A French woman bought herself a blackboard to learn to read the Revolution. She put it in a house in Aguascalientes and threw herself on top of

it thinking that if she did she'd learn better. As she discovered nothing, she threw it away. Then the animals retrieved it and returned it to its place, swearing that they would never again take it to the pawn shop for a dumb Frenchwoman to buy. Now Blackboard laughs every day. Sometimes, he gets drunk and starts shouting, but the next day he's black, shiny and original again like the first day.

13

BOOZER

1962

The lift motor began to hum. A fan in the ceiling emitted a stream of deliciously cool air. The moving cabin started its descent packed with people of diverse races; black, yellow, brown, red, white, cinnamon, copper. The lift operator was a mulatto: big, exuberant and full of life. The Tower of Babel began to descend from the 18th floor of the Havana Riviera. When I left my room heading for the lift, mellow, modulated horns were rendering " 'Til there was you" in the golden tones of the Big Band Jazz. I felt as if I were gliding over an ice rink. The hotel lobbies, the corridors, the landings, the reception rooms were all carpeted in a soft brown that melded with the liquid chocolate tones of the music. When I awoke it was late. The sun had filtered secretly over the sea and the stereo was playing "Glory of love". I went to the bathroom, washed my face and surveyed it at length in the mirror (more clichés). I was here at last. The bloke in the mirror was me, the same person, the same dumb short-sighted face, the Lenin-style beard that joined up with the moustache. From behind thick pebble glasses my oriental-looking Indian eyes peered back at me; crafty little buggers. The stereo started up "On the street where you live". My ablutions followed the rhythm of the soft music. I patted gently under my eyes with the towel, smoothing the first wrinkles that were beginning to show: how dare they, damned cheek: rubbed my Lenin beard where the water had accumulated and dried my forehead carefully to remove the shine, all the while whistling "Glory of love". Then came the main ceremony of the washing ritual: I combed my hair with extreme caution so I wouldn't leave a handful of it in the comb. Every day more and more falls out. It's got to be treated with care. This bathroom is great, terrific, like something off a film set. The mirror that reflected my marvellous mug, my lovely likeness, my beauteous boat was immense, like a lake. At the bottom of this lake was a pale pink room, full of tiles and glass. The bath and shower were encircled by a wall of sliding glass. Carpets, strange appliances that emerged from who knows where and were used for who knows what purpose hung from the walls. A fan: a daft air-conditioning contraption. Shiny towel rails: lanolin lotions and baby soft potions (darling, how absolutely fabulous!) I can't remember what else now. My face set in the middle of the lake, without my specs (I'd taken them off to wash it), began to emerge more clearly, my chinky eyes surveyed me, analysed me, scrutinised me with minute attention to detail: James Bond, TV version. The stereo played the Leo Face arrangement of "Me and my shadow". At first the trumpets carried the melody fortissimo, then, after a drum roll, the saxophones came in and the harmony mellowed to a deep blue velvet. Against the slow background beat of a single drum played with the brush the xylophone came to the rescue of the dying note changing slightly the texture of the sound. Then the saxes came in again rhythmically / sounds like Glen Miller, I thought. When the music became a single wall of sound with full orchestra (it seemed to be a forties arrangement) it left both me and my shadow imprinted, eternalised for an instant in the vast mirror of a Havana hotel bathroom. At last I was alone, free, far from my mother / Mother, leave me alone, let me live: Joyce: Ulysses / far from all I had been before, after and always, alone with myself, with my thoughts, with my bearded chinky face, with my myopic eyes, with my doubts and ambitions, with my secret and public desires, far from that day when I realised that I didn't have a father, when I went to school and the teacher, the "Miss", asked me who my father was, what his name was, and I realised that I didn't know, that I'd never thought about it, that nobody had explained it to me, that I was six years old and it was my first day at school, that I'd been thrown into the world without a father, not knowing where I came from or where I was going. I didn't know what to answer and, as my tears began to flow, I started to wet myself. I felt that all the children were watching me and I was there in the middle of the classroom like a murderer, like a condemned man, like a criminal whose crime was not having a father. The teacher looked at me with her squinty eyes and repeated the question / What's your father's name? / Then I felt the blood rushing to my head flooding me with a strange heat, I felt that my face was about to burst, I felt the taste of the tears that were running down my cheeks (*I should have put 'flowing': I'm making concessions to the reader: you're welcome!*), I felt something warm creeping down my legs, steaming, burning, humiliating. I closed my legs, pressing them tightly together, but it was too late, my bladder muscles had yielded to the pressure of the question. It was all too much for me. I shouldn't have cried, men don't cry. That's what my mother had taught me. When she hit me, she shouted / Don't cry, be a man, men don't cry / I tightened my jaw and loosened my bladder. It didn't matter if I peed, the important thing was not to cry. But I did both and there was no way I could stop the liquid flowing from either end. From that day onwards, I began to wet the bed every night. I was fourteen and I still went on wetting the bed / Miss, that boy's wet his trousers / There's always one traitor, one snitch, right from an early age, never mind the nationality, they're all the same, there's always one son of a bitch who'll betray you, inform on you, rat, squeal, split, spill the beans, tell tales. Being an informer, a stoolie, a nark, a grass, is the oldest profession in the world alongside that of the whore. They're lousy, mother-fucking bastards. The teacher's squinty eyes lit up and she stuck her face into mine, / What an execrable piece of filth / Up yours, I thought quickly, since I didn't know what execrable meant but suspected it might be rude / Disgusting, filthy, vile, little savage / That I did understand. My legs began to tremble and I let out all the reserve, all the residue of pee that remained in my bladder. Then I glanced down at my short trousers (that was another of my mother's dirty tricks making me wear short trousers until I was fourteen) and I saw the urine, the holy water, liquid effluent, golden rain descending, running, dripping, trickling between my skinny bare legs. Then I stopped crying and began to feel an intense bitterness towards my mother. What was it to have a father? I'd never needed him, I didn't know he existed, didn't know his name, or his face, or where he came from, or what he was like or his fingerprints. He didn't exist. What they called a father didn't exist for me. I only had a grandmother, a mother, a maiden aunt and a little sister without a willy. I knew this because one day I lifted the blanket that my mother covered her with and I saw that she didn't have one like me, it had been cut off. But what old squint-eyes asked, I didn't know. Who, or maybe what, was a father? Did you eat it? What with? Tortillas? Why were all those kids laughing at me? Did I have a clown's face perhaps? Did I make a mistake and say something funny, like when you say a tongue twister too fast: I'm not a pheasant plucker, I'm a pheasant plucker's son and I'm only plucking pheasants 'til the pheasant plucker comes: all those shitty kids laughing at me / Fuck off / Oh you uncouth little boy. On top of everything else, you're rude to other pupils. Come here, I'm taking you to the toilets / Squint eyes pulled me by the ear, almost yanking it off completely and, lugging me by the lughole, dragged me, hauled me, heaved me, kicking and struggling at her side, towards the bog (boys' bathroom, she called it). When we were alone in the convenience, the in-convenience, with me all tearful and wee-stained, sniffling, snivelling and ponging to high heaven, and her totally frustrated, she looked at me furiously, the bloody woman must have been an old maid, and in a state bordering on hysteria gave me a stinging slap round the face. Then she grabbed me from behind by the hair, lifted me on to the washbasin, and pushed me up to the mirror, squashing my nose flat against it / Look at yourself. Aren't you ashamed, you disgusting little reprobate? / I looked at myself at length, intently, my slanty eyes sank into the lake and behind me was reflected the opaque glass that concealed the shower and the tray. Then I grabbed the towel and rubbed it over my face drying my tears. I was alone, free, far from the teachers, from my mother, from all that I had been up until that moment. I left the bathroom. "On the street where you live" was finishing. It was an arrangement by Chapel with the Big Band Jazz based on the xylophone. Its melody provoked an unknown pain. I had never been alone before. "On the street where you live" changed its tone. The xylophone faded and the brass came in with their moody syncopation, the percussive sound plunged deep into my veins, the hi-fi raised my spirits and the supersound made my senses vibrate. I went to the window that looked over the sea from the 18th floor. A duo of trombone and sax ending with an A sharp on the trumpet made me hallucinate. Gazing out from where I was standing, the horizon was all the same, the decor of the room merging with the sea. Everything was blue, I felt wet, swimming, bathing in a blue immensity. I turned over, sprawled languorously in a vast bed, covered by a sea-blue bedspread. The room had a blue carpet, padded, soft and fluffy. The brass rocked me, lulled me, then I threw myself, dived, liberated, joyful, ecstatic, euphoric, into the sea, it was soft and springy. I rolled over as the melody of "On the street where you live" came to an end on a double drum roll. I opened my legs, smoothed my fingers over my chest and my arms, ruffled my hair, caressed my stomach, my balls, my legs, I was alone, I could do whatever I liked, strip naked, wank, leap, sing, talk to myself, laugh, cry, hop on one foot, balance on one hand, cartwheel, spin, pirouette, somersault. The bed sank and rose beneath my weight, spun with me, stopped, the water entered through my pores, the sun was finally sinking. Then I felt hungry. I hadn't eaten since I'd arrived, my nerves wouldn't let me. When I left the room, "'Til there was you" was starting. The slow blues with xylophone and bass saxophone slid over my skin in long glissandos gliding over the brown carpet that covered the 18th floor. I knew the words of the song in Spanish. Outside my room in that silent, solitary corridor where I, too, was alone and where all one could hear was the hotel muzak, I began to dance and serenade myself softly whilst I waited for the lift to arrive.

come to me
my belovèd
for I love you
I'm waiting for you
and never
never more

shall I forget you ... The lift was full and the words went on ringing in my head whilst a murmur of alien tongues accompanied the descent of the moving cabin. When we reached the first floor, the doors opened and, as we got out, the last strains of "'Til there was you" diffused, merged and were engulfed by the noisy, heady rhythm of a cha-cha. The hotel lobby was swarming with people. The first thing I heard was the bongos. They dominated, controlled, commanded all the rhythm. They imposed the inflection, the language, the cadence, the idiom of this miserable country. People passed, came and went, came again, had intercourse (social), laughed, talked loudly, softly, inbetweenly / Hi man, what's new? / In the centre of the lobby, like a vast skating rink or dance hall was a labyrinth of armchairs of every conceivable shape and colour. They formed an inextricable spiral in the centre of which was set a New Year's Wagon piled high, overflowing, spewing ornaments, baubles, gourds, bongos, maracas, coconuts, palms, nuts, sugar cane, yucca / Yuc-ca, he-ca, she-ca / My dear, I've just got to tell you / hey, come and listen to this. What do you think? / Allow me to present my partner / You have to do it with enthusiasm, with aplomb, comrade / People passing, singing, leaping around, and the bongos bug, bug bugging buggering. I began to push my way through to the dining room. I was about fifty paces away but it took balls to get through. I started to push / pardon me, excuse me, may I get through please? / Always the word "please". We must have been born servile. From the moment I arrived in Cuba I realised that, here, no one listens to us, no-one is aware of our presence, no one takes a blind bit of notice of us. We speak softly and carefully, timorously, our terror showing in our eyes. I first noticed it when I got to the hotel. Whilst we were on the trip round Havana and the guide was rabbitting on in a dull monotone, nobody uttered a word. We sat silent looking out, gawped, gawked, gazed, amazed, dazed, fazed. When we passed through El Foxa the little old peasant woman who was travelling in the same car as us was so agog she almost left her dentures embedded in the road. In other words, nobody uttered a dicky bird. When we got to the hotel some coffee-skinned character began to ask who all those red, tatty, ancient, discoloured, new, yellow, blue, cases, baskets, bits and pieces, odds and sods belonged to / What chaos! What a mess / What a pain in the bum that black guy is / What awful luggage / Nobody could find his gear. The mulatto was in a strop, probably because he couldn't hear anything above the din / Comrade, could you speak up a bit, I can't hear a word you're saying / What's the matter with your voice, young man? / When the guide with the folder returned after filling in the register with all our details, the pandemonium began to assume some order. No one listens to us, no one is aware of our existence. We are always apart, timid, huddled together in a group, drinking: all the girls sitting in one corner watching and us standing in a line whispering, nudging, goading, ribbing each other, egging each other on / Why don't you ask her to dance? / Well, why don't you then? / I can't dance but you can / The girls had been sitting there from when the party had started, from three in the afternoon, from years before, from the time when we formed The Club. From the day when I went to my first party, my first booze-up and Alicia surveyed me through half-closed almond eyes from where she was sitting alone, watching me. The marimba was making a stab at playing "Give me a kiss, a kiss to build a dream on, and my imagination will move mountains." My legs were trembling. I was fourteen and couldn't dance. I was an absolute wash out. I felt like peeing, crapping myself, running away, shouting, screaming. I felt the blood rush to my face burning it scarlet, then drain, leaving it pale and distorted. My eyes boggled, black buggers, my lower lip trembled, my teeth chattered, my hands sweated. Alicia got up and slunk over to me. The marimba was halfway through the piece so there was still time to dance. But I didn't know how. Alicia showed me, took me by the waist / I'll lead, don't be shy / swung me back and forth, pushing me / Go on, now you / We were always in a line, all of us just standing, no one daring to go first. Us on one side, the row of rat-arsed machos, and them on the other, the young whores. It never varied. They put up with it three times and then they laid into us. Three Saturdays of silent boozing. Nobody speaks. No one opens his mouth. Not a word. Sod all / They're a load of drunken bums / degenerate swine / cheeky little sods / stupid berks / We can't hear you man / Speak up man! / Nobody notices us. They don't even realise we exist. I began to push aside the people who were jostling past. I looked in my pockets for the meal tickets, yellow for breakfast, pink for lunch and green for dinner. I needed the green ones. I'd left them in my room and going up all those floors, getting back into the lift, listening to the gringo Sixties music on the modulated frequency of the CMQ and going into that blue room done out in the style of the George Raft heyday all over again was a bind, so I just kept on going. Beside the dining room was a small bar that I hadn't noticed when I entered the hotel. From it issued the rhythm of a Cuban bolero, a whine, a negroid soul sound / Never has ivy clung closer to a wall / It came from a small raised stage set up behind the bar where there usually hung a mirror so that inebriates could watch themselves get plastered. On this diminutive dais, three mulattos were playing guitars and maracas in a style copied from Los Panchos but in a purely Cuban adaptation / wherever you may be you will hear my voice calling to you with my song / All around, like in a variety theatre, little round tables with black and yellow seats continued the unbroken spiral that began in the lobby. How people got into it beat me. The human torrent came and went, ate and drank, boozed and belched, chattered and shouted, ate and drank, chewed and swallowed, came and went, sat and stood again, hummed and sang / stronger than pain, our love entwines us like ivy / The trio strummed and, with sweeping arpeggios, modulated up a fifth to begin the second section / wherever you may be you will hear my voice / I sat at the bar and ordered a cuba libre. I was alone in the midst of thousands of people *(another dumb cliché)*. A sense of freedom surged from within me. I had finished with all the control, the repression the commands, the compulsion, the tears, the entreaties, the prayers, the sulks, the smells, the shouting, the beatings and my mother's whippings. I was on my own. Free at last. I was alone, forced into the little cupboard under the stairs, barefoot, in the darkness. From there I could hear the murmur of the voices of the rest of the pupils. From the moment I started school the teacher put me under the stairs, in a little room that they'd improvised to keep the cleaning things in, and barred the door with a chair so I couldn't get out. The first time she did it, I was afraid of the dark. I began to see spiders, centipedes, cockroaches, vipers, dragons, venomous snakes, scorpions, all kinds of terrifying things and I began to sweat with panic all over, my hands, my buttocks, my forehead, my armpits. I wanted to scream, but my voice wouldn't come out, it stuck in my throat. I clenched my fists tightly, digging my nails deep into my palms. The floor was chill, icy, freezing cold. I couldn't see and I couldn't move. Outside I could hear the murmur of the teacher's voice as she taught the lesson. I would have liked to say I was sorry but I stuck it out. When she opened the door the entire school was lined up ready to go home. It was midday, and they had to recite the angelus in front of the big picture that hung outside the Head's office / Suffer little children to come unto me / I couldn't move. I was stiff, rigid, immobile, paralysed both inside and out, hating, hated with a loathing that would last all my life, but I remained silent. She handed me my shoes / put your shoes on and stand in line / Later, I grew accustomed to the punishment. As soon as she entered the classroom she'd point to my place. She didn't have to say a thing. I left my desk and went to the little door in the corner. Before going in, I took off my shoes and left them on her desk. Then I opened the door and took a quick shufty to see if there was something to sit on. Then darkness, peace. The noise of the school at lessons began to diminish, to fade into a vacuum. I was alone in my lair, my tower, my monastic cell and my imagination began to take over. I felt free, liberated. Sometimes, I'd have a quiet wank and since I was too young to come I left no stain to betray me. I always wanked the moment I was inside so there'd be no danger of the teacher coming back unexpectedly and catching me playing with my python. The world began to recede. The murmur of the teacher's voice faded, sinking into the void. I sat on a box, put my head between my arms and began to gallop on a white charger with wheels on its hooves and we rode and rode through an immense field of green, blue and orange that continuously expanded and evolved. Purple hued mountains thrust upwards forming ravines down which my trusty steed sped whilst behind us ran my mother, my grandmother, my maiden aunt, the schoolteacher and my little sister with no willy, all trying to catch me (Mother leave me alone, let me live) shouting, running, howling, begging, weeping, shrieking, imprecating, but my horse was swift, huge, many hands high with a long steady gallop. Sometimes it flew and then the women dwindled into insignificance, to nothingness, and I began to laugh. My peals of laughter dissolved, evaporating into the clouds. My horse leapt from one to another, pushing its way easily through the cotton balls until we reached the rainbow and slid down it. When, at last, we made it to the other side and climbed off the violet, the women had vanished. All that could be heard was a vague distant murmur. Then I spurred my horse on to go even faster. He began the descent galloping at top speed. He soared and plunged, faster than the air, faster than the speed of sound, faster than the speed of light. I felt the wind on my face. I closed my eyes and went sinking into a deep black whirlpool that calmed me, soothed me. I put my head down between my arms but the noise persisted. I couldn't detach myself from it. After a long while, the teacher opened the door and the glare of the light and the volume of noise left me stunned, motionless, disorientated for a moment, with my heart pounding and my hands trembling. In the school yard the good pupils, the well-behaved ones, were already starting the incoherent rambling: The Angel of the Lord announced to Mary: By the work and grace of the Holy Spirit: Mary full of grace, the Lord is with Thee. I climbed out, took my shoes from the teacher's desk, put them on and joined the flock. I had lost my freedom, my solitude. The litany began: The Lord is with you: / calling you with my song, stronger than pain our love entwines us like ivy / The drink went down a treat refreshing my oesophagus and my stomach, rushing to my veins, swelling them and infusing them with instant heat and strength. The ice clinked in my glass. There was loud clapping and the trio of mulattos acknowledged the applause, holding their guitars to their chests and bowing. They went off and returned. The applause continued. Again they went off and once more took a bow, smiling broadly, opening their big wide mouths to reveal huge equine teeth. They came (or went) for a third time and that was it. I had a second drink, now with less relish but with more calm, with greater panache. I felt that I was someone else, someone who was not me and yet, at the same time was me and five or six or ten others. People were beginning to get tight and the noise level was rising, outside of the bar the sound of the bongos was increasing, diminishing, swelling, intensifying and dying away. I turned my back to the bar, leaned on it indolently. I'd almost downed the cuba libre in just two gulps. At the most, only one sip remained. Before swallowing it, knocking it back eagerly, I made myself comfortable, settled my spine against the hard wood of the bar and checked out the scene around me. The crowd of people was all the same. I couldn't distinguish any one of them from another. It was like a monster with a thousand faces that might consume me at any minute. The smoke rose and disappeared who knows where, it formed silhouettes, monstrous shapes that mutated a second after absorbing the air, (or being absorbed by the air?) and, escaping through the door, vanished, followed by the dull murmur of the crowd, the monster with a thousand heads, that drank mechanically from the glasses, clinking the ice, (the body language is a cliché in itself so don't blame me this time), knocked back a glass automatically, robotically, idiotically, without even feeling or savouring it, roared, hooted with laughter, crossed one leg, uncrossed the other, settled their bums on seats, lit up another cigarette or a cigar, unaware of having done so, inhaled the smoke with no visibly pleasurable reaction: vacuous, vapid, vacant machines that clicked their fingers, moved their lips, ordered another drink when the waiter arrived or merely gestured with one finger indicating from a distance that they wanted another round. Outside, the bongos were playing frenetically. Nobody was listening to them, except me. Only I noticed them, sitting alone savouring the last drop, the dregs of liquor that remained at the bottom of the glass. The women all smoked like whores. They let their hands droop casually, limp-wristed, open-palmed, inserted the cigarette loosely between the tendon of their fingers and then, in a manner they considered the height of sensuality, drew the cigarette to their mouths in slow motion, opened their dark fleshy lips like raw liver and put the penis into the orifice: thick-lipped black cock-suckers. After a languid suck they lowered the hand slowly, voluptuously, and expelled the stream of smoke in every direction through their moist open mouths. My eyes started to sting, irritated by so much smoke. I ordered another cuba libre and climbed in under the stairs. The murmur began to recede into the far distance. The crowd started to lose its shape and substance, the edges blurring. I could no longer see it. I was alone and free. That was what I liked. I liked a mass that doesn't think, that leaves you alone. I liked to watch it, touch it, fondle it, caress it, feel that it was mine, belonged to me. Its sound was distant, warm, pleasing. I felt at ease with it. It was like a monster which doesn't think but which acts. Like an unfinished painting that one is always composing, recomposing, destroying and recreating. It mutates constantly. It's a work which you erase and when you rewrite it find that you have written the same thing. It's always the same but it's different by the minute. Each gesture, each laugh, each belch is quite unlike any other. It's different from the one that precedes it. Each drink, each cigar, each inhalation, each exhalation are another and the same at the same time. Laughter reaches me but I don't hear it. I only perceive it for an instant and then I'm alone again. It's unlike my mother or my grandmother or my maiden aunt or my little sister with no willy who are always meddling in your affairs, bugging you, loving you and you loving them, putting up with them, but at the same time hating them every moment. They suffocate you, asphyxiate you, mortify you, imprison you with their love for you and with yours for them. I'm never going back. I'll never return to my wretched little Guatemala to sink back into that hole that destroys me, that despises me, that suffocates me. Guatemala where my mother's house is, where the schoolteacher and the priests are and all those stupid acquaintances and strangers who know you and whom you know, who think they have the right to tell you what you should do and what you shouldn't. I'll stay here or maybe I'll leave here before long and go on to some other place, to some other country where there exists an amorphous crowd of beings that laugh or cry, are dissolute or virtuous, silent or garrulous, that smoke Havanas or pipes, that drink whiskey or wine or beer but don't meddle in my life, that let me see them, observe them, paint them, efface them, possess them, abandon them, that have no particular face or laugh, that permit me entrance to their homes unconditionally, that allow me to leave without attempting to detain me, that let me be free without imposing their ideas, their ideology, their manners, their customs. Here I'll stay and from here I'll leave, but I'll never return to my mother's side, to my mother's country, to the country of my non-existent father, to my country where you can never be alone or free, because you know everybody and everybody knows you and you kill and are killed and you have to flee and go into hiding because otherwise they 'disappear' you they imprison you kill you torture you cut off your balls stab out your eyes cut off your left hand fuck you rape you attack your house steal everything that you possess never let you live in peace leave you no solitude advise you direct you tell you what to do and what not to do because they all know you and love you and respect you and meddle in your life and mortify you and kill you by degrees or with a bullet and where your mother is and the dictator of the day and the police who at any moment

and for any reason put your name on file persecute you pursue
you and kill you
    No
    Here I'll stay
    Sitting
    Drinking
    Listening to the bongos

Mexico, D. F., April 1968
Madrid, February 1970
Guatemala, August 1971

Notes

1. Rodrigo de Triana. The lookout in the crow's nest of Columbus' lead ship who spotted land.
2. quetzal – the currency of Guatemala.
3. Guatemalan novelist and Nobel Prize winner.
4. FAR – Fuerzas Armadas Rebeldes (Rebel Armed Forces).
5. Rafael Carrera, ruler of Guatemala 1839-65.
6. Mano – Guatemalan death squad.
7. Corín Tellado – Romantic fiction equivalent in Spanish to Mills and Boon.
8. José Miguel Ramón Ydígoras Fuentes, president 1958-63.
9. Without papers or a fixer there was no way of getting a fixed job.
10. Marco Antonio Yon Sosa (194?-70), a guerrilla leader whose father was a Chinese merchant.